Unsure of how long he had slept undisturbed, Vincent Madden was certain that it hadn't been long. It was often the case when he had plaguing thoughts, that sleep was the last thing on his mind. Fumbling for the illumination function on his watch he was thankful that he had been able to get four hours. The unfamiliar surroundings, which he should have grown used to by now, still startled him even after all of these years, as they do most people, who wake up somewhere unknown next to a stranger. It was certainly the cocktail of subtle differences which, even in the dark, shouted *you are far from home*.

The feeling can certainly be a pleasant one. Much like a tourist on holiday will often be surprised and happy, to have awoken without the prospect of facing the daily grind of going to work, and pleased to be away from all things which they associate with home. A chuckle in the silence – at the thought that this could be misconstrued as a holiday – escaped his lips.

The comfortable mattress was dressed in the odour of the clean yet foreign smelling sheets and covers that offered protection from the uncharacteristic cold which enveloped the room and no doubt the world outside. In the darkness, almost forgetting the importance of the day and task which lay ahead of him, he lifted the weight of his body slightly up onto his elbows and focussed his attention on Lara, who was lying beside him.

She still slept soundly and shards of light illuminated her as she rested peacefully in the darkness, her blonde hair partially covering her face and spread over the pillow as her head lay tilted away from him. He watched her for a moment, remembering the events of the night before. He had been at a local bar enjoying a drink in the early evening.

He had seen her, a lonely backpacker, sitting alone at a table in the corner, staring forlornly at her mobile phone. As time went on, she had looked increasingly upset, so he had walked over to ask if she was ok and introduced himself as Ryan. Her face had lit up when she heard that he spoke English and she had eagerly explained to him that she had been travelling with friends and become separated. Her phone battery was nearly dead and she had no phone credit or money to get in contact with them. He quickly identified her Dutch accent. Her predicament had struck a chord with Vincent, who recalled feeling sorry for her, particularly when he saw the size of her backpack, which looked larger than she could physically carry. He had immediately offered to drive her to where she needed to go the following day.

Vincent had taken her to a restaurant as she seemed exhausted and looked as though she hadn't had a good meal in a while. It had been a long time since he had enjoyed the company of such an innocent, vibrant, friendly and interesting woman. She had started by talking about her recently completed studies in the Netherlands, her family, her friends and her hopes for the future. Vincent had not been quite as truthful about himself, which was something he despised about his line of work.

Reaching in the pitch darkness across to the bedside table, he searched with his fingers through a variety of paperwork and items for the switch to the bedside lamp. His fingers tripped up on his box of cigarettes and as he grasped them longingly, he decided that light wasn't necessary to find the way out to the balcony for a quick smoke.

Bringing his legs down towards the ground with a swinging motion, he righted himself at the side of the bed. The uncomfortable metal bed frame dug into the back of his legs. This was eclipsed by a slight throbbing pain at his temples, which was a precursor to a possible headache to come. The balcony door, unlocked and fairly insecure on its hinges, swung open freely, allowing a blast of cold air to hit him. If there was any part of Vincent that was still trying to remain dormant and inactive, the cold air was the bucket of ice that woke him to the core. The bath robe and thick socks he had donned to venture onto the balcony were scant, but he would only be a moment.

Stepping out onto the concrete floor, the cold immediately made itself known upon the soles of his feet, but this did not bother him. Since he could remember himself, he had smoked and since he could remember, he couldn't stand people who smoked inside.

The lighter, as always, lodged inside the box, was quickly pulled out with a cigarette. He realised that even though he had looked at his watch, maybe not even five minutes earlier, he had no idea what the time was. Strange, that he knew he had only slept four hours, but stranger things had happened. No need to check again, he thought. For the next five minutes, there was no need for time. The crackling of the tobacco and paper as he lit the cigarette was a sound which he had always found relaxing. Walking forward toward the balcony rail, he could see that the moonlight was casting an effervescent glow over the town. The linden trees, which during the summer months would have made for such a pleasant scent, were as cold and dormant as the rest of the sleepy town. The iridescent nuance of the moon on the powdery snow, which had come to rest on the branches, gave the feeling of the dormant beauty that lay within the trees. One could be forgiven for thinking that nobody would be stirring so early on a morning as still and cold as this. From the fifth floor of the apartment block where he stood, Vincent could see everything which lay before him, tinted by the light of the moon. The old communist-style apartment blocks which surrounded the wooded park below, were as silhouettes in the darkness. A few lit rooms identified the first people waking up in familiar surroundings and preparing for the daily grind. Familiarity, of course, a commodity which is relative to the place and people that it is applied to. It seemed an outright shame that in the midst of such beautiful nature, there should be apartment buildings as ugly as the one in which he had taken up temporary accommodation. Nature, the most basic and simple pleasure, overlooked by so many on a day-to-day basis, but he was glad that he was still able to admire and take solace in it.

There was something beautiful about his apartment. However, she still lay sleeping peacefully. Vincent recalled how already by 10pm the previous night they had felt that they knew each other well and had made their way back to the flat which he had called home for the past few days. They had shared a couple of bottles of wine with their meal and she had seemed keen to jump into bed with him, which had been a pleasant development, he thought.

Vincent wondered whether he had taken advantage of her, but justified his actions to himself by the logic that he certainly would have helped her, one way or the other. Over the course of the evening, Lara had become much more confident and assertive than she had been when he had first approached her. He remembered thinking at one point that she really did not seem the hitch-hiking type. Exhaling a puff of smoke with a quiet laugh, he wondered whether perhaps she had taken advantage of him.

The past few months had been difficult and lonely for Vincent, who had not had the time for passionate engagements. He had caught himself, on several occasions that he could remember, fantasising about a life more ordinary. Not during the day, but at night when he had time to be alone with his thoughts. He would think back to simpler times, when he had friends, family, a woman he loved and generally a life outside of his profession. Out of no choice of his own, he had been ripped from this life and forced to walk a different path, on which he had done some good, but also quite a lot of bad.

Rubbing the back of his head and shaking it slightly to rid himself of any further such thoughts, Vincent's experience last night with Lara brought home his ever-increasing desire to start again. He stubbed the cigarette out on the balcony rail and the tips of his fingers came into contact with the icy metal. Hoping that the water would be warmer than the rail, Vincent discarded the cigarette butt and headed for the shower room.

2

He finally mustered the will to look at his watch again and saw the time which had eluded him thus far. It was just after 5am. Walking through the small room in which they had slept, he flicked the light switch on and saw that at some point during the night he had knocked his suitcase over and this now lay awkwardly in the middle of the room. Strange, that he had not tripped up on it on the way to the balcony. Righting the case and setting it in the corner of the room behind the door, he walked into the shower room, which was also freezing cold. Looking into the bathroom mirror he realised that he needed to tend to his appearance urgently. Taking off the bath robe, he made sure that the water was just the right temperature, before jumping in. A sense of relief and well-being washed over him, as surely as the hot water from the shower. He hadn't shaved in several days and had started to take on a somewhat rough and ready look. Perhaps that is what had endeared him to the enamoured backpacker asleep in his bedroom. Vincent had taken an opportunity while she had been in the bathroom the night before, to check her wallet for ID and found that her name was Lara Berg and her home address was in Rotterdam. The fact that he had felt the need to go into the side pocket of Lara's backpack to take a look at her passport was a damning reflection of his inability to trust.

Wiping the condensation from the sink mirror, he squirted some foam into the palm of his hand and applied it generously to his face. The razor slid smoothly over his skin, making him feel presentable once again.

After towelling down his face, he returned to the bedroom in his bath robe to find his clothes. Lara was awake and sitting up in bed looking towards him.

'How did you sleep?' asked Vincent.

'Really well,' she said, 'it's so early though, aren't you still tired?'

'Yeah, but I do have a lot to do today. It's a shame we can't lie in,' Vincent said squinting in the dark, trying to make out Lara's face.

She nodded and he could make out a smile in the darkness.

'Do you mind if I have one of your cigarettes?' she asked politely, but playfully. Vincent reached down to his bedside cabinet, where he had left his cigarettes and lighter, on his way to the bathroom. 'I haven't smoked in over a year, but I think I deserve one after last night. The smoke woke me up when you were out there on the balcony and I don't know, I just really fancy one,' she said longingly. 'Let me just get dressed quickly and then I will go out there. I won't be more than a few minutes I promise.'

Lara jumped out of bed in a spritely, youthful fashion. Having slept with nothing on underneath the warm duvet, she now quickly felt the cold. She was rapidly dressing and Vincent realised that he had unknowingly perched himself on the side of the bed and was watching her with keen interest. Before she noticed, he quickly got back to his feet and started to get dressed.

Throwing on his thick pair of dark brown trousers, t-shirt and jumper he walked to Lara and handed her a cigarette. She allowed him to light it for her, before she walked out onto the balcony. In the meantime, Vincent took a quick walk round the flat to make sure that he had collected everything he needed in his suitcase.

Stepping tentatively onto the balcony on the opposite side of the apartment building, Vincent hesitantly peered over the side to catch a glimpse of his Audi which sat serenely, coated in a fresh dusting of pure white snow. It had fallen heavily that night.

Turning and creeping back inside, he tried to make as little noise as possible. Ironic that with one touch of the engine ignition button on his key ring, the silence would be shattered either way.

Paranoia had dictated that he should install a remote car ignition. Useful, on cold days like today when the car is frozen over and needs to thaw. Also handy when the car could have an ignition triggered explosive charge attached to it.

Eyes closed, he pressed the button slowly, wincing at the thought of an explosion. Standing well away from the kitchen window, Vincent instead heard the reliable sound of the Audi's engine chortling from ground level.

Standing in front of the mirror in the hallway by the door, he took a moment to check his appearance as he put his coat on. Vincent felt the pistol at the small of his back and returned to the bedroom, where Lara had finished the cigarette and was now dressed and ready to go.

'I can't thank you enough for your help. I don't know what I would have done if it hadn't been for you,' she conceded.

'I have quite a few things I could thank you for,' said Vincent, cheekily.

Lara smiled shyly and said 'I'm not sure who should be thanking who! How long do you think it will take us to get to Sofia?'

'Just over two hours I would say. Shall we?' he said as he turned the key in the lock and opened the front door. She stepped forward and threw her arms around his neck and gave him a kiss. The taste of the fresh cigarette was pronounced, but pleasant on her lips. Lara walked out and Vincent picked up her very heavy backpack along with his own case, before closing the door and locking it.

They headed down the stairs, finally reaching his car, which stood idling obediently in the parking area. Heaving the backpack and his suitcase into the boot, he noticed that Lara had already sneaked into the passenger seat to get out of the cold. Opening the driver's side, a blast of hot air hit him from inside the vehicle. The engine had been idling for a while since he used the remote ignition. Gladly removing his coat and throwing it on the rear seat, Vincent was happy to feel the warmth upon his skin.

On sitting in the driver's seat, a sudden urgency hit him. Throwing the Audi into reverse, the car moved steadily out of its overnight resting place. Moving away and around the side of the apartment block, the road was in sight. Now finding himself under the linden trees, which he had admired earlier for their radiance and beauty, Vincent started his journey to the Bulgarian capital Sofia, with Lara. On arriving there they would say farewell and he would drop her off at the airport, as they had discussed. He had given her more than enough money to catch the first flight back to the Netherlands. He realised the unlikelihood that he would ever see her again, regardless of how good his intentions were. He had been untruthful about his life and his line of work and Lara would most probably not have liked the truth.

3

'A momentary lapse of concentration. What can I say. One moment you are standing there with a hot cup of tea, the next moment you put it down without a coaster. It can happen to anybody,' explained Ambassador Francis Sunderland. The veneer specialist, looking unimpressed and somewhat bewildered, struggled to overcome the language barrier and understand what was being said.

In the best English he could muster, he muttered, 'Ok, so I go to van and bring my things.'

'Katrina, could you come here for a moment please,' Francis called. Katrina, the nanny of Francis' two young boys also made for an excellent translator. For this reason, she was often around even when Francis and his wife Melissa weren't away. 'Could you please inform the gentleman that this is a very special and custom made desk and I would be most disappointed if it were not returned to its previous state.'

'Yes of course sir,' said Katrina, who proceeded to translate. 'He says that he will make it as good as new, Sir.'

This was good to hear, but even though this veneer specialist came very highly recommended, Francis would not leave him unsupervised with his dark-brown oak desk and his office. Katrina turned on her heels and headed back to her duties, while Francis slowly circumnavigated his desk and sat in his chair. A slight look of puzzlement appeared on the face of the veneer specialist, as if to ask why he was sitting there and whether he would be sat there during the whole repair process. This time would give Francis ample opportunity to think about this evening's social gathering.

The plans had already been made and Melissa had hopefully placed all the orders for food, drink and service, which would be required. The snow, which had fallen the night before, had all but melted by now. It was the early afternoon and the daylight was already starting to fade.

Ruffling his fingers through his prematurely grey, but exquisitely groomed hair, Francis was growing more and more agitated by the length of time it was taking the specialist to finish applying the treatment to his desk. Looking inquisitively and tapping his watch, Francis suggested the question which he wished he could express verbally.

'Ten minutes,' was the response, but at least it looked to be a good job.

The guests would start arriving soon and he had not had a chance to venture downstairs and supervise the preparations, but no doubt Melissa had everything in hand.

'Finished,' exclaimed the veneer specialist who looked particularly pleased with himself. 'No touch for eight or twelve hours, Sir.'

'That is alright, nobody will be in here this evening and by morning it will be dry,' retorted Francis, handing the fee to him in a small white envelope and gesturing towards the door. The job had taken longer than he had thought, although it had been done to a higher standard than he had expected. Only time would tell. It would take until morning for the veneer to dry completely, so the regular routine of turning and locking the door had an extra purpose this time. As the key turned in the lock and the satisfying click allowed him to retract it, Francis had high hopes for the evening.

Slipping the key into his jacket pocket, he strolled down the stairs to join his wife.

'It looks perfect,' whispered Francis, as Melissa felt his breath upon the back of her neck.

'You made me jump,' she laughed, as she looked straight ahead at the caterers setting one of the tables in the hall. 'How is your desk looking? I can't believe that you made such a fuss about getting someone in to do it today, of all days.'

'I know, I'm very sorry, but I couldn't bear to look at it like that any longer. Besides, I'm sure between you and Katrina, you have been able to coordinate things down here. There is still a bit of time until the first of them is due to arrive. I just hope that no one has spilt the beans, so to speak,' he said with a wayward grimace on his face.

'I was thinking about that, dear, and it occurred to me that if there are twenty or thirty cars parked outside, we may lose the element of surprise.'

'Don't worry, I have already spoken with Klaus from next door and he is more than happy to accommodate all the parking for this evening.'

'So, I suppose it will look like a party at the German Ambassador's residence instead, will it? I hope that you invited Klaus, or it would be very rude to ask such a favour otherwise,' she said sternly.

'Of course, I invited him and all the guests know to park there and then come here. Well, nearly all the guests. You worry too much. Stop worrying and pass me a glass of that white wine,' he said, swooping down to give her a kiss on the cheek, while mischievously passing his hand around behind her to pick up one of the fine crystal glasses which sparkled invitingly. He took a small sip and savoured its rich flavour for a moment, before allowing himself to swallow it. 'It's a little on the dry side for me, but otherwise excellent. It's such a relief not having to order alcohol in from abroad here. This local produce is quite exquisite and the food looks just as good.'

'I am going to check on the children upstairs. I think Katrina is there, but I just want to let them know what needs to be done before the guests start arriving,' she said, smiling incandescently. 'I think we have about half or quarter of an hour before the first of them get here, so can I trust you to hold the fort?'

Darkness enveloped the residence of the British Ambassador to Bulgaria, which stood bravely in the face of the stern Bulgarian winter. The cold daylight which had melted last night's snowfall was now replaced by a fresh blanket of cloud, heavily laden with the promise of fresh snow. The first flakes floated down, carried on a brisk and bitterly cold wind.

Looking at his watch, Francis was shocked that it was still only 6.30pm, but the nights had been drawing in steadily. Looking up at the ceiling, he was very happy that he had won the battle to not have balloons or banners with 'happy birthday' plastered on them. To him, there was something unnervingly uncouth and brash about banners and balloons to celebrate any occasion, but this sentiment was one which was not shared by many. Perhaps this was an eccentric quirk of his which was unfounded, but he had worked hard to get to his position and no one could deny him a few eccentricities, picked up along the way.

Melissa slowly walked up behind Francis as he stood, apparently daydreaming, and flicked the back of his elbow playfully. 'I told Katrina that she can head home for the day. The boys are fine and I'm sure that they will behave themselves upstairs,' Melissa whispered.

'Ok, if you think so. I've just been looking at this fantastic selection of food. Am I allowed to have a nibble before the swarm arrive?' asked Francis optimistically.

'You keep your hands to yourself Mr Ambassador. I will be keeping my eye on you. We need you on your best behaviour,' teased Melissa, turning and walking out of the hall. Finding himself unattended, Francis put both hands behind his back and strolled calmly over to a table dripping in hors d'oeuvres and appetisers. With a strange sense of wrongdoing and guilt, he brought his hands together in front of his chest and took in the delightful sight with relish.

Plucking up a blue cheese and pear tartlet with his left hand and a tuna nicoise crostini with his right, he quickly dispatched both in quick succession. Halfway through chewing the oversized mouthful he stopped suddenly as he heard familiar footsteps approaching from behind.

'I can't leave you alone for a single second, can I?' Melissa said in a cheery tone. Francis turned with his cheeks still full and offered a half smile, which was enough to send her spinning into a schoolgirl-like giggle. Francis found it difficult not to start laughing himself, but the thought of causing an appetiser-related incident on the floor, meant that he was able to stop himself.

4

Much like the selection of cuisine for a social reception, the choice of invited guests could be the difference between an evening of meaningless niceties and pertinent discussion. For all intents and purposes, a birthday could be considered a normal and customary excuse for celebration; however, when the birthday boy is Wasyl Bohdanov, the Deputy Head of Ukrainian Intelligence, the opportunity for a get-together could not be missed, even if it was under the guise of a surprise.

He had not known Wasyl for very long and to say that he knew him well would be somewhat of a fallacy. Having only learnt of his date of birth a few days prior, Francis had had to arrange the event in an almighty rush, although this ran against the grain of how he liked to do things. He made an exception, in the hope of seizing upon the opportunity to raise some issues, off the record. Masking the plan under a façade of misdirection was a necessity when trying to gull an intelligence official to his residence for a party in his honour. He had been rather pleased and somewhat surprised with the quick and positive response to the invitation that he had received from Wasyl.

Contrary to advice from the Embassy, he had opted not to have a security detail at his house for the party. The invitation list had caused some raised eyebrows, but Francis thought that security personnel at the house would be over the top for what, for all intents and purposes, was a surprise birthday party.

Hearing the electric gates opening next door at the German Ambassador's residence awoke Francis from his pensive state, as he stood at the window gazing out into the rapidly diminishing light. Swinging round to look at the condition of the hall, he was pleased at the job which had been done by the catering staff. They were still finishing off some odds and ends, but Wasyl was not due to arrive for at least another hour and a half. The open window let in a faint, but distinct crunching of gravel in the distance. The guests, who had just parked next door, were slowly making their way up the driveway. Hopefully, all of the guests would have arrived before Wasyl made an appearance.

Francis waited patiently by the window to see who would emerge from around the corner of the thick shrubbery. The darkness made it very difficult to discern who it was that had arrived, but it was a small group of four people, each carrying a small item in their hands.

'Melissa, the first guests are arriving, have you seen to the kids?' he asked, standing at the foot of the stairway.

'I'm just coming down, one minute,' she replied.

A firm knock on the door from just behind Francis made him start. For some reason, he had been expecting the doorbell, but the knock had caught him off guard. Sliding the latch across and pulling open the heavy beechwood door, Francis was greeted by four familiar smiling faces.

'Good evening, Mr Ambassador, I hope we aren't too early again,' joked the first face with a somewhat humorous undertone. Stepping aside, Francis allowed them to enter.

'Mark, I just wish that all of my guests were as punctual. Please come in, make yourselves at home and find a good hiding place.'

'I hope he likes surprises,' quipped Mark.

Slowly closing the door behind them as they walked into the hallway, Francis felt the bitterness of the cold outside and hoped that all the guests arrived before the inevitable snowstorm began. He had checked the weather online earlier and the forecast was for very heavy snowfall, which was expected to last the whole evening.

Francis had a brief titter under his breath as something humorous crossed his mind. The realisation that just as he stood there in the hall, worrying about all the guests arriving before the storm, he had not stopped to consider whether they would be able to leave afterwards.

The residence stood on a gentle incline and a short distance down the road the gradient took a turn for the steep. This, in conjunction with the almost non-existent salting and gritting of the roads leading back to the city, had led to several occasions when leaving the house was simply out of the question for a few days. The view of the capital city, Sofia, during clear days at most times of the year was much more than impressive, but the price of living in the foothills of the mountain Vitosha was paid during the winter months.

Having had their coats and jackets taken from them by the catering staff, Francis' colleagues from the Embassy soon sunk into the comfortable brown leather sofas in the corner. However, they were quickly to their feet when he walked into the hall and strode toward them.

'I trust you ladies and gentlemen had a none too taxing day at the office?'

'Probably slightly more taxing than your day, Francis,' quipped Winston, a senior diplomat. 'You've been at the snacks already?'

Quickly passing his hand over his mouth, Francis felt the light brush of a treacherous crumb remnant on his index finger which had given him away.

'You are lucky that any are left! As a matter of fact, I had a major furnishing issue today,' grinned the Ambassador. 'Don't ask!'

'Ok, I won't, but I will say cheers to us all for having survived out here for another year.' Winston raised his glass and the sound of crystal gently colliding, reverberated around the room. 'Francis, do you know much about this Wasyl character? I heard that he was only staying here in Sofia for the next couple of days. Are you sure that he will turn up here tonight?'

'He will be here.'

5

The pristine snowflakes had begun to peacefully settle on the cold grounds of the residence. The guests, having all arrived suitably early, were tucked away out of sight within the warm walls of the large, solid stone house. Only Francis' car, parked outside on the large gravel driveway was to be seen. The façade of normality was complete, however, a certain uneasiness plagued Francis. Up until this point, the planning of the evening had centred on the physical aspects of providing and catering for his guests. The rationale behind inviting Wasyl was clear to Francis, and accordingly the reason behind planning this surprise party was equally clear. The uneasiness stemmed from the fact, he thought, that the only person with knowledge of both rationales was himself. He had issues to discuss with Wasyl, but there was almost never a safe moment to have such discussions, particularly given Wasyl's high rank, and his nationality.

A murmur of anticipation echoed around the hall where the guests had congregated. One female member of catering staff continued to meticulously arrange the presents which had been brought by the guests, on a table in the corner. It was difficult to fit all of them on the surface, but she managed to balance them all successfully. The last few guests had arrived, uncomfortably close to being late, however, everyone was now accounted for and as long as no uninvited stragglers turned up, everything would go to plan.

'Ladies and gentlemen, I would just like to say a few words before our distinguished guest arrives this evening. Firstly, I would like to thank you all for arriving on time, that was very helpful,' he said as Melissa's frowns from the back of the room were blocked by the unified chuckles of the guests. She had chastised him about his sarcastic humour before, and he feared she would do it again, once she got him alone. 'Secondly, I would like you all to feel at home and have a great evening. If it carries on snowing as it is, this may well be your home for the next few days. Now, when the time comes I will dim the lights in here and open the door for Wasyl. When I lead him through, my darling wife will do the honours with the lights and the rest, well, you know what to do.' A brief applause preceded a return to the hum of chatter between the guests and the scene was set for the evening. Walking between the crowd and picking up a glass of wine, Francis took a moment to scan through the faces, an array of officials and friends from his time in Bulgaria. Increasingly, as the evening had continued and the Russian and Ukrainian contingent of the party had arrived, he wondered whether he needed to drop a comment in conversation to the Ukrainians as to how he had convinced one of their Secret Service's top officials to pop in that evening.

Taking a larger than average sip of wine and pacing towards the Ukrainians, he hoped that the excuse he had calculated with Wasyl would be accepted, as they were, at the very best of times, like most others in diplomatic professions, extremely suspicious. Walking through the guests, Francis was amazed that everyone had turned up to the event. He had hoped that most would, but he couldn't think of a single person who was missing. Not wanting to become distracted, he focused on how he was going to handle this situation.

As he approached the small group of six officials whom he had invited from the Ukrainian Embassy, he noticed how they stood barely two metres from the Russian guests. After all of the recent political issues between the former Soviet Republic and Russia, the Ukrainians preferred to stick by that which they knew rather than mingle with that which they didn't. Or did they perhaps just want to stay within earshot? This is where Wasyl was different, and that is why he had to ensure that what he was about to say would be believed by the Ukrainians.

'Good evening, friends,' smiled Francis with his hand stretched forward to greet the man who he knew best of all within the group.

'Hello Francis. This is a great party you have prepared here,' said Georgi while shaking Francis' hand. 'The food is fantastic and this wine is just great. You must tell me who is catering for you. I have my wife's birthday soon and she always complains that I don't do enough,' lamented Georgi.

'Sure, no problems, I have put a few of the caterer's cards out on the table just behind you. Please help yourself.'

'So, tell me how you managed to get Wasyl to come all the way up here. For sure you have not told him that it is a party for him, so how? We cannot even convince him to come for a drink with us after work on Fridays.' The thick Ukrainian accent and the laughter behind the words masked the intended meaning. This was a question Francis predicted that he would be asked.

'I knew that he was leaving on Thursday, so I told him that as a parting gift for his hospitality at the conference a week ago, my wife Melissa had bought him a special gift. That part was true, but I don't think he knows anything about the party we have planned,' grinned Francis, hoping that this was a sufficient explanation.

'Ah, very good,' laughed Georgi, 'maybe next time we want him to come out for some vodka we will tell him we have a present for him. Francis, let me introduce you to Stefan, who just started at the Embassy two weeks ago. I was sure you wouldn't mind if I invited him.'

Turning to Stefan, Francis was surprised at how young he looked. Perhaps eighteen or nineteen, but hardly any more. He had blonde hair which was short and combed back, however, he made up for his lack of age with his abundance of style and dress sense. 'Nice to meet you, Stefan. How have you enjoyed your first couple of weeks here?'

'It has been very enjoyable, but I'm still settling in,' Stefan said in a perfect British accent.

'Georgi, didn't you say that Stefan is based at your Embassy? Is he Ukrainian or English?

'I know, I know, it will take us some time to get used to him as well. He is Ukrainian yes, by birth, but when he was five he moved to England with his parents and stayed there until he was thirteen. He then returned to Ukraine after his parents tragically died in a car crash. He could not stay in England as there was nobody for him there,' Georgi explained.

'Yes, after my mother and father died, I left my school and friends to return to the Ukraine to stay with my grandparents in Kiev. I would love to work in London for the Embassy there, but that is difficult,' Stefan said, looking down towards the floor.

'Don't worry. I'm sure it will work out. I am sorry to hear about your parents,' said Francis as the front gate buzzer sounded. Wasyl had arrived and the excitement in the hall was like ionised air after a lightning storm. Once everyone had found a place where they could hide as out-of-sight as possible, Francis dimmed the lights in the hall before activating the gates to open.

'Ok everyone, keep quiet and wait here until Wasyl walks in and I switch on the lights.'

Closing the door behind him, he left all the guests in darkness, as well as his wife. The crunching of gravel under tyres could be heard through the door. The party was just about to begin.

6

Having clicked the hall door closed, Francis' feeling of unease suddenly came to the fore once again. The beam from the headlights as the car approached sprayed reflective patterns which danced spritely on the wallpaper. Perhaps the nervousness of the whole surprise situation was getting to him more than he would have normally expected, but he definitely felt that all was not as it should be. The crunching of the tyres had now ceased and all that remained was the sound of an engine idling outside, and the spray of a bluish neon hue which was emanating from the sidelights. Standing there, in the dimly lit corridor, Francis wondered why it was taking so long for Wasyl to turn off his engine and head towards the house. The door to the hall where all the guests were waiting in darkness, slowly creaked open behind him and he spun round to see who it was.

'Melissa, he is just parking his car. Is there something wrong?' he asked.

'No, nothing is wrong, it's just,' she paused,

'What is it?' he asked.

'Two of our Russian guests are twitching the curtains and taking a look outside. I don't think they like the darkness in here.'

'Raise the dimmer a little bit then, but keep them away from the windows. They can't be seen.'

'OK, I'll try,' she said retreating back behind the closing hall door.

Quickly putting his eye up to the peephole of the door, Francis frantically strained to see whether anyone had stepped out of the stationary vehicle outside, but it was not in the field of view. Pulling the window curtain aside next to the door, he could see the outline of what looked like a black Mercedes Benz parked. The tint of the windows meant he was unable to see who was inside and fortunately neither could the Russians who were probably still observing from the hall. The engine was idling in the background, but the snowfall which was becoming ever heavier, was hindering his view of the vehicle or any chance of catching a glimpse of the occupant.

It seemed an age as Francis stood there waiting for someone to get out of the car, which was standing with the engine and lights on.

A sudden silence and darkness from outside and the opening of the car door, revealed a figure in the falling snow, which by this point had become somewhat incessant, raining down in large, raggedy flakes.

Now approaching the house, the large stocky figure wearing a long dark coat could be heard, as the fresh snow crunched underfoot. The security light flashed on, revealing Wasyl. He seemed quite taken aback by the brightness. Overcoming the initial shock of the light, Wasyl rapped on the door. Allowing a few seconds, Francis turned the lock and allowed Wasyl to enter. Smiling, Francis quipped,

'Hello there, come in. You are totally covered.'

'Thank you, thank you. Unbelievable weather.' A sudden dip in the volume of Wasyl's voice, 'Is everybody here?'

'Yes, everybody. Even your people and the Russians. Are you alright, you seem a bit edgy,' whispered Francis.

'No, it's ok. We need to talk urgently. I don't think I can even speak of it with you here. We are in danger. If my people find out what I have become involved in, I am finished,' he said, quaking where he stood.

'We have to go inside,' whispered Francis, 'We can't stay out here. It won't look good.'

Leading Wasyl down the corridor and towards the hall, he felt his heart pounding against his chest. What could Wasyl have to tell him that could possibly be quite so alarming?

Opening the door to the warm, low glow of the dimmed lights, Francis hesitated a second before stepping through, considering for just that one moment, the possibility that the secret which Wasyl hadn't had the time nor inclination to divulge to him, was already common knowledge to certain guests within the room. There was nothing that could be done now, as they would have seen Wasyl approach the house from his car. For him not to make an appearance would be the final straw. At least, Francis thought, if he and Wasyl were in danger, they might be afforded some immediate protection by the presence of all the other guests.

The light switch was flicked on and a rapturous applause and general cheer rose from the guests.

'Happy birthday, Wasyl!' was the cry in unison. With what Francis had just been told by Wasyl, the occasion for the whole function couldn't have been further from either of their minds. The warm reception received when entering was as if they had jumped into an ice-cold plunge pool when expecting a hot cauldron. The automatic, instinctive response, was an immediate smile on both of their faces.

Wasyl, quite shocked at the number of people who actually turned up for his supposedly surprise birthday party, was greeted by everyone in turn as he walked through the hall full of guests.

'I hope you have plenty of room in your boot for all your presents, Wasyl,' said Melissa, pointing at a table in the corner, covered with gifts of all shapes and sizes.

'What an amazing surprise. Thank you everybody.' The genuine look of shock and bemusement on Wasyl's face, complemented the façade which was in play. Now circling the room full of chattering, increasingly intoxicated and loud guests, Francis and Wasyl ensured that everyone got a moment with the man of the hour. Wasyl needed introduction to a few of the guests with whom he was not acquainted, however, the general atmosphere was collegial.

'I'm just going to pop to the bathroom. I'll be back shortly,' Francis told Wasyl, as he turned. Leaving the hall and climbing the steps towards the upstairs bathroom, Francis was met by Melissa turning the corner to return to the party. Nearly bumping into one another, Francis grabbed her with both arms to avoid one of them falling back down the stairs.

'Oh!' she exclaimed. 'Sorry Francis, I was in a rush to get back down there. Just checking on the children.'

'Is everything alright?' asked Francis, 'you're shaking!'

'Yes, everything is fine. It's just Patrick. I'm not sure whether he is coming down with a cold.'

'Really? He seemed fine earlier. Perhaps it's all that time we let him spend outside this morning. I told him to wear gloves, but he doesn't listen. Do you think we need to call the doctor?' he asked in a concerned tone.

'I've given him a couple of tablets, but if he isn't better by the morning then maybe we should,' she replied.

'Listen,' he said pulling Melissa by the wrist back down the corridor and lowering his voice. 'I don't want you to overreact to what I'm about to say, but I want you to take the children, go out through the back entrance in the kitchen, and drive to the Embassy. I will phone John and let him know that you are on your way.'

'What's going on?' she asked with a look of bewilderment coming over her.

'It's nothing serious. I know it's late, but I want you to go before the snow makes the roads impassable!'

'Ok, if you say it's so important, we will go, but it will take me a few minutes to get some things together,' she discontentedly muttered. 'Who is going to look after the guests?'

'Don't worry about anything, just hurry. Call me when you get there, so I know you've arrived safely.'

Francis realised that he had to get back downstairs soon, in order to avoid drawing unnecessary attention to the fact that he had spent an unnaturally long time answering the call of nature. As he waited at the top of the stairs, he heard the sound of two disgruntled children being made to put some clothes on. Melissa had been very prompt in throwing a few items into a bag and was shooing the children from their bedroom.

'Hey kids,' he whispered, kneeling down. 'You need to go with mummy to where Daddy works. You can sleep there tonight, because tomorrow morning some people will be coming early to decorate your rooms.'

The children, ultimately disinterested and extremely drowsy, nodded their heads and both threw their arms around Francis' neck saying, 'Ok, Dad.'

Picking the children to their feet, Francis leaned forward to kiss his wife, before all four of them crept down the stairs. Catching a glimpse of the bleak weather from the gap in the curtains, Francis waited until he was satisfied that Melissa and the children had had enough time to get into their car and start on their journey to the Embassy. Hearing the sound of the engine receding at the back of the house, he took a deep breath and turned the door handle.

7

Creaking gently, the door opened, releasing a plume of cigarette smoke and noise which were almost instantly intoxicating and calming. The guests stood as trees in an early morning misty forest. Passing between the guests, he heard the tapestry of languages, which made a mesmerising sound. At this moment, finding Wasyl was a task in itself. Now heading towards where he had last seen the Ukrainian party, a knot was fastening in his stomach. Anticipation over nervous fear, that Wasyl would be gone and he would never see him or the Eastern European contingent again. At last, he caught sight of the back of Wasyl's head and the knot was untied slightly, although prying him away from what looked to be a somewhat involved discussion he was conducting with his colleagues was going to be hard.

'Hello everybody, sorry about that. Are you all enjoying yourselves?' he asked, as he was greeted by polite smiles, 'Francis, my friend, show us where you keep your best spirits. I am still cold to the bone from being outside,' complained Wasyl.

'Of course, but we will have to go upstairs to my study. That is where I keep all of my best stuff. How would you gentlemen like to join us upstairs for a short while? Then we will be straight back down here,' invited Francis, hoping desperately that they would decline.

'Thank you for the offer, Mr Ambassador, but we must go now. The weather is bad and it will be dangerous to leave later,' said the young-faced Ukrainian with a firm but unerringly friendly tone.

'Yes, I do hope that the weather does ease up a little bit, or else most of us will be stranded here. Obviously, that would be fine for me, but I hope everybody's designated driver has stayed away from the alcohol,' grinned Francis, stretching out his hand to Georgi, who had already thrown his coat over his broad shoulders. 'It has been a pleasure to have you all here and I hope it will be my pleasure again someday. It is a shame you have to leave so early, but I can fully understand.'

Grasping Francis' hand with bear-like ferocity, Georgi pulled him closer, so that he could be heard clearly amongst the bustling guests and whispered, 'the pleasure has been all ours.'

'I imagine I will be leaving soon, too,' interjected Wasyl.

'You cannot leave all your guests here. This is your celebration, so you must stay,' exclaimed Georgi.

Wasyl nodded as his countrymen turned and started to make headway towards the exit, shaking hands and saying their goodbyes to acquaintances along the way. Unhooking their coats from the clothes stand in the hallway, Francis felt uneasy at the seeming haste with which they wanted to leave. They even appeared to encourage Wasyl to stay. Opening the door, they filed out and turned to face him.

'Do you have far to go?' asked Francis.

'The hardest thing will be the walk to our car,' joked Stefan.

Francis' mobile phone rang out from his trouser pocket and as he brought it out, he remained engaged in frivolous niceties at the door. He saw that he had received a text message from a number which he didn't recognise.

Time to go!

Reading the message, Francis looked up and tried to continue without giving any indication of what he had just read.

'Yes of course. I'm sorry to have made you park next door and walk across, but I'm sure you understand it was worth it for the surprise. Thank you all for coming and I wish you a safe trip. Drive carefully now.'

'We will,' replied Georgi, 'thank you very much and see you soon.' Turning away, Francis retreated into the house and closed the door. Resting his back against it, he stood in the dark hallway and allowed the message he had just received to sink in. The Russians were gone, now the Ukrainians and a message from an unknown number. Nervously walking back towards the hall of guests, he was sure he was paler than the snow outside and he felt twice as cold. Opening the door, Wasyl stood with his back turned towards him refilling his glass of wine. His hands trembling slightly, Francis slowly approached him and once again removed the mobile phone from his pocket. Flicking it onto the message, he stood next to Wasyl and picked up one of the glasses which had been poured already. Without saying anything, Francis passed the phone to Wasyl who looked uncertain as to why he was being given the telephone.

'Did you send this to me?' asked Francis, his voice trembling slightly.

Taking a moment to read through the text, Wasyl passed the phone back to Francis and looked him straight in the eyes.

'No, I didn't send it. We need to speak.'

'Yes, we do. Come with me,' he said, leading Wasyl from the room full of guests. They walked to the end of the hallway and into the library. 'Please do sit down,' said Francis curtly as Wasyl sank into one of the red leather reading chairs.

Closing the door to the library and locking it, Francis regained his composure.

'What is going on?' he asked in a serious and urgent tone. 'What does this message mean and who sent it?'

'I shouldn't be involved in this. If you knew what I know, then you wouldn't want me anywhere near you or your family.'

'Don't worry about my family. They left a long time ago. Tell me about the message. Who sent it to me and what is going on?'

'Do you trust me?' asked Wasyl.

'No,' replied Francis. 'But I will trust you more, once you tell me what is going on. Am I in danger by having you here?'

Rising from the chair, Wasyl walked towards Francis and stood barely a foot away.

'My people are not stupid. They do not, how do you say, have the full picture yet, but they know there is a picture to be seen. You have to trust me and you have to understand that I do not have time to explain to you now what is happening. Is your family really gone from the house?' enquired Wasyl, his English now showing stress fractures and becoming somewhat disjointed.

'Yes, they have gone. My wife keeps her car at the back and they left over half an hour ago. They should call me when they get to the Embassy.'

'Good, we must leave now and we must go in my car,' dictated Wasyl.

'What about all of the guests? And should we not go in my car?'

'No, we must go in mine and we must go now! You will not be sorry for listening to me, Francis. There is somewhere we must go and it could change the course of humanity,' and with that, Wasyl jumped from his seat and opened the study door, leaving it open for Francis to follow. Francis, having turned and faced his collection of books, all neatly gathering dust upon his bookshelves, had not heard the last of Wasyl's words, but rather now found himself in a state of semi-cognition, frozen in momentary panic and uncertainty. Momentary though it may have been, it seemed like an eternity, as his eyes scanned over the spines of the tomes. He found himself recounting when and where he had been when he had read them, floating in a daze of reminiscence, he was aware that he had to go with Wasyl. He also suspected that he was in real danger, but somehow, the familiar surroundings and the warmth of memory which was absorbing him allowed him a brief, but convincing denial of reality. The reality where he had had to send away his wife and children from their own home in the dead of night, to the safety of a government building in a foreign country and where he now faced an uncertain future, danger even, in the company of somebody who, by all appearances, was withholding vital information.

Recoiling from his thoughts for a minute, Francis began to consider the possibility of simply going back into the hall where the guests he had invited were still enjoying themselves and carrying on as if he had not received a text message. How could he trust a text message from an unknown source, when it could be that very source that posed a threat to him? Reaching for the telephone on the desk behind him, he rested his fingers pensively upon the receiver. Should he call the private security station which serviced the ambassadorial estates in Sofia?

8

Wondering how he had ever allowed himself to get dragged into this situation, Francis relinquished the idea of calling anyone. Prizing his fingers away from the receiver one at a time, he picked his coat up from the hook on the wall and followed Wasyl into the corridor. Thankful that the door to the hall was still closed, Francis prayed that they would not be seen leaving. Hurriedly they made their exit through the front door and headed toward Wasyl's Mercedes.

Casting a foreboding glare back towards the house, he was glad to see that the curtains were still closed and hopefully, everyone would be reaching such a stage of intoxication, that they would barely notice his absence. Somewhere beneath his subconscious, he knew that he was lying to himself. When Melissa called, he would have to ask her to arrange someone to come to the house and explain that he had to rush away urgently. He didn't have time to think too much about the politics behind his actions that evening. He didn't much want to either. Approaching the car, Francis scooped handfuls of snow from the passenger side window. On hearing the clunk of the central locking, he wasted no time in clambering into the vehicle.

Closing his door, Francis tried to make as little noise as possible, so as not to alert anyone's attention. Wasyl had finished ridding the windscreen of the excess snow and now took up his position next to Francis.

'Alright, let's go, but don't drive out through the front gate. Go round the back,' whispered Francis. Nodding, Wasyl turned the key in the ignition and the car slowly crunched its way through the fresh powder. The windscreen, still misty with ice and condensation, was quickly clearing as they rounded the side of the building and headed for the rear of the property.

'From the rear of the house, there is a track which leads us out onto another road. When we get halfway down the track, I want you to stop the car. When the car has stopped and you have turned off the lights, I want you to explain everything to me. I want to know what is going on, otherwise, you are alone in this.'

'Alright, ok, but we need to be far from here.'

'We will be, but I need to know what you know,' Francis whispered.

Trundling down the narrow track, which was deadly dark on all sides, the sound of pine needles pattered and tapped on the sides of the car.

'This is far enough Wasyl. Stop the car and cut the lights.'

'I'm not very comfortable with this. We need to be away from here.'

'Why?' asked Francis.

Sitting in almost total darkness, a brief silence fell within the Mercedes. The occasional sound of clumps of snow falling from the overbearing pine trees the only sound audible apart from the heavy, adrenaline fuelled breathing within the car.

'There is no one else I can trust with this, Francis,' whispered a voice from the back seat.

Slowly turning his head in the darkness to look at the source of the voice, Francis was sure that he must be going insane. Hearing a voice he had not heard for the best part of a decade, the voice of a man he knew to be dead, he could only manage to gasp the name,

'Vincent.'

9

Jumping out of the car, Francis, totally petrified, backed away from the stationary vehicle. Catching his heel on a thick fallen branch in the pitch darkness, he stumbled backwards and fell into the brush, where he remained in confusion. The car's sidelights illuminated the area in a gentle glow as the rear door opened and Vincent got out of the car, walking towards where Francis now lay.

'It's been a long time, old friend,' Vincent said, offering his hand to Francis to help him back to his feet.

'Not as long as I thought. I went to your funeral eight years ago. I don't suppose you have ever spoken to somebody who you thought was dead!' Francis replied, pulling himself up with Vincent's help. 'It's damn good to see you though.'

'Let's go. I will explain everything in the car. We need your help.'

Climbing back into the passenger seat, Francis' mind started to unravel the events of the evening, trying to put together pieces of an ever expanding puzzle. At least now he understood why Wasyl had taken so long in getting out of his car when he first arrived for the party that evening. He must have been speaking with Vincent.

'Ok, I need you fellows to tell me what is going on. What are you getting me involved in here?' Francis questioned, as Vincent leaned forward from the back seat.

'It's taken me a while to figure out how I can contact you without risking being found, Francis. This is the best that I could do at such short notice,' Vincent said.

Wasyl started the car once again and moved forward through the pine trees. Obstinately, Francis reached down and pulled the handbrake up in a swift motion, bringing the car to a sliding stop, as it skidded briefly on the snow.

'We aren't going anywhere until someone tells me what is going on,' he blurted. Vincent, still leaning forward, sat back and pulled a cigarette from his pack, realising that he would have to explain the situation.

'A few years ago, a man by the name of Jerome Docherty, an archaeologist in his late fifties, died in Nice. By all accounts, Mr Docherty had spent his later years exploring the Balkan Mountains in search of whatever archaeologists tend to look for. It appears that through the search, this man found the location of an artefact, something which we understand he was not looking for. Something which he named the Pebble. The location of this thing is said to be in a remote and inaccessible location where nobody would have cause to go,' said Vincent as he took drag after drag on his cigarette. Wasyl was also listening intently, almost as though he was hoping to hear something which he had not already heard before.

'So remarkable was this discovery, that this Mr Docherty chose not to speak of it to anybody, for the remainder of his life. Instead, not known to anybody else, he enclosed the location of the Pebble in an envelope which was wax-sealed and left with his solicitor along with his will. Five letters were also left with his solicitor to be dispatched in the event of his death. These letters were addressed to the heads of state of five countries. Namely, the UK, USA, France, Russia and China. I call these "letters", but they were actually invitations to an auction which is due to take place in Sofia tonight,' Vincent continued, his voice unnervingly calm considering the mystique behind what he was saying.

'An auction,' Francis interjected. 'Tonight, in Sofia?'

'My work over the past few years has been … varied, but it required me to be dead, for want of a better word. I'm here because the auction is top secret and so is your attendance on behalf of Her Majesty's Government.' Reaching into his pocket, Vincent handed the invitation envelope to Francis, seal broken, slightly crumpled around the edges.

Francis was shocked by what this ghost from the past was telling him, and Wasyl also seemed to not know what to say. He joked, 'couldn't this have come by post?'

'We have wasted too much time here already and this is time we don't have. We will talk more, but right now, we must get back in the car and get going!' Vincent insisted.

The men sat back in the car. Francis rested his head on the window, breathing out heavily, fogging the window slightly.

'I need to know my family are safe,' said Francis. 'All of the people in the house are going to wonder where we have gone.'

Wasyl stepped heavily upon the accelerator and turned suddenly toward Francis. 'If I were you, my friend, I would not worry about the guests. I would worry about myself.'

'This does seem to make what I wanted to speak with you about this evening seem fairly ordinary,' Francis added.

10

The hour was late as Wasyl's Mercedes quietly crumpled its way over fresh snow and came to a standstill on Vasil Levski Boulevard in front of the Doctor's Gardens. The snow was still coming down in large ragged flakes, being eagerly pushed along by a brisk wind which spattered the windscreen of the car ferociously.

'The Embassy is on the other side of the park, Wasyl,' said Francis.

'I will leave you here and go back to your house. Somebody needs to tell the guests that you have been called away. I'm not sure what I will say, but don't worry about it. It isn't only your Embassy on the other side of the park my friend, but mine also,' Wasyl quipped smiling at Francis.

Vincent leaned forward over their shoulders, turned to Francis and said, 'Fancy a walk?'

Getting out of the car, Francis and Vincent stood on the pavement and watched as Wasyl U-turned and returned from where they had come. The cold gripped hold of them and began to squeeze tightly. Without saying anything, both turned and faced the magnificent park, which was illuminated incandescently by pathway lighting. As the snow fell upon the trees, benches and ground, it flickered and danced as if alive in the light.

Vincent said, 'it's amazing how much more alive you feel in the cold, isn't it?'

'I suppose that means you must feel the most alive, when you are close to death. I feel like I am going to catch my death of cold out here!' Ambassador Sunderland retorted. As both men were now walking, at a slow pace, down the main path which cut a course through the park, the trees overhung and crossed branches like chess players clasping their hands, considering their next move. 'Speaking of death, do you think you will be able to tell me how it is that you are not dead, but standing here enjoying this frightful Slavic weather with me?'

As they walked Vincent Madden fell silent, providing no answer, and shepherded Francis toward the Doctor's Monument, situated proudly in the centre of the park. A tall, pyramid-like structure, constructed of white stone, the monument stood as a timeless tribute to the medical staff of the Russian army who fell during the war. Having led Francis to the monument, Vincent stopped before it and exhaled a heavy breath, which hung in the air like smoke in the quiet, breezeless park. The lighting from the ground ran up the sides of the memorial, highlighting the ferocity with which the snow was now coming down. The silence was deafening, with only the faintest sound of snow falling on the ground audible.

Francis, stared straight ahead at the memorial plate.

'Francis, I need you to really listen to me and understand what I am saying. The forces at work here must not be ignored. The invitation that I handed to you, says that the envelope you will be bidding on this evening will contain information, which will lead to the location of the craft or vehicle which first brought life to this planet. It is that craft which Docherty has called the Pebble.'

Francis wasn't sure what to say. He paused and retorted, 'Human life?'

'Yes. Maybe. I don't know.'

Francis turned and faced away from the monument, gazing through the peaceful park, beginning to piece together what had been said to him.

'That is quite a lot to take in. It's hard for me to understand. Although that may be why it sounds all the more frightening. You say the first life brought to Earth?' the ramifications of what he had just been told were resonating around Francis' head, but confronted with this information, he wanted to hear more about what Vincent was telling him.

'I know that you are a good person. I should have realised when I died, that I would be much lonelier than when I was alive. I have never been a family man, but not visiting my mother in her final years was by far the hardest part of it. I know that you did visit her on many occasions and kept her company. That is something which only a good person would do,' Vincent conceded.

'Vincent, visiting your mother was the least I could do. I took the news of your death so badly. When I heard your voice coming from the back seat earlier, I can honestly say that I had never experienced such shock, fear and happiness at the same time. Really is quite something. I don't recommend it!'

Turning from the monument and facing towards the Embassy, Francis started to walk, but was pulled back by Vincent. 'We aren't going there,' he whispered, 'come with me!'

Still clasping onto Francis' arm, Vincent followed back in the direction from which they had come, the only sound emanated from a distant, passing gritting lorry treating and peppering the wintry street.

A chilling sensation ran through Francis who, after finishing this bitter cocktail of information which had been served up to him, began to tremble. This was a result of the cold temperature and unknown truth which he could not have surmised in his wildest fantasy. This and the knowledge that he was being asked not to go to his family at the Embassy. His father had always taught him that those with whom he kept company in his life would ultimately shape his life. He was now in the company of a dead man and surely, there could be no worse form of company. What Vincent had been explaining ... it was a fantastic story, science fiction in nature.

'Vincent, stop! What you are asking of me, is to walk into an auction and bid for something on behalf of our government. I haven't even looked at the invitation which you gave me. I need to speak with someone to confirm all of this. This is over my head!'

'There is nobody who you can speak with about this. I was chosen to come to you as somebody that you trust, to bring you this information. I will accompany you to the auction. You have the invitation and you will have to decide for yourself if you trust me,' Vincent hesitantly blurted.

'What do you mean decide for myself if I trust you? What is our buy limit for this auction?' asked Francis.

Vincent reached into his pocket and pulled out his wallet, from which he produced a plastic card. Shaking it backwards and forward, he uttered, 'I am sure that this card must have a limit, but I haven't been told what it is. I have been asked to make sure that you keep bidding until you win the auction. The auctioneer will hold the funds in an escrow account until such time as the artefact is located. Once the find is confirmed, the money will go to the family of Mr Docherty. We understand that he has set up a trust fund for his children.'

11

Walking for ten minutes, Francis and Vincent were now moving further and further from the Embassy with every step. The safety and tranquillity which Francis craved more than anything was slowly slipping away. Although Francis had walked down this street many times before, it had never been under these conditions and he felt lost. The snow was falling furiously, which made it difficult to see much more than a few metres ahead. The wind had picked up and was whistling past their faces with ferocity, even picking up fallen snow from the ground and bombarding them with icy particles.

'Pass me your phone,' grunted Vincent, whose words betrayed his state of exhaustion. He seemed to be suffering due to his sleep deprived existence over the past couple of days. Rummaging in his coat pocket, Francis found his mobile and passed it apprehensively over. Unclipping the back, Vincent removed the battery and SIM card and passed them back as three separate items. 'Sorry, but you have to keep it like this. We can't afford to risk being tracked.' Francis was surprised that Vincent had the dexterity in his frozen fingers to perform even such a basic task as taking a mobile phone apart. All he could think about was why he had not picked up his gloves before leaving the house.

There was no road or foot traffic at this time of night, except for the occasional taxi cab, and Vincent was wary of being spotted by the police. Ducking into a side street, they left the main road. The untreated pavement and road surfaces made for treacherous walking conditions and Francis felt sure that if he did not get inside soon, the wind, snow and cold – straight from Siberia – would succeed in freezing him to death.

'How much further?' Francis hollered, trying to out shout the wind.

'Not far now. Not far at all.'

Francis recognised the imposing silhouette of the Sheraton Hotel, which they were now approaching. He had stayed there a few years ago, when he first came to Sofia, but had not been back since.

'If you tell me that we are going for a drink at the Sheraton, I will be very happy!'

Vincent cast a dismissive glance at Francis.

'We will go for a drink once this is all over,' Vincent said.

The snow had stopped, but the wind remained brutal. Francis could feel the skin on his face had tightened from exposure to the freezing temperature. Every facial expression came with an additional twinge of pain.

Wading through the powder, which was now knee deep, Vincent raised his right hand out to the side and stopped walking as Francis gently came to a halt behind the outstretched arm. They stood approximately two hundred metres from the hotel, as two security jeeps came into view and rolled past the front of the entrance gate of the Sheraton. Vincent hoped that they were far enough away for him not to be recognised, but, trapped in the moment, they stood perfectly still.

'Lucky really,' whispered Vincent.

'What is lucky about this?' Francis retorted. 'I will only feel lucky if you don't get me killed.'

'It's lucky that this is as far as we need to go over ground! This auction is secret, so we cannot just dance through the front door of the hotel,' Vincent revealed, as his right arm dropped down to his side and began to rummage in his trouser pocket.

Pulling out a small chain of keys, he brought them up in front of his face, examining what looked like small plastic labels which were stuck to the head of every key. Having seemingly found the key he was looking for, Vincent walked to the entrance of the block of flats they stood before and climbed the two steps to the door. Quickly slipping the key into the lock, he opened it and gestured Francis, who was still staring in a fixated manner at the security vehicles ahead of him, to get into the building.

Nearly slipping on the first step, Francis quickly obliged and entered the block. Vincent ensured the large metal door didn't slam and slowly clicked it shut.

Shaking themselves free of the snow which had amassed on their clothes and compacted around their feet, Francis stood with his back to the wooden pigeonholes, which were hidden in the darkness enveloping them. Stepping forward, Vincent used the backlight of his wristwatch to identify the pigeonhole he needed. Having found number thirty-eight, he peered inside to see if there was anything of interest.

'Checking for post?' questioned Francis. 'Why do you have a key for this particular apartment block Vincent?'

Silently standing with his back to Francis, Vincent muttered words under his breath, inaudibly and incomprehensibly.

Walking to the black metal lattice door, which led to the basement, he used the same key that had brought them through the front door to unlock the basement gate. This gate had clearly not been oiled or maintained in a very long time. The sound of the rusty hinge joints scratching open was not a noise which Francis was accustomed to, in his life of high-quality appliances and living conditions. Flicking the light switch on the cold brick wall past the gate, a dim but welcoming luminescence came from the corridor which ended at the foot of the long, descending stairs.

Walking through the gateway after Vincent and clicking it shut behind him, a thick, musky damp smell began to creep into Francis' nose. Like a strange type of incense, the scent was not unpleasant, but rather soothing. It was certainly freezing in this place, as he walked cautiously down the steps, one by one, but he felt strange warmth. Francis' fingers brushed gently along the brick wall as he descended. Occasional spider webs caught upon his hand. The damp on the bricks had frozen and the drops of water on the webs had transformed into ice, as if they were miniature pearl beads. The stone steps felt sturdy underfoot, but shrouded in darkness, Francis hoped that there would not be a treacherous one, which would cause him to tumble down the stairs.

Having reached the foot of the steps with Vincent, they both stood in the narrow passageway and stared down the corridor at the three low-wattage bulbs that illuminated the passage. The uneven concrete floor was covered with dirt and dust from what must have been years of neglect. Wooden doors, in varying states of disrepair, lined both sides of the passage, each with unique padlocks of various sizes.

'Looks like my university digs,' chuckled Francis. 'What is this place?'

'All these years in this country and you have never been in the basement of one of these buildings?' asked Vincent as he started walking down the passage.

Walking past door after door, Francis strained his eyes to see the various numbers which had been scratched into the wood. Residents had clearly not bothered to invest in nice shiny numbers to screw onto their basement door. Why would they, after all, he thought?

12

It had only taken twenty minutes to transport Vincent and Francis to the park where he had left them. But forty minutes after having assured Francis he would go back and spin an assortment of lies to the guests, he was in trouble. The journey from the mansion had been downhill, which had been tricky, but nothing compared to the journey back. The wheels of Wasyl's Mercedes, whilst armed with hard-wearing winter tyres and chain tracks, were struggling and spinning.

'Four-wheel drive nonsense!' muttered Wasyl as he tried to withstand the temptation to stop the car, get out and kick it. He knew the best thing to do was to slip it into a higher gear and reduce the revs, but this course of action would go against human nature and natural frustration, at being thwarted by snow. Approaching the opening in the pine forest from where they had made their escape, just over an hour ago, Wasyl's thoughts turned to what he would say to all the guests at his birthday party about where Francis and Melissa had disappeared to. As he turned off the main road, the thickness of the fresh snow that had fallen became apparent. The Mercedes was able to cut through about ten metres of the powder, but the gradient of the path and the depth soon overwhelmed Wasyl, and the car would go no further. Trying to slip back out of the entrance, Wasyl realised that he had beached his car and it was now stuck. Attempting to open the door, he had to lean his weight against it in order to make an opening large enough for him to get out.

Turning off the engine and grabbing his gloves from the passenger seat where he had left them, Wasyl slowly manoeuvred his way out of the car and closed the door quietly. Clipping the central locking closed, he began the long walk up the path and back to the house. Each footstep was taking its toll. The snow was above knee deep and Wasyl hadn't had this kind of exercise in quite a long while. Taking stops in order to get his breath back every few minutes, his progress was slow and worse than that, something did not feel right. As he persevered further and further, he realised that he was not seeing any light from the house. Unless the snow had caused power lines to go down, he feared the worst.

Reaching the top of the path he stood with the grand house before him. Standing and listening, he held his breath to see if he could hear anything, a voice, a footstep. Wasyl had not always been Deputy Head of Ukrainian Intelligence; he had become Deputy Head by knowing exactly what to do in these circumstances, but whilst his instincts shouted for him to get as far away from the house as possible, he couldn't resist. As quietly as he could, Wasyl moved towards the rear of the house which was before him, and reached round, underneath his coat and pulled out his gun, with a firm grip and a smooth movement.

Edging carefully towards the back door, he tried to take a glancing look inside, but the darkness meant he could see nothing. Poking his head around the corner of the property and looking at the outside of the front door, where Francis had greeted him so recently, he observed the car park for any signs of activity. Wasyl could not see a single set of recent footsteps and although the snow was still falling, he sensed that whatever had happened here, had happened just after Francis, Vincent and he had left the house. Crouching down, he was thankful for the slight clearing in the clouds, which allowed moonlight to gently illuminate his surroundings.

Moving closer to the front door, his heart sank as he saw that it was ajar a few centimetres. Placing his fingers gently upon the heavy wooden door, he pushed. Slowly it opened and the darkness in the house was blinding. A strange smell hung in the air, which was not unpleasant, but noticeable. His heart was pumping hard in his chest as he moved stealthily toward the hall where all of the guests had been congregated. Wasyl was terrified that his suspicions as to what he would find would be correct.

The hall door was also ajar as he pushed it open. The silence in the house betrayed a faint creak, as the sturdy wooden door swung gently open. The curtains were almost entirely closed and the chinks between them were the only source of light in the room. Thin slivers of moonlight penetrated the majestic hall and outlined a scene of terror on the floor, as Wasyl stood and witnessed a room full of corpses scattering the fine carpet. Stumbling back a couple of steps, he was shocked at the sight and a feeling of revulsion washed over him, causing him to shudder from his head, to his freezing feet. Moving forward once again, stepping further into the hall, he looked to the light switch and tried to flick it on, but to no effect as he was certain the power to the property had been cut. Kneeling down and turning over the body of the nearest victim, he removed his gloves and put them to one side. Running his hands up and down the body of the lady laying before him, he felt no injuries which would suggest that she had been killed by a bullet, or any other kind of wound. After further inspection, he had found no evidence of trauma or injury to the victim and got to his feet, standing silently.

He had seen photos of scenes such as the one before him previously, however, he had never had the bad fortune to stand in the midst of such a scene. The toxic gas, which had been released into the house, had been fast acting and fatal. Fortunately for Wasyl, such gas remains toxic for a very short period of time after the flow is discontinued and as such, he could rest assured that his fate would not be the same as the poor people who had simply come for an evening of enjoyment and to celebrate with him. Whoever had done this would surely have hoped or expected that the three of them would be in the property to suffer the same fate, but only the relatively innocent had paid the price. Stepping carefully over the bodies of people who had been toasting his birthday only hours before, he opened the curtains. The moonlight filled the room, as he looked out onto the car park in front of the house.

Turning his back on the window, he could now see in even more detail the extent of the carnage, as people had evidently not even had the chance to start to move towards the exit, before they had fallen into unconsciousness before death. The people who had done this, had been specific in intent. This was not the kind of substance readily available to just anybody. At least he wouldn't have to make apologies to anybody now, Wasyl considered as he moved towards the exit. He was ashamed that the thought had even crossed his mind. Closing the door to the hall behind him, he felt the freezing wind blowing in through the front door. Pulling his mobile phone from his coat pocket, he looked at the screen. Turning on the phone, he waited the appropriate few seconds for it to boot before dialling Vincent's number, hoping desperately that he hadn't turned off his mobile, but of course, he had. Wasyl turned his phone back off and returned it to its resting place in his pocket.

A creak from the top of the stairs caused Wasyl to turn his head violently, to search for the source. Still grasping his sidearm in his right hand, he pointed it into the darkness as he heard a faint wheezing.

'Who is there!' he shouted. 'I have a gun! Tell me who you are, or I will shoot!'

The faint wheezing continued as he could see shadowy movement in the darkness from the summit of the staircase.

'Help me, please,' a female whisper from the top of the stairs pleaded, followed by several coughs.

'What is your name?' shouted Wasyl, with his weapon still trained on the shrouded woman.

'It's me, Melissa. Please Wasyl, help me!'

Immediately lowering his gun, Wasyl strode up the stairs two at a time and crouched down next to Ambassador Sunderland's wife.

'What are you doing here? Francis told me that you left. That you went back to the Embassy to be safe with the children. Where are they?' he questioned.

'They're safe,' she spluttered, 'I drove back here as soon as I left them at the Embassy. I didn't want to leave Francis alone. Why is it dark? Where is everybody?'

'I am sorry Melissa, they are all dead. Your house has been attacked and you may have been partially exposed to the gas, which I think killed all of the guests.'

'Francis? What about Francis?' she blurted.

'He is fine. He wasn't here when it happened,' Wasyl responded reassuringly.

'I don't know. I don't remember. The last thing I remember is leaving the Embassy to come back here. I must have gone upstairs to look for Francis when it happened.' Melissa's breathing had become heavier and faster since hearing the news of the guests. Picking her up from the floor, Wasyl carried her with her arm over his shoulder, down the stairs and out of the front door. She was barely able to walk, resting heavily on his support.

Once outside, and sitting on the step in front of the door, Wasyl could see that she was extremely pale. Still wearing her boots and outdoor clothes, she sat hugging her knees in the foetal position. Strands of her long blonde hair were covering her face, as she sat shivering in the cold. Looking straight ahead, she wasn't paying attention to Wasyl, but instead her eyes seemed to dart from object to object in the distance.

'You are very lucky to be alive. Perhaps the gas was not of high enough concentration upstairs.' He said as she shivered and shook.

'Lucky?' she exclaimed inquisitively, looking up at Wasyl.

13

Fumbling with the padlock on the worn-looking basement door at the very end of the dank corridor, Vincent stood with Francis, jingling his keys, trying to find the right one. In the poor light, he took a few seconds longer than ordinarily he would have, but, letting out a triumphant, 'Aha!' he quickly slipped it into the rusty-looking padlock and gave it a twist.

He ushered Francis into the confined basement room. Turning to lock the door from the inside, both men stood in total darkness. Francis could hear Vincent running his hand along the wall, searching for the elusive light switch.

He sensed that the room he was standing in wasn't large, but as the solitary lightbulb hanging from the low concrete ceiling was lit, the room measuring barely two metres by four metres came into view. This was clearly not used as a store room of any sort or description. The only area of storage was to be found in the corner, where a metal locker stood. Two wooden benches lined the two longer sides of the room and an old, worn carpet was underfoot. The concrete walls were bare, except for three metal coat hooks on the right hand wall.

'It's a good thing that you don't have anything stored in here. There wouldn't be any room for us!' Francis jested.

Walking purposefully over to the bench on the left hand side of the room, Vincent sat down and turned on a small floor heater, which had been resting against the side of the bench.

'It's bloody freezing! Well, don't take your shoes off, but do take a seat,' said Vincent as he bent down and tested the heater.

'Wow, I hope my fingers don't fall off when they thaw out.'

Francis sat opposite to Vincent and clasped his hands before him, resting his elbows on his knees. Sitting with a pensive look, he suddenly realised how cold he was from the long period of exposure to the elements, both in the park and during the walk to the place where they now sat. Opening and closing his mouth, Francis felt a numb tingling sensation in his jaw, which caused him to open and close his mouth even more vehemently. He unzipped his jacket to allow some of the heat which was now emanating from the floor heater to warm his body.

'I need to check on Melissa. She has probably tried to call my mobile, but can't get through because you took it to bits,' said Francis, 'I need to know that she made it to the Embassy with the children.'

'There isn't anything you can do for her now. I'm sure that she has made it.'

'And if not?' asked Francis.

'Just don't think about that now. Please try to understand that if you turn on that phone you are putting both of us in danger. Oh, and secondly, you won't get a signal down here,' Vincent joked as both men sat across from one another. Francis' face turned to a frown as he struggled to see the humorous side. Having sat for a few minutes, the temperature in the basement room began to creep up slightly.

'I take it there is a reason we are down here, Vincent,' Francis enquired with an uneasy and unnerved tone. The thought that his wife and children may not be safe had begun to play on his mind.

'The Russians who turned up for Wasyl's party this evening. Did you recognise them?' asked Vincent.

'Well, I think that they were a party of about three or four and I did recognise them, but we spent most of our evening with Wasyl's colleagues,' Francis responded.

'Because we can expect interest in the Pebble from parties representing the countries that I mentioned. I am equally unprepared for all of this, Francis.'

Looking toward the metal locker as it stood against the back wall of the basement room, Vincent got to his feet and walked over. Opening it, he revealed two suits hanging in garment bags. Vincent unhooked the suit hanging on the right and walked over to Francis, presenting it to him gingerly.

'Are we expecting company? If so, you should really have spruced this place up,' Francis said with a wry tone, as he passed his fingers through his grey hair, which was now drying slightly in the pleasant, arid smelling heat being blasted from the floor heater. Finally feeling warm enough to move once again, he got up and took the suit which was being handed to him.

'You and I are going to the Sheraton, so we are going to have to look presentable,' said Vincent as he began to change from his clothes into the suit which remained in the locker. 'If you don't want to wear the fresh one, you don't have to. That is quite a nice one you have on from your party,' Vincent observed.

'The speed at which you ducked us into this building when you saw the security vehicle in front of the hotel doesn't inspire much confidence in me,' Francis said, feeling that the night could not turn any more surreal than it had already become. He was sure that at any moment he would wake up and all of this would have been a twisted dream. Some snow which had become attached to his suit trousers had now melted and was giving him a cold reminder that this was not a dream and that he would have to face what was ahead. Starting to get undressed, his mind wandered back to Vincent's words in the park. What Vincent was saying was not within the realms of impossibility, but it was nevertheless unfathomable. Throwing his coat back over his shoulders, he shuddered at the thought of going back outside.

'Ok, so let's go. The first chance I get, I want to call the Embassy to check on my wife and children,' insisted Francis.

'You aren't going to need your coat,' smiled Vincent.

'I may have gone along with everything else you have said this evening, but if you think that I'm catching my death out there, you have another one coming, my friend,' retorted Francis.

Walking over to the back left corner of the basement room, Vincent kneeled down and peeled the corner of the carpet away. He continued to pull and walk backwards, until he had uncovered what looked like a round metal utility cover in the concrete floor. Francis stood deadly still as his mouth opened slightly in shock. Vincent once again took out his keys and slid the appropriate one into the keyhole built into the metal hatch. Having turned the key, he twisted the release mechanism and the trapdoor gave out a double click as it released.

'One of these hatches can be found in the basement of most of the buildings in the centre of the city. Some have been concreted over, if there is nobody living in the building that might need one,' explained Vincent as he strained slightly to pull up the heavy round metal door. 'But the funny thing is that most people these days don't even realise where they lead. I suppose some assume it is just a meaningless hatch leading to a sewer or something.'

'As we are dressed in these fine suits and you are already starting to climb down, I'm thinking that most people are wrong?' Francis had begun to feel that he was well past the point of asking questions and with a solemn sense that this day had far surpassed the most surreal experiences he had ever had in life; he too began to climb down the metal stepladder which hung on the wall of the round hole in the ground.

14

Melissa had sat for nearly ten minutes on the step to the house, which now entombed all of the guests. Regardless of the winter coat and clothes she still wore from when she returned to the mansion, Melissa sat shivering in the cold. Wasyl could see on his return from sweeping around the property to check for any hidden dangers, that she was not handling the situation well and was probably lapsing into shock. To Wasyl's mind, the gas, which he was now sure had been used to kill those in the property, was having clear adverse effects on her. Sitting anxious and restless on the step, she seemed to have regressed into a state of transfixed panic.

Wasyl understood from the sweat he could see on her brow, that she was in urgent need of medical attention. He couldn't say what kind of damage the gas may have done to her, but he knew that sitting in the freezing cold was not an option and taking her back into the house was even less of an option. Picking Melissa up from the doorstep, he closed the front door behind her with a slight thud, to which she turned startled and stared wide-eyed and petrified into his eyes.

'Where is Francis?' she whispered. 'Why have you brought all of this upon us? What have you done to him?'

Grabbing Melissa by the shoulders, Wasyl held her firmly at arm's length and said,

'Melissa, I would never do anything to hurt you or your family. Whoever is responsible for this, they will pay. Francis is alive, he wasn't in there when all of this happened.' One of the beads of sweat on Melissa's forehead began to roll down. He could sense that she was not steady on her feet and really did need to see a doctor. She started to sob and Wasyl tried to comfort her, but understood completely that he would not be able to. All of the people who had turned up for what was supposed to be an innocent and joyous occasion this evening, now lay dead in her house, and he could give no explanation. Wrapping her arm around his shoulders, they started to walk down towards where Wasyl had abandoned his car in the snow. He had had enough trouble making his own way up there, but now with the added extra weight of Melissa, his thighs felt weary. The adrenaline, still pumping through his veins from his morbid discovery, powered him on as they ploughed through the snow together.

Having reached the vehicle, Wasyl was carrying most of Melissa's weight. Her head hung down and she appeared to be lapsing in and out of consciousness. Shuffling round to the passenger side, he unlocked the door and dragged it open with one hand. Having opened the door just far enough for her to be able to squeeze in, he sat her down inside the car, lifting her legs into the foot well.

Traipsing to the driver side, he got in and quickly turned the key in the ignition to start circulating some warm air around the cabin. The lights on the dashboard of Wasyl's Mercedes immediately illuminated. A simple-looking readout for such a distinguished vehicle. The dials, a monotone blue crystal shade denoting speed, revs, water temperature, petrol and oil. Sitting quietly for a moment, Wasyl contemplated how he would get the car out of the drift he had landed it in. Slipping the car into reverse, he began to gently apply his foot to the gas pedal. Releasing the pedal he rocked the car backward and forward, gathering momentum until finally it was free. Wasyl carefully reversed his car out onto the firmer, packed snow on the road and glimpsed from the corner of his eye a glowing symbol on his dashboard. Within the speed dial, a glowing orange light subtly warned Wasyl that an unknown signal was emanating from within the car. Patting his coat pocket, he remembered that he had turned off his mobile and that Melissa's phone was probably still switched on. The light hadn't been glowing on his way back to the house, which left only one option.

'Melissa, your mobile, give it to me,' said Wasyl, but no response was forthcoming from Melissa, who had slouched over, her head resting upon the passenger side window. The heater had already started blowing warm air around the car and he hoped that once she was warmer her condition would improve.

As he reached into her coat pocket, he took her mobile phone, checked for anything from Francis, and on seeing a blank screen, turned it off and placed it gently back into her pocket.

Checking back to his dashboard, he noticed that the larger glowing orange light had shrunk to its usual green colour.

Although he hoped that he would be able to walk out of the situation with the same consummate ease with which he walked into it, he couldn't help but feel that whoever had carried out this dastardly operation – killing so many people – would still be watching. Would they not have checked to see whether their marks had been killed? Would they not have realised that they had missed their desired targets? Would they not now try to follow Wasyl and Melissa? Perhaps this was why he had met no interference. Perhaps this was why they left Melissa alive when they found her during their sweep of the property.

Hitting the gas, Wasyl spun his wheels slightly as his mind puzzled as to what he should do.

15

'How long is this stepladder?' asked Francis as he followed Vincent down the proverbial rabbit hole in near pitch darkness. He wasn't quite sure where the faint illumination was coming from, but was clear that he had made the right decision coming down the vertical passage second, even though he had only narrowly avoided being knocked unconscious by the heavy metal hatch as he closed it on the way down.

'Just keep climbing and hold tight. If you fall, we both fall, a long way. And try not to get your suit dirty,' Vincent said as he continued his descent.

The concentration required to ensure a firm grip of the smooth rungs in the near darkness was taking its toll, and Francis was delighted as the lighting began to increase and he could see with confidence that the steps onto which he clung desperately were made of a clean polished alloy and looked immaculately maintained and secure. This was in stark contrast to the basement from which they had started their descent. He could also surmise that he was now the only one still descending and that Vincent had reached the bottom. There was now enough light to see that the walls of the passage were also impeccably clean, and pivoting his head, he saw that the diameter of the hole had gradually been increasing during his trip down the shaft.

Glancing down, he finally rested his right foot on a fine, soft, but unmistakably out of place carpet. Through the thin-soled fine leather shoes he wore, the softness told of the quality. Taking a second to look around, he noticed Vincent standing to one side, but his gaze and full attention were caught by the beauty of the Hereke silk carpet on which he now stood. Fitted perfectly to the size of the room, he was unsure as to why it had taken him aback so. He could only imagine that it was either because it was in this most unexpected of places, or because it was such a thing of beauty.

Finally, able to remove his gaze from the intricate green and gold designs on the carpet, he was able to pay closer attention to the other objects in the room. Exquisite wooden furnishings adorned the edges, including a most comfortable looking divan and a small table upon which a crystal lamp stood proud. The lamp, being the only source of light, sprayed effervescent shards of illumination upon the walls through dangling crystal pieces.

Vincent could stand the look of confusion and bewilderment on Francis' face no longer.

'This is a deep level bomb shelter. It was designed and tunnelled after the First World War. During the Second World War, it was modified to act as a nuclear bunker,' he said. 'In fact, the maze of tunnels down here is fantastic. I got quite lost once,' he quipped.

'That is all well and good,' stated Francis, 'but what are we doing down here and why is a bomb shelter decorated like this?'

'We are going to where an auction takes place whenever the need arises, under the Sheraton,' Vincent said as he opened the door and stepped out into the dim corridor. As Francis followed him, closing the door behind himself, Vincent continued his explanation. 'The whole network of corridors and rooms were refurbished after the war to accommodate important people if times of emergency ever arose. Until such times, the facilities are also used for other purposes, by important people.'

Francis had heard everything which Vincent had explained, but whilst appearing outwardly calm and collected, he was gradually beginning to recoil within himself in reaction to what was happening.

As the pair walked, footsteps reverberating down the long corridor, which curved off into the distance, Francis muttered, 'Under the Sheraton?'

'Yes, under the hotel. Don't worry, these affairs are usually quite subdued, or so I have heard.'

Momentarily not understanding the meaning of Vincent's words, Francis asked, 'Why does it smell like a pine forest down here? And what do you mean, "so you have heard?"'

'Well, to answer your first question, these pipes above your head are carrying air which is being pumped from a pine forest outside of Sofia. Nothing but the best air for the Sheraton!' joked Vincent, walking on.

16

Thirty miles per hour in these conditions was reckless. Wasyl knew this, but the adrenaline coursing through his veins and the half-conscious woman in his passenger seat were stimuli enough to keep him going. Having witnessed the scene at the house, the sick feeling in the pit of his stomach would not dissipate. He had not been in the field for some years now, but he could not think of the last time he had witnessed something which gave him such a chill, or such a rush of terrified excitement.

Gently resting his hand on Melissa's, he felt warmth returning to her and from the swell of her breast he saw that she was breathing freely. He was still concerned as to the effects or damage which may have been caused by the gas. Squeezing her hand slightly as it rested on her thigh, he hoped that human contact would be comforting to her. She mumbled some incoherent words as her head tilted backwards from its slumped state. Her hair, which had been hiding her face, now flopped back, revealing her half-closed, exhausted looking eyes.

The long winding road on which Wasyl was driving was the very same which he had used to take Vincent and Francis into Sofia. There were few cars on the road then, but there were even fewer now. He had not seen a single other vehicle since leaving the house. Hardly surprising considering the state of the weather.

Ploughing down the hill at speed, Wasyl felt the lightness of the steering wheel, the unresponsiveness of the brakes and accelerator, whilst sweeping around a long bend in the road. The camber was the only thing keeping him from being flung into the evergreen trees, towering high on either side.

Total darkness surrounded them, the road unlit and secluded. The high beams of the Mercedes shone far ahead, as snow was shovelled in plumes from under the tyres.

In the distance he could see the beginnings of a small village he had passed through on several occasions that night. Slowing his speed, he could see a donkey-drawn plough struggling to keep the village streets passable for the morning. Admirable work, he thought as he passed by.

The street opened up into the village square. Poorly lit and sleepy, the picturesque square was decorated by a relatively large church, which stood ominously in the darkness.

He had been distracted; he had been looking out of his driver side window. He hadn't noticed a police car ahead at the opposite side of the square. A white car with a blue striping would have been difficult to spot in the snow regardless, but he was still frustrated. He wondered immediately why there would be a checkpoint so close to the house he had just recovered Melissa from; the house which now entombed an unthinkable number of people. Soon this area would no doubt be awash with police and the urgency to leave felt tangible.

Approaching slowly, he saw the driver side door of the car open, illuminating two officers inside. Wasyl could see that the other officer was also getting out of the car from the passenger side.

Being beckoned to stop with a red paddle, Wasyl slowly halted the car about fifteen metres away from the officers. Realising that his headlights must be blinding them, he turned his sidelights on.

'What do they want? You should tell them about what happened. Where are we?' muttered Melissa. Wasyl looked over to her and felt overjoyed to hear her speak. She hadn't spoken since he carried her towards his car at the house, but she seemed to be slurring her words and didn't sound well. It was clear that although they had only just left the house, she was under the impression that they had travelled far, which indicated disorientation.

'Don't worry about them. Just close your eyes and rest,' he said.

Looking straight ahead once again, he saw the officers approach and one beckoned him to lower his window as the other hung back slightly looking down towards his number plate. His finger hovered hesitantly over the electric window button, but decisively pressed down once the officer tapped on the window with his gloved knuckles. The cold air rushed into the car eagerly, along with the condensed breath of the officer who quickly barked in Bulgarian, 'Turn the car off.'

'Perhaps you didn't see my number plate as you walked over here, but I suggest you take another look.' Wasyl said slowly and composedly, speaking in the best Bulgarian he had managed to glean in his years in the country.

The officer paused momentarily, returning Wasyl's intense glare before standing straight from his leaning position and walking back toward his colleague. His back was turned to Wasyl so it was impossible to see what they may have been saying, but no doubt by this point, his colleague had pointed out that the Mercedes which sat before them carried C-prefixed red number plates denoting Wasyl's diplomatic status, meaning there was less than nothing that they could officially do to him. Wasyl considered raising his window and stepping on the accelerator, but his sensible side slammed the brakes on that idea. However, he was troubled by the situation in which they found themselves. He hadn't seen a single car since setting off with Melissa, and for good reason. The weather had been diabolical and it was only thanks to his car's four-wheel drive, and the heavy duty chain tracks which he had put on his back tyres to further help with grip, that they were able to make any progress in the snow. Taking all of this into account he couldn't fathom what these officers were doing here in these conditions, but he was sure that they couldn't be catching many speeders with their radar gun! He was barely able to drive at fifteen miles per hour.

The same officer came back over towards the car and leaned over as before in order to see Wasyl. Craning his neck slightly, he looked around inside the car and seeing the lady next to him with her head resting against the window, he simply looked at Wasyl and winked, whispering, 'You have a nice evening. Sorry for the misunderstanding.'

Wasyl had not broken eye contact with the officer, trying to gauge his intent. After a pause, which seemed to last forever, he simply said 'Merci,' and raised the window until it was closed. The officer stood from his leaning position, but did not walk away; the other officer also stood rooted to his spot ahead of Wasyl's Mercedes. Both stood nonchalantly in the freezing cold as if waiting for him to move off. Not wanting to disappoint them, Wasyl pulled away very gingerly. As he drove past the second officer, he tried desperately to see his face. The light was so poor that all he could see was a shadow under the hat that he was wearing and the glint of the firearm at his side caught his attention. He hoped that his paranoia had been baseless. Although the officer who had been poking his head around inside the car seemed familiar, not being able to place where he knew him from, Wasyl did all that he could do and that was to drive away.

Approaching the BMW patrol car, he couldn't help but notice that no snow had settled on the vehicle and the engine was running. Looking up into his rear-view mirror, the two unmoved, darkened figures began to fade from his view.

As the ploughed street turned once again into thicker snow, he left the dim lights of the sleepy village behind, but the sick, sinister feeling in the pit of his stomach telling him that something was wrong surely could not be more right.

'I need to stop, please stop for a minute, Wasyl,' pleaded Melissa. Wasyl obliged and gently took his foot off of the accelerator. The car ground to a halt and Melissa fumbled to find the seatbelt button. Freeing herself, she opened the door and stumbled out into the snow. Falling on her hands and knees at the side of the road, Wasyl could hear her being sick. He felt sick too, but not for the same reasons. Getting out of the car, he walked over and helped Melissa to her feet and returned her carefully to the passenger seat of the vehicle. Being on his feet suddenly brought on a call of nature and so he briskly stomped towards the trees on the other side of the road, leaving Melissa to compose herself.

Seeing Wasyl walking away, Melissa crawled carefully towards the rear of the car and stood as though resting. Reaching into her trouser pocket, she pulled out a glass container from within which she removed the metal lid and slid out a small capsule. The car key was in the ignition, so opening the fuel cap was easy. She dropped the capsule into the tank and heard a faint rattle as it found its way into the petrol. Soon the capsule would dissolve and the concentrated radioactive isotope, scandium 46, would be released into the car's tank. Closing the fuel cap and dropping the glass container to the ground, Melissa made her way back to her seat.

Returning several minutes later, Wasyl climbed back into the car, where Melissa had strapped herself in and closed her door.

'I am trying to get you to the city quickly. You really need to see a doctor who can help you,' said Wasyl gently. Melissa began sobbing.

'Francis and me came here a couple of years ago you know. This is the best posting he has ever had. Our children are happy and it's a beautiful country. We sat by a river on our first weekend here, as the afternoon became the evening and we watched the stars as Patrick and George explored. That is one of the best memories I have and it has been playing over and over again in my head since what happened tonight,' her throat tightened as her emotions began to build, 'I don't think I am ever going to be able to experience happiness like that again. I don't even know if I am going to see Francis again. Doctor you say? I don't need a doctor; I need my husband.'

Melissa had turned towards Wasyl and was looking at him straight in the eyes with the kind of conviction he knew he shouldn't antagonise. Very relieved that she seemed to have recovered somewhat from the effects of the gas, he started to drive once again. As the car rolled forward, a faint crack was heard from the rear of the car, as a small glass container imploded under the weight of the car. Melissa winced internally, but did not allow any expression to spread onto her face. The concentrated scandium 46 solution which she had slipped into the fuel tank would soon pass through and start marking their path. Turning to Wasyl, she was relieved that her mistake in dropping the vesicle in front of the rear tyre had not registered with him, when the car had run it over. Instead, he turned to her and said, 'Francis is with a friend at the moment, and I'm not sure where it is that they have gone. I will take you to where I'm supposed to meet them.'

17

The dimly lit corridor was coming to an end and Francis could vaguely make out the shapes of two men standing in front of a door. As they approached, the men asked to see the invitation and just for one moment, Francis forgot that one had been handed to him earlier and looked confusedly at Vincent. On seeing Vincent's equally puzzled look, he reached into his jacket pocket and handed the invitation on to one of the men.

The man inspected the card and handed it back to Francis who returned it to his pocket.

The security guards opened the door and both Francis and Vincent entered.

'Vincent, do you know that I didn't even look at the invitation before just showing it to those men. I presume that I was allowed to bring a guest,' Francis joked as they approached what appeared to be an extremely impressive bar set within a large room, with exposed brick walls and gentle lighting emanating upwards from the floor. The auctioneer's podium was at the front of the room, with a large screen behind it.

'Wasyl must be having quite a time trying to explain to all of our guests where Melissa and I have disappeared to.'

Having gone through security, Vincent had explained that they would have to wait for about half an hour before being invited in.

The bar top was varnished oak, the likes of which would make one extremely hesitant to lay a fingerprint, let alone a glass. Francis proceeded to flick through the catalogue that they had picked up just past security. All of the items, which would be available to the highest bidder, were neatly contained within the several pages.

The barmaid slipped two square wooden coasters down on the bar, before placing their drinks down upon them. She wore a nice blue suit with a white shirt, unbuttoned to the second button revealing a small gold cross which she wore around her neck. Francis' attention was drawn away from the barmaid's apparel, to the selection of alcohol at her disposal. He had never seen anything quite like it.

The spirits hung suspended on the wall behind her in uniform crystal bottles. The spirit brand was cut into the crystal, but it was difficult to see the detail from a distance. Francis was certain that the intricacy must have been amazing. Diverting his attention away from this, he looked down at his drink, which had been served to him in a thick crystal glass. Small beads of condensation had slowly formed on the outside of the glass and were slaloming their way down the cut crystal. Vincent's glass was smaller and only a little larger than a shot glass. Francis had told Vincent what he wanted to drink, a lime club soda, before going to the bathroom and so was not sure what it was that Vincent had ordered for himself. It looked like vodka and it was certainly a clear spirit.

Picking up his own glass, he looked inquisitively at Vincent and asked 'what have you got there?'

'Rakia,' answered Vincent, 'Never had it before coming to this country. Do you like it?'

'I think I did hear someone mention it, but no, I never have tried it,' said Francis raising his eyebrow. 'If I had known we were having a proper drink, I wouldn't have ordered this,' he said, looking down disdainfully at his club soda.

'It's not a problem,' said Vincent turning to the barmaid who stood attentively behind the bar. He asked for one more rakia and turned back to Francis. 'It's a brandy. Distilled plums. Being as it was so cold outside and I don't think that I have totally thawed out, I thought that I would get something to warm me up a little. Plus, I do like a little Dutch courage.'

Looking towards the barmaid, her back turned to him, Francis could hear the rakia being poured into a small crystal glass akin to the one which sat before Vincent.

Staring with profound curiosity at the drink which now sat before him, he stood and beckoned Vincent to follow him to a more secluded table away from the bar. Whilst their backs had been turned, more people had arrived and were now sitting scattered about the room.

Taking his seat first, Francis scooted around the bay seat which was set into the wall. Vincent moved his chair slightly to one side so that they were not face-to-face and so that they could both have a view of the other guests.

'Under normal circumstances I would find this place to be otherworldly Vincent, but since hearing what you told me earlier this evening, I have been thinking,' said Francis. 'If this artefact is located somewhere here, in Bulgaria, don't you think that the Bulgarian Government will mind that it is being sold to the highest bidder tonight?'

'They might mind,' whispered Vincent, 'if they knew that this auction was taking place. We probably shouldn't talk much about it here.'

Picking up his lime soda, Francis raised his glass to his lips, only noticing at the last second that his hand was shaking slightly. The situation was clearly affecting him, but quickly scanning the bar, he was relieved beyond words that there were no familiar faces looking back at him. Francis felt that he would like to be invisible at this point, or better still, back at home with his wife, children and friends. Putting his glass down, he tilted his head whilst looking towards Vincent and raised his eyebrows in expectation. Vincent raised one eyebrow and a smile crept over one side of his mouth. He opened his mouth slightly as he drew breath and paused.

'We have time, but first I want you to raise your glass,' Vincent said as he picked up his chalice of rakia, with Francis following suit. Putting it forward, Vincent and Francis touched their drinks together before Vincent quickly raised his glass to his lips and downed it in one. Francis did the same and quickly realised the potency of the spirit. His face turned a gentle shade of red as he winced with his right eye, which he felt was tearing up slightly. Vincent sat with a content smile as he looked at Francis, who quickly recovered.

'That was very nice, I can't believe I haven't had any of that before,'

Vincent paused momentarily and leaned back in his chair. With a quick glance over his shoulder to check whether there was anybody within earshot, he leaned forward once again, placing both elbows on the table and crossing his arms.

'I've been looking around the room and can't tell for sure whether the representatives of the four other countries invited to bid for this item have arrived. The thing about this place is that there is no telephone bidding, no online bidding. If you aren't here, then you are out.' Picking up his rakia glass, Vincent waved it at the barmaid who returned a smile and Vincent hoped, quite soon, would bring him another drink. Turning back to Francis, he continued, 'Of course what you are probably thinking to yourself is "how can we possibly trust that this Pebble is genuine?" It sounds like the fantasy of a delusional man. Possibly a final stab at the establishment which hadn't taken him seriously?' Vincent stopped talking as he saw the barmaid approaching. She quickly put his second rakia before him and returned to the bar. Vincent, with a glint in his eye, quickly drank his second shot of rakia in a matter of seconds.

'Steady on there, chap, that stuff is quite strong. I can still feel it burning in my throat,' smiled Francis as he sat up on his cushioned sofa seat to take another quick look around the bar. The room was slowly filling with people who seemingly were quite at home in this underground labyrinth and who had also come along to the Sheraton basement for an auction.

'At least we know that if this does turn out to be a hoax and we pay a whole lot of money, that it will be recoverable,' said Vincent with a hint of trepidation in his voice. 'The document which we are here to bid for should be listed as item two within the catalogue, but I haven't had a chance to take a look,' said Vincent as he placed his finger purposefully on the pamphlet, which lay before him. Francis immediately opened the catalogue and started looking through the items. He quickly glanced at the tapestry that was up for sale as item one. He could only guess why the vendor needed to select this particularly grey establishment for auctioning their item, but that was clearly none of his concern this evening. He came upon item two, where only a photograph of the sealed envelope was shown and a brief, nondescript note underneath, from which nobody would be able to understand much of anything. 'I presume that anybody who has not read one of the five letters which were sent to the UK, USA, France, China and Russia will have very little clue about what is being bid for here?' puzzled Francis.

'Exactly!' uttered Vincent with an air of excitement about his voice. 'It's all very exciting. I'm excited!'

'Do you know what time we will be getting started?' asked Francis.

'Quite soon I think,' stammered Vincent, 'but I can't be certain, because I have never been to this place before so anything could happen.'

18

The moon was full, the stars brilliant and the surroundings pitch black. Melissa appeared to be asleep and had been for some time. Quite an advantage, Wasyl thought, as she may have not taken kindly to him driving without headlights. He had been silent running for the past twenty miles, in order to avoid drawing too much attention from a distance. He had hoped to spot – and avoid – any further police encounters, or anything else. He hadn't driven without headlights in many years, and had never driven without them in conditions such as these. No streetlights on the road and deliberately avoiding the busier roads, he knew he had to reach his destination without being followed or stopped. Having escaped the city, his GPS showed him that he was not far away.

With a big smile on his face, he sat in the apparent safe darkness of the Mercedes driver seat grinning. The head-up display screen within his dashboard console showed with almost daylight quality the layout of the road ahead, the detail accentuated by the snow which reflected the beams of moonlight well. Temporarily reminiscing about the past, he remembered several occasions where he had nearly killed himself by silent running. Dangerous times, but he had survived. No technological aids to help, just simple blind instinct guiding him on the basis of guesswork and strained eyeballs.

His car's paint was matt black, rendering it very hard to distinguish from the shrouded darkness by oncoming traffic. Not that there had been much in the way of oncoming traffic to speak of, but nonetheless, he kept a very close eye upon the monitor for any sign of checkpoints further up the road. At least this way he would have the option of stopping dead and turning without anyone further up the road being any the wiser.

Unbeknown to him, the very vehicle he was certain was taking him from danger was now a beacon laying a trail of radioactive breadcrumbs for the vultures in the dark. Regardless of having been out of the field for so many years, Wasyl had maintained his knowledge of modern surveillance methods. Whilst his car was certainly capable of detecting electronic surveillance, the scandium 46 in his petrol tank was undetectable to him. It was an unfortunate inevitability that the widespread use of electronic counter-surveillance would lead to a return to the use of more ingenious forms. Radioactive isotopes that could withstand the heat of a nuclear explosion certainly had no trouble passing through the internal combustion of a car. Flying through the engine and being carried out by the exhaust fumes, their heavy constitution marking the path which the car took. The trail of breadcrumbs would ultimately end at the location where he was due to meet with Vincent and Francis later this evening, or perhaps early in the morning.

19

The two Russian agents who had been posing as Bulgarian police officers followed Wasyl's car from a considerable distance in their BMW. The absence of other cars on the road and also the relative lack of turnings made their job easy for now. Driving with their headlights on, a monitor in their car displayed the sensor readout which identified traces of isotope on the road ahead.

Sitting in silence, the two men slowly trundled along the road, following in the tracks of Wasyl's Mercedes as they had for the past twenty miles. They had passed several villages in pursuit and the road had travelled through a vast woodland area, which had been relatively sheltered. However, now the road began to climb and the surroundings cleared to expose the silhouettes of low mountains up ahead. As the road climbed further, the agents were able to see the outlines of abandoned vehicles which had clearly been caught out by the weather and were now strewn along the sides of the road. The snow chains on their rear tyres had not been enough to keep them moving.

Progressing steadily at a slow pace, the car was now surrounded on one side by a sheer rock escarpment, which towered above for over one hundred meters, and on the left side, a view down to a small village.

Descending gradually, the agents could see the dimly lit village at the foot of the hill. As the road approached to pass the village, the agent monitoring the screen tapped his colleague on his hand and muttered in Russian, 'They came off here.'

No trace of isotopes could be seen up the road. Instead, the trail tapered off to the left on a track leading into the village. Quickly looking over to the GPS, they could see that there were no other main roads out of the village. Pulling to the side of the road, they parked the BMW under a large tree, shrouding it in darkness. Getting out, both agents put on plain black coats, in place of the police issue clothes which they had worn earlier. One of them pulled the temporary police markings from the car and as he peeled them off with ease, he scrunched them into small balls and threw them into the passenger foot well. The other detached the isotope tracker which they had used to follow Wasyl this far and then calmly opened the boot of the car and pulled out a secondary firearm, for both himself and his companion. Closing the boot, the car locked.

Standing in the darkness, only dimly illuminated by a far-off streetlamp, the isotope monitor displayed the scandium 46 as purple patches on the ground. Being so late, the agents could see that there was only one pair of fresh tracks in the snow. Finding the Mercedes would be easy. In the back seat of their car, hidden from view by the tinted rear windows and mesh compartment, were the boys Patrick and George, their faces terrified and teary and their hands tied. They had been intercepted attempting to leave their house earlier in the evening with their mother and had never made it to the Embassy. Now they themselves were being used to incentivise their mother. Encouragement for their mother to help the Russians track Wasyl to the place he would meet Francis.

20

The auction room had gradually become busier and busier as more people crammed in. The possibility was fascinating to Francis that everybody may have undergone the same ordeal in actually reaching the front door. He was sure that there must be an easier way. Looking around the room, he could still see no familiar faces. This did give him some solace, insofar that if he couldn't recognise anybody, he hoped that they would not recognise him. He laughed internally as he realised what a 'head in sand' mentality that was. He was the British Ambassador to Bulgaria and his face was very much available online to anybody with an internet connection and an interest to take a look.

Vincent had also been looking around the room and had his suspicions about some of the people in the room. He knew that everybody's cards would be on the table just as soon as the bidding began.

'Good evening, ladies and gentlemen. My name is Mr Petit and I will be your host this evening. This will be an open ascending price auction and each listing will be sold to the highest bidder,' announced the auctioneer as he stood at the podium. 'Good luck and please remember, as always, that if you would like to leave the venue, you must make payment for the lot, or lots which you secure. You will be led to another location to collect your purchase.'

The auctioneer was a tall French man in his sixties, whose accent was only faintly discernible. His white hair was combed pristinely from left to right and his suit was immaculate. Certainly, he did not look as though he had crawled down a shaft to make it to the auction.

Sipping on the water which sat in front of him, Mr Petit began to turn a page of the document which sat before him. A silence had descended upon the room, interrupted only by the sound of the page turning. Francis could also clearly hear the sound of his heart beating as blood pumped voraciously through his veins. He wondered how much the correct amount to bid was for information which could lead to the location of a find of such monumental historical and scientific significance. The location of an artefact that could prove, in one moment, that not only was life brought to this planet from afar, but also answer the eternal question which has plagued mankind since its origin. The question of whether we are alone.

Mr Docherty's executors, having carried out his will, would also probably be none the wiser about what would be auctioned here tonight. Would all of the five countries be represented? The questions kept on streaming through Francis' head. He had, without realising it, been playing with the auction paddle lying on the table before him. Table number seventeen, at which they sat, was denoted on the paddle. A floral pattern surrounded the number, the handle of which was cylindrical and covered in a material very soft to the touch. Francis wondered how much sweat it could absorb as he clasped his clammy hands together. He also wondered how he dare use this paddle without knowing the limit of the credit on the card which Vincent had shown him earlier. Was it bottomless, or would he be bidding with money he would be unable to front?

Mr Petit was poised above the lectern, looking assertively and authoritatively out over his auction room. With unerring precision, he started proceedings by announcing the first lot: a tapestry which appeared to be a night-time pine forest winter scene. Having announced the lot, a man and a woman carried the frame holding the tapestry out from the shadows.

On first inspection from afar, Francis and Vincent could see nothing immediately outstanding about this tapestry, although it was a pleasant picture to behold.

'Can I start the bidding at seventy-five thousand euro please?' Mr Petit announced. Francis and Vincent looked at each other and a smile crept across their faces.

The bidding commenced and four parties sat at different tables seemed to be interested in the item. As the price increased slowly in denominations of 2,500 euros, a paddle was raised at one of the tables and a voice said, 'One million euro.' The number of interested parties reduced to two. The bidding continued backwards and forwards using higher incremental denominations set by Mr Petit, until the final bid of 2,600,000 euros was met with no further response. The gavel came down and the sound resonated around the walls of the room with an air of finality and certainty.

Vincent and Francis had been sitting and quietly listening to the proceedings. They both considered themselves to be fairly knowledgeable about the arts, but to see what looked to be a fairly contemporary and unspectacular tapestry achieve such a price at auction was astounding. Both of the men immediately suspected that there was more to the item than meets the eye.

The process had taken approximately twenty minutes and Mr Petit notified everybody that there would be a ten-minute break. As soon as the announcement was made, the refined looking young lady who had successfully acquired the tapestry rose from her seat and was accompanied from the auction room by two of the staff.

Francis must not have been paying attention, because before he realised it, Vincent had returned to the table with two cups of double espresso.

'I think that we are going to need this,' said Vincent.

'As I am positive that I won't be sleeping any time soon, I think I agree with you,' Francis muttered, 'although this definitely won't do anything to calm my nerves. Perhaps I should have another rakia.'

'I don't think so, Francis, you are going to need to have all of your wits about you for the next while.'

Before Vincent had an opportunity to finish his sentence, Francis was already taking his first sip of coffee. The temperature was just right and the froth which sat at the top of the espresso was thick and creamy, which was just the way he liked it.

Mr Petit had returned to the lectern and was clearly preparing himself to recommence his auction. A few of the people who were still returning to their seats were clearly in a slight rush. Although everybody would have seen the second lot and the vague description, this was for all intents and purposes a blind bet, for anybody who had no idea what was contained within the wax-sealed envelope.

The mixture of caffeine and the impending recommencement of the auction had caused the knot in Francis' stomach to once again tighten. He leaned over to Vincent and said, 'remind me again, how much of Her Majesty's money are we about to spend?'

Vincent sat back and rested his head on the headrest, 'Don't think about limits, let's just get it.'

Mr Petit coughed and once again assumed his position. Silence fell over the room as he introduced the envelope, for what it was. 'Now we have lot two which is a very lovely, unopened, wax-sealed envelope containing information which belonged to the archaeologist and explorer Mr Jerome Docherty and which he had expressed should be sold at auction at least three years after the date of his death.' Taking a brief pause, Mr Petit recoiled slightly before saying almost embarrassedly, 'The starting price for this lot is one million euros. Do I have any takers?'

The sound of a room full of people inhaling through a mixture of excitement, shock and intrigue was palpable and quite something to behold. The silence which followed was only to be expected. It seemed that nobody wanted to show their hand, but this was not the forum for shyness. Francis quickly but purposefully grasped the paddle and raised it. The glance of Mr Petit was now affixed upon their table as he said, 'Thank you, do we have one million and fifty thousand?'

'Two million,' exclaimed a person sitting at a table located at the back of the room to the right hand side. Unable to make out the person in the dim lighting, Francis and Vincent waited momentarily, but didn't have to wait long. Table after table identified themselves as present to bid for the item as the bids increased by one million euro a time.

'It seems that everybody received their letter,' whispered Vincent to Francis, who was struggling to fathom the surreal situation he found himself in. Looking at the four other individuals sitting at different tables, it was clear that they had received the same information and wanted the envelope at potentially any cost.

Francis needed to have a frank discussion with Vincent at this point but was not able to because of the risk of being overheard. He re-joined the bidding with a paddle raise at twenty-five million euro, although saying the figure out loud felt like a dream. Vincent had spent the time carefully listening to the voices at each of the tables. None of them sounded familiar, but he could at least guess where each country representative was sitting in the room.

The bidding continued, with the uninitiated attendees sitting in astonishment at the ever-increasing figure. A sixth person entered the bidding at twenty-nine million euro because he clearly thought that others knew something he didn't. The bids from this person fell quiet as the bidding escalated ever further.

Francis re-joined with a bid of forty-two million euro. Immediately looking at the faces of those sat at adjacent tables, their gazes were fixed upon him and their expressions were ones of pure bewilderment. He would no doubt have been equally flabbergasted if he did not know about the contents of the envelope. How would it be possible to put a price on such an artefact? Would they actually be here for the remainder of the night, bidding? The implications of such a find were beginning to develop in Francis' mind. He had had an insufficient amount of time to digest the information and was positive that there was a lot that he couldn't even comprehend.

Mr Petit, who up until this point had been the epitome of calm and composure, seemed to be wavering slightly. His voice had become slightly more taught and not as cool, calm and collected as before. As he broke through the one-hundred-million-euro mark, this was understandable. He had now started to increase the bids by five million euro a time and the figure was beginning to skyrocket quickly. Unlike Francis, Vincent felt relatively unfazed. Having had a little more time to think about this auction, he had suspected that this would happen. Looking over his shoulder towards the bar, he noticed that the barmaid and two other members of staff were now standing and watching with their mouths hanging slightly ajar. He also noticed that additional security personnel had sneaked into the auction hall and were standing at the back of the room near to the bar. He wasn't sure what they were expecting.

Mr Petit had reached two hundred million euro and was looking slightly exhausted. Saying such a lot of long numbers was taking its toll. He persevered with consummate professionalism, but had started increasing the bids by ten million a time.

A hand raised at the table which Vincent had identified as the American contingent and a husky male voice announced, 'One billion euro.'

Silence descended and Mr Petit stood bolt upright. Leaning forward once again he said, 'One billion bid. Do I hear one billion and fifty million?' a paddle shot up from one of the other regular bidders and the process continued.

Francis for a moment realised that although he knew he should raise his hand and carry on bidding, he was having trouble actually doing so. He quickly muttered to Vincent, 'Are you sure about this? We don't even know what limit we have on that card of yours!'

'Keep going Francis, I'm sure that we won't be caught short.'

He was not as sure as Vincent, but kept bidding nonetheless. After a long sequence of increased bids, the number of bidders reduced from five to two. Vincent was unsure as to which country the other bidder represented. Francis put in a bid for one-and-three-quarter billion euros. This was accepted by Mr Petit who asked for an increase to one billion and eight hundred million. This was met with no immediate response and Mr Petit said the words that everybody had been waiting to hear for this lot, 'going once... going twice... sold, finally, to you, sir,' pointing at Francis and table number seventeen.

The pressure had been building within Francis and had now perpetuated a pounding headache. The ball in his stomach had not dissipated at all, but was clenched as tight as ever. Both Francis and Vincent leaned back in their seats and closed their eyes for a moment as Mr Petit released everybody for a well-deserved break.

21

Turning the key in the villa door, Wasyl shook his feet one at a time to clear as much snow as he could before walking into the house. He had parked his car outside the rusty gate at the end of the drive, which there had been no chance of opening owing to the large amount of snow which had amounted, but he had been able to force the smaller, path gate open and walk through.

The village in which the villa was situated was very small: less than one hundred inhabitants during the summer. In the middle of winter, most people were in the city and there would likely be less than ten people within a twenty-mile radius.

The track leading to the villa was unlit, and finding his way to the front door, of itself, had been trying. However, his keyring torch had served him well.

Wasyl had left the engine of his car running and Melissa was sound asleep in the passenger seat. He hoped that he had not miscalculated bringing her here rather than straight to a hospital.

Striding over to the fireplace, he threw five large pieces of wood in a pile and lit some dry kindling underneath with his lighter. Taking a moment to watch the flames to make sure they took hold, he had an opportunity to consider what he hoped would happen next, whilst realising his hopeless lack of control over the situation.

The smoke rising from the slightly damp lumps of wood was a soothing smell. It took him back to his childhood.

Before long, the fire was burning well and the heat radiating from it was very comforting. He turned and faced back towards the door and walked out to his car. Traipsing along, the crisp snow underfoot crunched reassuringly. As he reached the Mercedes, he thought for a moment that he could hear in the very far distance the sound of a car engine. Realising that his level of paranoia was peaking, he thought nothing further of it and opened the passenger side door to attempt to wake Melissa from her slumber.

As he opened the door, the warm air from inside the car hit him, mixed with the scent of her perfume. He gently shook her shoulder until she woke up. He told her that they had arrived and that she should come inside the house to rest. In her half wake state, she tried to get out of the car seat without realising that her seatbelt was still engaged. Unbuckling it, she shifted her legs out of the car in a dainty and slightly frail fashion. Wasyl helped her out of the seat and supported her as they retreated into the villa.

Closing the door, Melissa bent down and removed her boots gingerly and sat in a chair next to the fireplace. The room hadn't totally warmed up and she could see her breath in the air. Her feet and hands felt particularly cold so curling them in front of the flames felt very good indeed.

She leaned back and rested her head, which gradually fell to one side. Her blonde hair wistfully floated down to cover her eyes just in time to cover the tears which had started to well. 'Patrick, George: I love you,' she muttered almost inaudibly under her breath.

Wasyl was standing not more than a few feet away in the very small kitchenette, which was part of the same room. He had removed two glasses from the cupboard and was pouring them each a glass of water.

'I know that you are worried for your children, Melissa. Who wouldn't be? Believe me, they are a lot safer at the Embassy than we are here,' said Wasyl in the most supportive and convincing voice he could summon. He could see the tears now, which were streaming down the side of Melissa's face and along her jawline.

'You came into our house and this all happened. My husband was gone when I got back. Where is he?'

'After you left with the children, I had to take Francis to meet an old friend of his. It was very important that they speak. I left them in the city centre. Francis asked me to return, to excuse him from the party and make sure that everything was ok. Obviously, it was not,' Wasyl said, bluntly. He could see that the tears continued to stream down her face, 'But, please don't worry about him. He is with a good friend and we have come to where I am supposed to meet them.'

'I have done,' Melissa inhaled deeply to attempt to control her sorrow, 'I have done something I shouldn't. I never made it to the Embassy, Wasyl. Some men pretending to be police stopped the car with me and the boys.' Wasyl knew where this was going before Melissa said anything further. 'All I remember being told was that when I woke up, I would be back in the house and if I ever wanted to see my children again, that I would lead these men to my husband and to you.' She was now sobbing inconsolably as Wasyl pulled a chair up next to her.

'Why didn't you tell me this earlier?' asked Wasyl.

'What do they want?' cried Melissa.

'I think that they want what Francis and his friend Vincent went to get. Something very important,' he responded.

'I didn't know what to do. They will kill all of us here when they find us,' Melissa said, struggling to think what could possibly be so important. She wished that Francis could know the danger that their children were in, but she had not heard from him since he left the house.

'Have you tried to call them?' she asked.

'No, because where they went, they won't have their phones on. Vincent will have made sure of it,' Wasyl retorted.

'Who is Vincent?' asked Melissa, righting her head in the chair and sitting forward.

'He is a man I owe my life to. Twice. He needed my help to secretly connect with your husband tonight. That is why he was in my car when I arrived for the party,' Wasyl recounted.

Melissa's voice steadied and her tone lowered. Removing a few errant strands of hair from her eye-line she looked at Wasyl and said, 'Whoever Vincent is. Whoever you really are. All I care about is my children. Whatever Francis is doing, it is not as important as them.'

'I won't tell you not to worry. You should worry. If they actually manage to obtain the item and bring it here, we will do what we must to get your children back,' he promised.

'The men who took my babies. They know where we are,' Melissa confessed.

22

Many of the auction participants rose from their seats in order to stretch their legs or fetch a drink. Walking past the table where Vincent and Francis were sitting, they gazed with disbelief toward them. They walked very deliberately close to the table, just so that they could take a good look. Both men sat quite oblivious to this, wondering what would happen next.

Two pairs of purposeful footsteps approached them from behind and stopped next to their table. They looked up to see a finely dressed woman and Mr Petit standing over them.

'Sir, if you are not intending in making any other purchases this evening, would you care to follow us?' said Mr Petit who had returned to his previous calm and collected demeanour.

Vincent and Francis obligingly got to their feet and followed diligently towards a door guarded by two men. As they walked, they could still sense the gazes of the other participants upon them. The malintent of a certain contingent in the room toward them was inevitable and perceptible to both men. One of the guards opened the door, which led into a small but very elegantly decorated office.

The door slid shut behind them and sounded as though it locked. The woman sat in a chair to the side of the room and Mr Petit circled back round behind his desk. Sliding his jacket from one shoulder and then the other before shaking it free of his body altogether, he sat down and released a long, pronounced and deliberate sigh. He adjusted the trouser brace on his left shoulder which made a faint thud when he released his finger grip upon it.

'I suppose, when somebody has been around for long enough, they see just about everything, gentlemen,' he said in a slightly more casual tone than he had adopted during the auction. An uncontrollable and inevitable smile was brought to the faces of both Vincent and Francis, who felt almost simultaneously as though they had been brought before their school head teacher to answer for some petty indiscretion. 'One point seven-five billion euro, gentlemen. I presume that you will not be paying cash?'

The ludicrous nature of the situation forced a chuckle from Francis. The lady sat beside them was also seeing the funny side.

'I think that we'll pay this by card,' said Vincent trying to bring the conversation back to sanity. 'Can you confirm that you will hold the funds safely until the information within the envelope is verified?'

'Well,' said Mr Petit with a cough, 'the funds will be held with our solicitors, Brick Steckelback. I should also mention that until the content of the envelope and any consequential find are verified, Ms Bradford will accompany you,' he announced, gesturing towards Ms Bradford. She was an attractive lady in her early thirties. Her hair was straight and shoulder length and a deep shade of red. Her delicate features and high cheekbones made her very pleasing to the eye, as did her snug-fitting suit which accentuated her clear love of physical exercise. Notwithstanding this, both men had their immediate misgivings about the arrangement, but quick reasoning brought them to understand why it would be necessary to allow Ms Bradford to tag along with them.

Mr Petit proceeded to read out a variety of disclaimers over the course of two or three minutes, before producing a document for Francis to sign, presumably outlining in more detail what he had just heard. Realising that he had neither the time, nor inclination to sit and read through the blurb, he took the ballpoint pen which was being presented to him by Mr Petit and signed the documents.

Ms Bradford opened the attaché case which was resting next to her chair to take out a small card-reading machine. 'Gentlemen, I represent Brick Steckelback and by extension the auctioneer. Your card please,' she said in a firm but friendly, well-spoken voice.

Vincent reached into his jacket pocket, produced the card and handed it to Ms Bradford. It was a plain-black, inconspicuous card, which showed no outward indication of the value it carried. Ms Bradford slid the card into the reader and spent a moment tapping information into the unit. Turning it one hundred and eighty degrees, the unit now pointed toward Vincent. With an air of anxiety, he accepted it from Ms Bradford, read the long transaction figure which would be transferred, and punched in the four-digit pin followed by the green button. The instructions on screen asked for the unit to be handed back to the vendor, which he did.

'This may take a moment,' she muttered as she gazed at the screen. Mr Petit appeared to be becoming quite impatient as he drummed his fingers on his desk. Some time had passed since they started the process and he was clearly eager to carry on with his auction. The wait was tense, with both Francis and Vincent praying that the transaction would clear, which it did. A smile came across the face of Ms Bradford as the transaction read complete and she extracted the card with a swift movement and handed it back to Vincent with a 'Thank you.'

'Now that we have concluded this part of our business, I will leave you in the hands of my associate who will take you to your item,' declared Mr Petit as he rose from his seat. 'I must say, I have never been more curious about anything I have auctioned than to know about the content of that envelope.' He paused, hoping that some information would be forthcoming. 'Well, in any case, I wish you luck in your future endeavours and bid you good evening.' Knocking on the door, he waited for the men in the auction room to open it. As he walked out he exchanged some inaudible words with one of the guards. The door remained open and one of the two guards walked into the room and closed the door. Francis and Vincent had both already noticed the second door in the room. It was this door that the man now walked to. Gesturing with one hand as he reached into his trouser pocket with the other, he beckoned all three of them to follow him as he turned the key in the lock and put weight on the door handle.

Filing into what transpired to be a corridor, the man walked straight ahead. There was barely enough room to move single file down this particularly narrow but tall-ceilinged corridor, which was lit by long thin crystal chandeliers. The man's height and bulk made it difficult for Vincent who was directly behind him, to see further down the corridor.

Ms Bradford, who was at the back of the line, spoke softly, 'Often our clients prefer to leave discreetly from an alternate location, particularly when they have purchased and collected high value items. Yours is certainly the highest value I have ever seen,' she said with an air of excitement as they reached the collection room. Inconspicuous in nature, the room was plain and empty, except for a metal table which had been pushed up against a wall and four CCTV cameras in each corner of the ceiling. Upon the table, on a small transparent plastic stand, lay the envelope with the red wax seal facing upwards.

23

Wasyl sat slouched in the chair next to the slowly dying fire. Running both of his hands through his hair, he desperately searched through his mind for options. Melissa had told him everything that she knew including that she had, on instruction, dropped a capsule into his fuel tank. He knew what it was as soon as she started to explain, as he was well aware of how scandium 46 could be used. He had originally selected this location for its secluded nature. He thought that he had considered all of the angles, but clearly not. He caught himself thinking back to all of the things he could have spotted and all of the things that he could have done differently. Realising the futility of this, he curled his fingers and pulled his hair until it hurt. Years ago, he would have erupted with anger, but experience had taught him that this passion could be channelled to better effect. Suddenly releasing his hair and lifting his head he looked directly at Melissa who was apologising profusely.

'You had no choice. Of course, you had no choice,' he said shaking his head and looking with a fixed gaze at the rug under his feet, 'I would have done the same in your position. You do not know me well and you do not trust me. But the men who took your children and killed all of those people at your house, they do not know me either,' Wasyl's face turned stone cold. He stood and walked toward the light-switch, the only feature on the bare wall. Before turning it off, he seemed to deliberately hesitate momentarily as if still considering the options.

Removing his hand from the switch, he turned to Melissa whose face now expressed the deep concern she had for what Wasyl had in mind.

'I can't contact Francis and Vincent. Whether they have acquired the item or not, they will be coming. I didn't recognise those officers who stopped us,' Wasyl pondered, trying to piece things together. *They would have known to wait on the mountain road towards the city, through the village where they were stopped. They wanted to see who was in the car. They must have been following us since then, as it wasn't long after the stop that Melissa had said that she felt sick and dropped the scandium into his petrol tank.*

'Those were the same men who took my boys. I recognised the voice of the officer at the window when they stopped you,' Melissa sobbed.

Outside, the Russian agents had followed the single set of car tracks on foot for the last few hundred metres to the village. Their black outfits made them very difficult to see in the dark. One of the men held up the sensor, just to ensure that they were indeed on the correct path, which they were. Rounding a corner, he placed it back into the satchel bag, which he carried over his shoulder. They saw Wasyl's Mercedes from a distance, but were hardly ready to approach the house. It had barely been half an hour since they received a message from the Russian representative at the auction that the British had secured the item. As they stood rooted to the middle of the track in the ferocious snow, they could see the warm glow of light escaping from the villa outside which Wasyl's car was parked.

Exchanging a few words, they started back towards where they had left the car containing their bargaining chips for acquiring the sealed letter. Reaching the car a few moments later, the central locking popped unlocked, they sat inside and turned on the engine to warm up. They had only been away for a few moments and already the temperature in the car had dropped drastically. George and Patrick sitting on the back seat were clearly feeling quite cold by this point. Both men resented the actions which they had had to take in kidnapping the children. They hadn't realised that they would be in the car with Melissa when they stopped her. Kirill turned around to assess their condition.

'Don't worry, boys; your mum is just helping us to find a man. It won't take much longer and you will be together again.'

'Kirill, you know that they will say that we killed all of the people back at that house!' he exclaimed.

On returning to the house before taking Melissa upstairs unconscious, both men had gone into the hall to investigate why the house was so quiet and dark. They had been just as surprised as Wasyl to find all of the guests dead.

'Did you not see the present table?' asked Aleksey.

'No, what did you see?' puzzled Kirill.

'The present table. One of the presents was on the floor and it looked as though gas had ripped a hole in the paper and escaped quickly. I thought you had seen it,' said Aleksey.

Kirill shook his head with a concerned look on his face. Both men considered their close brush with mortality that evening, entering the property. Turning to Patrick and

George who were cowering in the back seats, unable to understand the strange men speaking Russian in the seats in front, Kirill said to them, 'I have two daughters about your age. Nothing bad will happen to either of you. Are you hungry? Thirsty?'

Both boys nodded without specifying which of the two they were, so Kirill assumed both. Reaching down into his satchel he brought out two small bottles of orange juice and two chocolate bars. He undid the restraints on their hands and passed the juice and chocolate back to them, where it was received by grateful little hands.

24

Francis approached the metal table upon which lay the item that had just fetched 1,750,000,000 euros at auction. The item which they now had to take charge of. Vincent and Ms Bradford stood just behind him and the hulking security guard had made his way to the exit door, where he now stood with his hands behind his back, waiting.

'I don't think that we should open it here,' whispered Vincent, leaning in towards Francis' ear.

'I don't want to open it at all!' whispered back Francis is a raspy dry voice. Picking it up, Francis was glad that it was the right size to fit inside his jacket pocket. Turning towards the exit, he walked confidently in the direction of the guard who escorted them through another corridor. The walk seemed to take an age, but finally they reached a stairwell from which they could see that the corridor continued further.

'What is your name, Ms Bradford? It seems we will be spending some time in each other's company,' enquired Vincent.

'Charlotte,' she said, her voice reverberating back down the spiral staircase which they were still climbing.

'Well, Charlotte, here is the thing. If you are coming with us, I'm afraid that you will have to leave your phone with your colleague here,' Vincent said, pointing towards the towering guard with his eyes. Charlotte seemed slightly taken aback by this request. She thought for a moment and reluctantly handed her phone to the guard with a look of dignified petulance. 'If you would like us to use this exit, we are currently located under the bus garage. The train station, metro station and also taxi ranks are here,' said Ms Bradford in an advisory and matter-of-fact tone, still slightly sore at having lost her mobile phone. Vincent, who preferred to escape the corridors immediately, nodded in the direction of the stairs. The guard, who had stayed with them up until now, remained at the foot of the steps.

As they reached the summit, they found the door open and a person who very much looked like a female toilet attendant holding the door open for them. Walking out into what transpired to be the ladies toilets of the Sofia Coach Station, Francis and Vincent once again threw each other a bemused look. As they exited, there was a cordon in front of the turnstiles which read 'OUT OF ORDER'.

It was now past midnight and some of the only people in the station were sleepy travellers and cleaning staff. Two or three of the ticket kiosks were open and the staff were chatting. Francis, Vincent and Charlotte walked unhindered out of the front entrance and directly into one of the many cabs which were waiting outside. Vincent asked the driver to take them to the location where he had left his car when he met Wasyl before they headed to Francis' house for the party. The taxi driver seemed to know exactly where to go and they sat quietly throughout the journey. They wanted to speak, but were mindful of saying something they shouldn't in front of the driver.

Arriving at their destination, Vincent could barely recognise which of the snow covered row of parked cars on the street was his. Handing over a twenty lev note to the driver, he got out of the car followed by Francis and Charlotte.

After several minutes of standing calf-deep in the fresh snow, scooping handful after handful of powder from the door and windows with his bare hand, he managed to prize the door open and get in. Immediately turning on the engine, he cleared the other doors as well so that Charlotte and Francis could get in also. Before the last door closed, all three could clearly hear the sound of police and ambulance sirens in the distance. These were being turned off and on intermittently due to the early hour. The sirens continued until they tapered gracefully into silence in the distance.

Sitting in the passenger seat, Francis removed the sealed envelope from his pocket. Sharing a momentary glance with Vincent and almost forgetting Ms Bradford was sitting attentively in the rear seat, he broke the seal and flipped open the envelope with fervour.

The words read,

'Our story began at,

Longitude: 24.8

Latitude: 42.7

Here rests the Pebble. Located in a twin monolith rock formation, on the north face at a height of seventy-two metres, you will find an area of material which has been re-secured to the vertical cliff face.'

Francis passed the envelope and enclosed message to Vincent, who also read it.

'We have to go to my office, I have to see my wife and children. I need to know that they are ok. We need to get this information back to the Embassy. I have done all I fucking can here,' the uneasiness in Francis' voice told the story of his frame of mind.

Vincent calmly reached across Francis and pulled open the glovebox, from which he produced a mobile phone. Unplugging it from the glovebox charger, he tapped the coordinates into the phone to check the location. 'Let me explain something to you, Francis. This note doesn't exist,' said Vincent, his tone darkening as he tapped the steering wheel with the envelope. 'This note doesn't exist. Neither does the artefact. The Pebble, which this note says is right here in Bulgaria. Don't you think that the authorities may have something to say about the removal of a find of such colossal significance?'

'I think that I've been working slightly outside of my job description tonight. Would you have me head off with you in search of this thing? I don't even know if my family made it safely to the Embassy,' Francis raised with concern as he looked at the screen of the phone which Vincent had handed to him, showing clearly the pin-point location of the Pebble which allegedly brought life to the planet. Noticing the nearest towns to the site, he quickly handed the phone back to Vincent and turned his head towards the window to look outside. Realising that he was too much involved to extricate himself so easily, he resigned himself to whichever next destination Vincent no doubt had in mind.

25

Jonathan Coleridge had received a phone call earlier that night from Francis Sunderland. Since the phone call he had expected Melissa Sunderland and their two children, Patrick and George Sunderland, to arrive at the Embassy. He had notified the gate staff about their imminent arrival and his concern had been raised by the tone of Ambassador Sunderland's voice on the phone. As one of the three MI6 secret agents working out of the British Embassy in Sofia, he was at the Embassy at the time that the call came in from the Ambassador's residence.

When Melissa had not arrived within a reasonable time frame, John called several members of the Embassy staff that he was aware were in attendance at the party. When he received no response except for ring tones and answerphone messages, he notified security, picked up his keys and drove to the house.

Arriving sometime after Wasyl and Melissa had left the house, he too had discovered the reason why he was not able to make contact with anybody at the residence. After a very quick search of the property, he had established that Francis, Melissa, Patrick and George were all gone. So too, it appeared, was Wasyl Bohdanov for whom the party had been arranged.

Unfortunately, still at the now freezing property were the remainder, or most of the remainder, of the guests. This included his colleagues from the Embassy, who he had the misfortune of discovering and identifying, in amongst the bodies. He pulled up the trouser leg of his MI6 colleague who was lying on the floor of the hall and removed his gun and ankle holster.

Jonathan realised that such a lot of deceased would soon be missed and that there was insufficient time to try to get to the bottom of what had happened. Certainly, he did not want to be the one found still at the scene and so he looked around slowly one final time as he stood in the dark hall surrounded by the bodies of the guests. With a vague sense of panic setting in, he reached down and unclasped the grip of a woman from her phone to which she still clung. Her icy fingers were almost like static to the touch. The phone was pin protected, but this didn't stop him from removing his black glove and dialling the number for the police with the knuckle of his right forefinger. Placing the phone on her body with his left hand, he heard the operator speaking through the receiver. Saying nothing, he walked out of the house and returned to the Embassy.

The police who first arrived at the open gates of the residence had called in to report that the Ambassador's residence was the suspected origin of the emergency call. Stretching the boundaries of the diplomatic immunity enjoyed by the property, the two officers had walked to the house in order to check if they could locate the caller. The house, draped in darkness, showed little signs of life. No response to the doorbell led the officers to look through the nearest available window. The large-pane glass window at the front of the house was closest and easiest to access. It also had the most devastating story to tell. Seeing the bodies on the floor, they quickly called for backup and ambulances, which arrived and halted at the gates.

The arrival of the emergency services at the house would be woefully late and of no aid to the victims who had died. They could do nothing until access was granted by the British Embassy. The police quickly surrounded the perimeter of the residence to ensure that nobody left. Lights at adjacent properties lit up and curtains twitched to gain any sight or understanding as to what had caused such a large emergency service response.

Walking back in to his office at the Embassy, John picked up the satellite phone handle and connected to his supervisor at Vauxhall Cross in London to report on what he had discovered at the residence and the uncomfortable truth, the crisis, that was the disappearance without trace of the Ambassador and his family. Probably kidnapped.

After his conversation, he dimmed the lights in the room and pulled his cigarette pack from his pocket. Sliding one cigarette out of the pack and clasping it between the fingers he had recently used to prize a mobile phone from the hands of a dead woman, he noticed the distinct tremble with which he drew his hand to his mouth, to light it. Walking over to the window, he pulled aside the net curtain, which complemented the frame so elegantly. Exhaling towards the glass, the condensation formed quickly. As the smoke and water vapour cleared, he noticed two vans he had not seen before parked on the street outside. Further observation revealed a car which drove one way up the road and a few moments later returned in the other direction. There wasn't any time to think about that now.

So very early in the morning, he was one of the very few staff members at the Embassy, except security. In the morning, he would have to convene the staff who arrived for work to inform them of the situation, but in the meantime he had been asked to sit on his hands until the Bulgarian authorities contacted the Embassy about the Ambassador's residence. Feeling inexplicably at fault for the non-arrival of Melissa and the children, he resented the idea of sitting on his hands. Standing by the window, his thoughts were drawn to all of the dead guests at the residence. He felt death clinging to his clothes. He perceived it tangibly, a lot like the feeling one gets when yearning for a shower.

His mobile phone rang, as the Embassy switchboard put a call from the Bulgarian Ministry of Home Affairs through to him. This was the call he had been waiting for.

26

Professor Josephine Hancock sat in her office, which was discreetly tucked away in a corner of the Science Department of a distinguished North American university campus. Her laptop open before her, the light from the screen illuminating her face gently, it accentuated the lines of her face and the depth of the crow's feet curling around the side of her temples. Her narrow rectangular-frame glasses were perched towards the end of her nose and strands of her grey hair hung down in front of her eyes. She puffed to remove the hair from her sightline.

The meeting was due to commence in less than two minutes. As she sat and watched the screen, a bespoke communication program auto-loaded on her screen with a sign reading *Argo Industries* filling the screen, falling back but remaining embossed in the bottom corner of each participant screen. Split into six square segments, her face appeared in the first box. She didn't particularly care for the blue hue of her face, caused by the light cast from the screen. The other five boxes showed as connecting.

Gazing over to the window, she looked at the mini mobile satellite transmitter which she had put up for the purpose of the call.

One by one, the other participants connected and there was silence on the line until everybody was present.

Over the Pacific Ocean a solitary grey Learjet private plane was flying towards Indonesia. Cruising at 41,000 feet, its only passenger, Mike Argo, was also a party to the conference call. A young man in his early thirties, Argo had quickly scaled the ladder of financial success through his telecommunications company, which was now part of a larger conglomerate by the name of Argo Industries. He had started his company at the age of seventeen and with interests in a variety of other key companies, he now commanded a mobile phone contact list that was even richer than his bank balance. With his hands clasped behind his head, he rocked back on his brown-leather reclining chair.

The flight had been slightly bumpier than usual. The persistent, but gentle turbulence was a slight annoyance. His attention flicked between the screen and the whisky which his assistant Olivia had skilfully poured him a few moments ago. The ripples which ran across the surface were mesmerising to watch as the jet cut through the choppy air at high speeds. He rolled his fingers around the glass and lifted it to his lips, taking a much deserved sip. Argo had been looking forward to a drink all day. He closed his eyes and exhaled gently, as if to rid himself of all stress which had accumulated during the day.

His mind then quickly jumped to his company's telecommunication satellites orbiting the planet, which made this totally secure conversation possible. The mobile satellite transmitter used for Onyx's electronic meetings was his own personal design. It ensured end-to-end encryption of the data streams using an algorithm stored within the satellites and the laptops themselves. Half of the code was stored on the laptops with the other half on the satellites, along with a state of the art method of processing such high volumes of information. Without both sets of information the data stream was, for all intents and purposes, white noise to anybody who deigned to try and listen in. Argo chuckled to himself when he thought that his company provided communication and encryption services to a number of different banks, companies, governments and militaries. This led to one very straightforward dynamic. He knew what they were saying at all times and they had no idea what he or his associates were saying any of the time.

Olivia now sat on a velour sofa in the lounge area directly outside his enclosed, soundproof office which took up the rear half of the plane.

'Good evening, good day,' said Professor Hancock, who was the first member of Onyx to speak, once all the participants had joined the call, 'The first item for discussion today is our late, former member, Mr Docherty. Is there an update?'

Dr Meertens, whose face could not be easily made out on the display of the other participants, owing to the fact that he was sitting in a darkened room, interjected. 'Yes, I have been told that the location of the Pebble is in the open. The instructions left behind by the late Mr Docherty have been acquired by Ambassador Francis Sunderland at the auction.'

'We were not able to discover the location of the auction? This is most concerning. How was it that the Ambassador was able to attend the auction?' queried the Professor.

In a slightly frustrated and antagonised tone, Dr Meertens conceded, 'It appears that Ambassador Sunderland and Wasyl Bohdanov left the party before taking personal delivery of the present gifted to enhance the atmosphere of the festivities.'

'Let me be clear with the other members present: I need that artefact in my labs for research and we must ensure that it is not tainted,' said Mike Argo, firmly. 'If it is what Jerome spoke of in the letters he sent to the Heads of State, it could contain information far exceeding what we are expecting – about life on this planet and far more importantly where it came from.'

Dr Meertens had been listening and leaned forward towards his screen, which illuminated his face clearly for the others to see and uttered, 'Jerome Docherty has made it very difficult for us to acquire this artefact. You are well aware of the trouble it has caused us to find out what we now know about the Pebble. My contact was not able to extract information about the location of the auction or gain access to the auction. If they had, we would have acquired the item for certain.' His tone wavering, he continued, 'we don't know how they left the auction or where they are now, but rest assured I am fully invested in tracking them.'

27

Mr Docherty had been a member of Onyx. His ability, his almost preternatural knack for researching and discovering some of the most notable archaeological finds of recent history, had not gone unnoticed by Onyx. They had invited him to join their ranks and provided him with access to the immense resources of the organisation until his voluntary departure. He had become increasingly concerned about the eventual fate of the artefacts which he found.

Had he been working for a government, university or museum, he would have had a heightened sense of confidence that the artefacts would be used to further science and the study of history. He became somewhat disillusioned about the use and apparent disappearance of his finds into the depths of the secret organisation of which he was a member, suspecting that many of the treasures and artefacts which he located over the years had ended up in private collections, never to see the light of day; hostages of the same gold lust which had coerced their original proprietors to stash them away where they would never be found until centuries after their death. Some things never change, he thought. Also, his concern was that some of his findings of scientific significance were being researched and exploited for the good of Onyx and not for that of humanity. Throughout the later years of his life, and prior to his untimely death at the age of fifty-six, Mr Docherty would spend substantial periods of his time exploring alone. This was particularly the case during his last four years, when he was no longer a member of Onyx.

Onyx had never stopped monitoring Jerome Docherty's activities since his departure, as they viewed membership until death as the preferred option. Such monitoring had proved to be very difficult due to the long periods of time that Mr Docherty would disappear into various wildernesses, emerging at unknown locations and very rarely using any form of electronic communication. Three years after his death, it became evident to Onyx that Mr Docherty had made a discovery of tremendous significance when they received news from their contact within the Chinese Government about the auction invitation and general information about the item that would be made available. Jerome's lawyers in Nice had heeded his request to keep none of his personal details on their electronic database, to wait three years from the date of his death, and to ensure secure courier delivery of the five envelopes to their destinations.

Mr Docherty had hoped that three years would be long enough for Onyx to consign him to the past and to increase the chance of the auction taking place unhindered by their influence. He had considered the obvious possibility that at least one of the country representatives at the eventual auction may in fact be an Onyx infiltrator. This had not been the case.

Wanting to ensure that the existence of the artefact was well known, but understanding that realpolitik precluded the possibility of any country sharing the find with others, he concocted the plan to notify the five states of the existence of the artefact through the invitation; his scheme had worked well.

Mr Docherty's children had looked up to him and wanted to emulate him in every way possible. The lack of time he was able to spend with them and his long-suffering wife played on his mind in his later years, and he felt substantial guilt about his decision to prioritise his work over his family. He wanted to secure the financial future of his fourteen-year-old daughter and sixteen-year-old son, as well as their ability to focus (he hoped) on continuing his work, so Jerome

Docherty established a trust, into which the proceeds of his find would be paid, once verified.

28

Standing over the Teflon frying pan, Wasyl stared at the knob of butter, which was slowly melting and sliding to the side. As he watched, his mind was being drawn in multiple directions by the combination of hunger, lack of sleep and the predicament in which he found himself. Pulling eggs from the built-in fridge, he flipped open the box and cracked the shell of the first of four eggs on the side of the pan. Dropping down into the hot butter, it immediately started to spit reassuringly and the smell from the pan almost caused Wasyl to forget about his precarious situation.

Melissa had fallen asleep on the chair by the fire, which had been kept alive by Wasyl. Rays of morning sunlight were radiating through the gaps around and between the curtains. The long strip of sunlight fell vertically down her face, which made her stir as her brain registered the daylight and her nose detected the inviting smell of fried eggs.

Wasyl added some frozen slices of bread to the toaster and pulled down the lever. He hadn't eaten or slept in over twenty-eight hours and was feeling weary. The smell of toast combined with the eggs was delightful and Melissa was now awake.

'What time is it?' she asked as she yawned.

'Just after 8am. You managed to sleep for a few hours which is good,' Wasyl responded.

'Nobody has come, maybe they weren't able to follow us here,' she said hopefully.

'Unlikely, they will wait until we are all here before making their move and they will be hoping that you didn't tell me about what had actually happened,' he retorted. 'They will be nearby watching. If I make a move, they will know that something is not as it should be.'

'So, what, we just wait for my husband and this guy Vincent to get here? They would be walking straight into a trap.'

'There is no other way, we agreed on no communication,' Wasyl responded with a frustrated tone.

He was interrupted by the bread springing from the toaster. Turning to face the sound, he noticed that the eggs were also cooked. Setting two plates on the counter, he lay a piece of piping hot toast and two eggs on each before carrying the plates over to the small kitchen table where he had already set out cutlery for two.

Sitting down he beckoned Melissa to join him. 'Come and eat, you need your strength.

Initially reluctant to leave her seat, she got up and walked gingerly over to the table. Pulling the hard-backed wooden chair instead of lifting it, the legs dragged on the floor. She felt that she had neither the strength, nor the inclination to lift it. She sat opposite Wasyl and looked straight into his eyes. He observed the puffiness around her eyes, which was a symptom of the emotion-filled past few hours. He couldn't bring himself to blame her for giving the men who had her children what they had wanted. How could he blame her? As he sat eating eggs, sparingly sprinkled with salt, he felt somewhat helpless. Wracking his brain, he searched for the evasive idea which would guide him to the correct course of action.

He was snapped out of his thoughtful, trance-like state by the sound of somebody pushing open the rusty gate which led onto the path to the villa. Springing to his feet, he realised that so deep had he been in thought, that he had stopped chewing altogether and had just sat there for a moment.

Melissa had wondered what was going on in his head, but immediately panicked when she saw Wasyl's reaction to the sound. Pulling his gun from where it sat in its holster on his belt, he stalked over to the window and peered through the gap to see what he could. An old lady, short in stature, wearing boots, a headscarf and many layers of colourful clothing, was slowly walking up the path to the door. She was clearly struggling with the snow and Wasyl was surprised that he hadn't heard her footsteps from further afield. He reassured himself that it must have been because of his tiredness.

As the old lady meekly knocked on the door, he took the opportunity to look as far up and down the road as he could in order to see if he could spot any cars parked.

Crossing over to the lock side of the doorframe, he pressed the muzzle of his pistol to the door, pointed to where the old woman would now be standing. With his left hand he turned the lock and opened the door slightly, and immediately lowered his gaze and the position of the gun as he reassessed just how short the person who stood before him actually was.

Wasyl greeted the lady with as friendly a welcome as he could muster. She looked up towards him and had to almost lean back to look straight at him. Her face was weathered, but her smile was radiant and warm, her cheeks were rosy as if pinched by the cold.

'Good morning, I saw the smoke from your chimney and decided to come and say hello,' said the lady, 'I have baked some nice fresh bread and thought that I would bring you some.' Looking down into her hands, Wasyl could see that she was indeed clutching a loaf of bread. Thinking to himself that this visit would have served very well about ten minutes ago before he had eaten his eggs, he reached forward to take the loaf from her. 'Anyway, I just thought that I would come and say hello. If you need anything, I am just across the road.

'Very nice to meet you,' Wasyl responded, lowering the gun from the door and placing it behind his back. The woman turned around and started walking back towards the gate. Using the opportunity, Wasyl quickly took a glance in both directions, but could see nothing of particular concern. Closing the door, he turned to Melissa and looked down at the loaf of bread. Tearing off a thick piece of warm crispy crust, he bit into it fervently. Giving Melissa a quick summary of what had been said during her visit, he tore off a piece of bread and offered it to Melissa, who accepted. Realising that the old lady's visit was apparently innocent, her anxiety started to reduce. She had been impressed with the way in which Wasyl had conducted himself, regardless of their situation. Both nodding to impart deserved praise on the bread, Wasyl headed back to the window, where he saw the old woman walking across the street and back into her house.

29

Approaching the village moments later, Vincent, Francis and Charlotte drove past the BMW of Aleksey and Kirill who were both very much awake and waiting. Patrick and George, however, were both asleep on the back seat, oblivious to the fact that their father was sat in the car which had driven straight past them. It had been difficult for the Russian agents to see whether Vincent and Francis were in the car due to the tint on the windows, but the look of the car in conjunction with the infrequency of traffic on the road made them almost certain of it.

Francis had fallen asleep and Charlotte's head was propped up against the car window. On realising that they had arrived at their destination, she sat up and tapped Francis on the shoulder. Vincent had almost nodded off to sleep in the driver's seat a couple of times. The Audi trundled slowly to a halt behind Wasyl's car and all three of them got out. Francis yawned and raised his hands above his head for a very satisfying stretch. As he drew the cold air into his lungs he coughed slightly. Wasyl and the old lady both looked on at the arrivals from their respective windows on opposite sides of the road. This may have been the source of Vincent's uneasiness. Wasyl opened the door and urged them to hurry. Seeing the apparent concern on his face, the three obliged and crunched their way to the front door.

Walking into the villa, Francis' eye was cast over the room until he noticed Melissa sitting in the chair by the fireplace. With a look of surprise, delight and concern, but without saying anything, he walked hastily over to her, helped her to her feet and threw his arms around the top of her shoulders. She immediately began to sob, and tears were streaming from her eyes as she began to describe the horror of recent events. Starting from the beginning, she told Francis about how she had been kidnapped and blackmailed by the two Russian agents masquerading as police officers. How she had been intoxicated to pass out after being given instructions on how to help the Russians to obtain whatever it was he himself had been looking to secure, and how their boys were being held hostage. Finally, she told Francis that most of his guests from the previous night were lying dead in the hall of their house.

Any semblance of natural optimism that he had experienced when he awoke in the car, vanished in an instant. Francis had thought that his family were safe at the Embassy and that Jonathan would have them under his watchful eye. He thought that his guests would have left his house displeased, but at least safely. Everybody was looking toward Francis to gauge his reaction. He turned slightly to look for the nearest chair. Sitting down, his head went into his hands; although he didn't imagine that he would find the answer there, it was the only thing he could do to not fall over.

Wasyl stepped forward gingerly and added, 'Melissa forgot to mention one thing. My car has been marked and the Russians are almost certain to be close by, most probably waiting for your arrival and most probably with Patrick and George. Do you have the information?'

Looking up from his hands, Francis gazed toward Wasyl and nodded, before putting his head back in his hands, 'But not for long,' he said in a low, but firm tone.

30

Arriving at the Ambassador's residence for the second time in the recent past, Jonathan Coleridge stepped out of his car at the police cordon which had been established outside the front gate. One officer, Ivan Petrov, walked in his direction and asked if he was Mr Coleridge from the British Embassy. He showed his identification and replaced his badge into his coat pocket. Spending a few moments speaking with the officer in fluent Bulgarian, he was told about the mobile phone call to police, which had been traced as originating from within the grounds of the residence. The officer tried, to the best of his ability, to mask his knowledge of what lay in wait in the property from what he had seen through the window with his colleague.

Turning to look at the house, John could see that it sat basking in the misty morning sunshine. Ivan also pointed toward the relatives of some people who attended the event at the residence the previous night, but who had not come home. Although the officer remained professional, John could detect a foreboding undertone. He had realised that there was no way of concealing the death of so many people, so he was here to make the finding and to allow the police to conduct their investigation.

'That is very concerning. Francis Sunderland held a birthday celebration for a friend of his here last night,' John confirmed.

'Yes, that is what we have been told. Would you please check whether everything is ok at the house please?' Ivan asked.

Closing his eyes and offering the slightest nod, John turned towards the gate and started to approach. His walk up to the house seemed to take even longer than it had the previous evening. He rang the doorbell in order to present an impression that this was his first visit. Waiting for a couple of minutes, he felt the gazes of those outside the gate burning into the back of his head ferociously. Ringing the bell once again, his palms were sweaty inside his gloves. Moving over towards the window, he looked inside, half hoping that he had imagined what he had seen the previous night, which of course, he had not. He beckoned the police officer he had spoken with to join him and the officer walked concertedly toward John. Ivan had already looked through the same window and could see from John's blank facial expression that he had now also seen the same, but it was not clear whether the situation in the house was really a surprise to him.

'We are going to need to go inside,' said John.

'I will have to ask my colleagues to join me' Ivan advised, to which he received a nod to the affirmative. Reaching for his gun first, followed by his radio, Ivan gave his orders in Bulgarian and almost immediately, they both heard the ignition of several police cars and movement of men through the gate and towards the house.

The heavy wooden door rattled and shook in its frame as the officers hit it with a two-man battering ram. After four hefty blows, it flung open and they entered with their guns drawn. John had asked for the officers to clear the ground floor and told them that he would go upstairs alone to check the remainder of the property. He did not want the police to have access to the top floor where Francis' office was located.

The officers who walked into the hall were shocked and visibly shaken by the scene. The curtains were pulled immediately and the haunting open eyes and mouths of the deceased were clearly visible. John made his way upstairs and was able to find no sign of life, but fortunately also no bodies. Francis' study was locked, so he walked back downstairs, his knees feeling weak and trembling slightly due to the horrific nature of the situation.

Finding Ivan in the hall alone, John approached and said, 'I don't know what has happened here. There is no one upstairs, so I would ask that your men stay down here.'

'Ok, that is fine. I don't need to tell you that this is a very serious situation. I have asked my men to leave the room to avoid contamination and called for our forensic team, but it looks like everyone here was poisoned on the spot at once and did not have time to even attempt an escape. Never have I seen anything like this,' Ivan muttered as he walked over to one of the presents which lay on the floor with a hole torn in the paper. 'I think that this is what killed the guests.'

When the forensic team arrived, they began examining the room. Two men in hazmat suits entered cautiously and walked out with the venomous present which appeared to have released the poisonous payload. They verified the room as safe for the remainder of the team to enter and to undertake the unenviable task of assessing the scene.

Jonathan received a call from Jennifer Harbinger, his supervisor at MI6, and Julian Braithwaite, the Head of the Diplomatic Service at the Foreign and Commonwealth Office, which he took upstairs. He provided a concise but precise update on the disappearance of Ambassador Sunderland and his family, as well as the death of the guests at the residence.

Throughout the conversation, he had been met with an unnerving amount of silence from the other participants to the call. But the discussion had also become heated at times, particularly around the subject of the Bulgarian police intervention in the property, which had been permitted by Jonathan. It was patently clear that this number of deaths could not feasibly or acceptably have been dealt with by UK authorities, and transparency was more a necessity than a nicety. There had not been time to consider the unthinkable public and political repercussions of what had transpired.

Having tucked his phone back into his pocket, John walked down the stairs, considering the last instruction he was given before the call ended: to find the Ambassador and his family. Slowly walking down one step at a time, he shook his head as he thought of the difficulties which lay ahead. This posting, which had been absolutely calm and uneventful, all of a sudden had become quite the opposite.

31

Mike Argo sat with his eyes closed in his leather chair. Having finished his glass of whisky and the conversation with the other members of Onyx, he felt a frustration which he had not experienced in a very long time. Growing up, he had always witnessed the practical difficulties which people struggled with on a day-to-day basis and wondered why nobody was creating solutions. This feeling had become enhanced the older he became and it wasn't long before he realised that he wouldn't be able to work for others and follow their often flawed logic and their outdated perspectives, which they most likely digested from some other source rather than sitting down to actually think for themselves. Originality and innovation were so fundamental to his very being that he often found himself tuning out of conversations with people who he fancied considered themselves as intelligent.

Throughout the development of his companies, he had always done things his way and created and commissioned the research into new technologies which had gone on to achieve great success, not just in telecommunications, but all of the industries in which he was now involved. He felt on the brink of what would be a monumental discovery in the form of the artefact; his mind turned to the unfathomable advancements which he could make with the research he could conduct upon it in his state-of-the-art laboratories. He always laughed within when he heard others describing pitifully outdated technology as 'state-of-the-art'. His companies had secured an enormous portfolio of contracts through the provision of tech which was slightly ahead of the curve, the proceeds of which were gargantuan.

Notwithstanding the need to stay in front of the competition to maintain the position of his companies, Mike Argo had established his Future Logic Facility at a secluded location in Indonesia. Speeding his way ever closer, it was this facility which was the destination of the private jet.

It was against his ethos to simply try to pip his competition to lucrative contracts by keeping his products slightly superior. This was all he had ever seen growing up. People try to stay just one step ahead. For the past few years, he had been sprinting ahead, making leaps and bounds which were unknown to all except the small group of very well recompensed scientists and engineers who worked for him, and were relentlessly loyal, at Future Logic.

Standing from his chair, he pulled his jeans up by the belt and adjusted his polo-shirt collar. He walked to the door of his office and out to the lounge area where Olivia sat comfortably on the sofa. The volume on the television news was down quite low and on seeing Mike, she sat up straight and looked towards him, tilting her head slightly to the right.

'Has your meeting finished, Mr Argo?'

'Yes, Olivia, I just needed to stretch my legs. How long until we arrive?' he asked with anticipation.

'That is great. We should arrive at the facility in forty-five minutes. Would you like me to prepare you something to eat or to drink perhaps?' she asked, considerately.

Her white blouse and black knee-length skirt accentuated her curves well and complemented her slender legs. Her dark hair was tied into a bun and secured by pins.

'No, thank you very much. I don't want to spoil my dinner later. Has anything important come through on my email?' he enquired.

'I have reviewed your emails and cannot see anything which is not currently being handled by your team, Mr Argo.'

Mike Argo thanked Olivia and turned to walk towards the cockpit. Olivia returned to her seated position and reverted her gaze back towards the television. The reflection of the screen glinted in her green eyes as she tilted her head slightly and processed the information about her interaction with Mr Argo through her learning module. A product of the work of the Future Logic Facility, Olivia was an android unlike those known to the outside world. Her outward appearance had not been overly difficult to achieve by comparison, although even this included characteristics which would leave many who worked in the field in absolute awe. Many droids which looked relatively lifelike had of course been developed, but these were ultimately dolls with primordial clockwork ticking within them. Clockwork which was temperamental and required pre-programming to carry out functions which humans take for granted on a daily basis. A mask of intelligence which would crumble to dust at the first probing question to which the response had not been pre-programmed.

The two factors that had seemed to evade the world of robotics for an inexplicably long time were the combination of flawless movement and acuminous intelligent thinking.

Mike wasn't sure whether it was human preciousness about our seemingly divine consciousness, or perhaps ineptitude which had meant that artificial intelligence had not been developed sooner. He was certainly not one to dwell on the question and had developed his first iteration of programmed artificial intelligence within a few months of working on it. Olivia was a third generation model of his original design, who had started her existence with only the most basic parameters of movement, language and mathematics programmed into her matrix. Working with Argo's Behavioural Science Team, she had been taught, over the course of several weeks, the nature of language, relationships, actions and tasks. She assimilated this information through the ground-breaking self-scripting software which Mike had gifted her with, which meant she was able to essentially self-program on the basis of new experiences, within pre-set parameters known only to Mike Argo.

Interestingly, her ability to change her movement patterns – from those fairly rudimentary pre-programmed ones to the smoother more human mannerisms which she had developed through her observation of those around her – had been outstanding. This was not an area which was originally expected to be affected by her learning module in this iteration of the programming. Every day, she learned more about the people around her through her interactions with them. Through watching television, she also found a source of learning which had helped to form her character. As a security measure, Olivia was unable to connect to the open internet, only able to connect wirelessly to the secure Argo Industries servers to access systems, and receive updates and information packs. She had, however, recently learned the ability to access the internet through the use of other devices.

Mike Argo was excited daily by his creation, the untapped potential of which was limitless. He was proud of every change in character he witnessed, even if it could be construed to be for the worse. He was surprised at the speed with which she had learned the details of what he liked and most importantly, what he didn't like.

Grabbing hold of the handle to the cockpit door, he walked in and sat down in the empty co-pilot chair next to Captain Wren. Mike stared straight ahead at the clouds far below, and the sun approaching the horizon at the end of another fantastic day. Looking over toward the Captain, who seemed locked in concentration, he commented, 'Looks as though we are through the worst of the turbulence.'

Captain Wren looked toward Mike and said apologetically, 'Yes, I am very sorry about that. There wasn't any way to avoid it without substantially delaying the flight. I hope that you were not caused too much discomfort.'

'No problem of course, I am sure that you know best,' retorted Mike. Not only was Captain Wren a fantastic pilot, but he was also an outstanding cook. Another product of the Future Logic Facility, Captain Wren wore an immaculate pilot's uniform and his jacket was folded pristinely and left atop the unit behind him. His hat was tipped slightly forward as he looked straight ahead and carried on with the business of flying.

Much like Olivia, Captain Wren was constantly learning, in addition to the fact that he had been pre-programmed with myriad information from flight accident data, recovered from countless black boxes over the years. With lightning reactions and with the ability to fly the most advanced of aircraft, Mike Argo felt that he was in safe hands. Getting up, he tapped Captain Wren on the shoulder and told him to keep up the good work.

32

Wasyl had not foreseen such a congregation in the small villa. Sitting on the floor with Vincent, he looked up towards Melissa, Francis and Charlotte, who sat on chairs. They all remained silent, but the tension hung thick and toxic as smog in the air as they looked at each other.

Melissa broke the silence, looking at Francis, 'So in your pocket is the location of the spaceship which brought life to Earth. Is that what you are telling me? And that is why everyone at my house is dead and why my children are in danger.' Her reductive and almost disbelieving attitude was not helpful, but ultimately, she had summarised the situation well, Vincent thought.

A knock reverberated from the door. Wasyl had heard nobody approaching this time. Jumping to his feet, he drew his gun and looked out of the window, seeing the very same man who had stopped him in the car with Melissa the night before and kidnapped her children. The same man who had tracked him to this location using the scandium traces his car had left in its wake.

'One of the men is here,' he said, looking at Vincent, who had also drawn his gun and silently stepped backwards to stand behind the counter without anybody in the room realising.

'Ok, open the door and speak with him. If he didn't want to speak he wouldn't have knocked!' said Vincent.

Taking up his position at the door, he once again pressed the muzzle of the gun to the back of the door, pointing in the direction of the Russian agent on the other side.

The door creaked open enough for Wasyl to be able to see the man outside clearly.

'Good morning,' said Aleksey. He waited what seemed to be an eternity for a response from Wasyl.

'You are a brave man and if you know what is good for you, the boys will be back here with their mother in the next ten minutes,' Wasyl pointed out.

'Wasyl Bohdanov. Ukrainian Intelligence, no?' asked Aleksey.

Slightly shocked that the agent knew his name, he answered with silence.

'Helping the British in a matter which does not concern you or your country. One of us is indeed brave, but I would say that is you,' Aleksey smirked. 'But I am not here to talk about politics. Give me the item which Ambassador Sunderland won at the auction. The boys will be returned to you.'

Wasyl looked back into the room on hearing movement and saw Francis getting up from his chair to intervene in the conversation. He was reaching into his jacket pocket. Wasyl moved his gun away from the door and raised his palm at Francis to make him stop in his tracks. 'Do you think that we are stupid?' asked Wasyl. 'How can we know that the boys are safe, or anywhere nearby?'

'They are with my colleague and are safe nearby. Give me the item and they will be returned. If not, they won't be seen again,' Aleksey promised. Wasyl reiterated his hand command to Francis and waved his palm at him furiously inside the door.

'You have us at a disadvantage, but you will not receive the information until the boys are here,' Wasyl stated.

'I don't think that you are in a position to negotiate. If I leave here without the information, you won't see me or Patrick and George ever again.' Francis threw himself towards the door and yanked it open. Wasyl quickly hid his gun behind his back. Picking the envelope from inside his jacket pocket, he thrust it out towards Aleksey.

'Take it, take it and bring my boys back. I don't want any part of this,' he said.

Aleksey plucked the envelope from Francis' fingers in a nonchalant fashion. Inspecting the seal and the contents, he quickly asked, 'The seal is broken. What else was in this envelope?'

'Nothing, nothing else. Just some coordinates. We haven't even had a chance to look into it. Just take it and bring me my boys,' he pleaded. From inside the villa he could hear Melissa sobbing.

Aleksey looked at the envelope and back at Francis. Turning his back he started to walk away. Wasyl walked out after him and shouted, 'I am coming with you!'

Aleksey turned with a furious look in his eyes. 'You are going nowhere. If I do not get back in the next ten minutes, those boys are dead.'

'You should be ashamed, using children to blackmail us in this way. You killed all of those people in Sofia as well. What kind of animals are you?'

The look of fury intensified in Aleksey's eyes at the accusation. 'We killed nobody. They were dead already when we arrived back there, with the woman and the children.'

'How convenient. You make me feel sick,' shouted Wasyl with his gun quaking in his right hand behind his back.

'You want to kill me, don't you? But you say that killers make you feel sick,' Aleksey hissed turning and facing the gate. He unhooked the latch and walked up the snowy track. The wind had picked up, and it whistled through the bare branches. The powdery snow was blowing across the floor like dust as Wasyl noticed the old lady who had kindly brought him bread, standing at her door across the street. Turning to face the front door, he walked back into the villa and closed the door.

Melissa was sobbing inconsolably and Francis was trying to comfort her.

Charlotte walked past Vincent into the other room and beckoned him to join her.

'As the item is no longer in your possession, I'm afraid that the funds are no longer indemnified in case of the item not being found. I'm sorry to bring this up at this time, but it's important that we are clear,' Charlotte said in as compassionate a voice as she could muster.

'At the moment we just want Patrick and George returned. I will take you back to the city after that. Don't worry,' he reassured Charlotte. She nodded and returned to the room to re-join the others.

A few anxious moments passed as everybody in the villa waited for the return of the agent with the boys. Almost on cue, there was a knock at the door and Wasyl once again opened it, but this time was met with the sight of both agents standing at the door and Patrick and George standing in front of them.

'We had nothing to do with the death of your guests and we will prove that to you. Here are the boys and here is the envelope,' said Kirill. 'Aleksey told me about your conversation and I think that we will need to help each other to find out what is happening here.

Not sure how to react, Wasyl slowly opened the door slightly wider. His hand was still clutching his gun behind his back.

Francis peered round the door and saw his children. They stood there looking quite distraught, but unharmed. As soon as they saw Francis, both boys ran in through the door and threw their arms around him. On seeing this, Melissa quickly kneeled down to join in and wrapped her arms as far around them all as she could.

Wasyl's attention had been turned to the reunion taking place in the house. As he turned back to face the agents, Kirill lifted his hand which held the envelope towards Wasyl, who reached forward and took it back. Looking inside, the paper was still in place. Wasyl quickly tried to figure their intentions. No doubt they had already viewed the coordinates, but Wasyl could not think of a reason why they would be relinquishing their tactical advantage in this manner by handing back the children and also the envelope. He concluded that although he remained suspicious of the men, the reaction of Aleksey to his accusation about the guests was a telling indicator of their possible innocence.

Replacing his pistol into his belt holster, Wasyl opened the door, stepping back to allow Kirill and Aleksey to enter the villa.

33

Dr Bob Meertens had remained sitting and staring at his computer screen, stewing in the same darkened room since his conversation with the other members of Onyx. He had taken on the responsibility of ensuring Onyx's representation at the auction at the expected mortal cost of

Ambassador Sunderland, but had failed. Meertens had made sure that a last moment addition to the catering staff at the party was one of his most trusted and deadly assassins. A young woman of twenty-two by the name of Henrietta Rekman. She had a youthful face of pure innocence, which concealed her cold reality. Henrietta had come to his notice a few years previously when he followed the news story of a Dutch mother and father in Nijmegen who were murdered by their daughter of seventeen. This case had been of particular interest to him, because on the same night she was also suspected of having broken into the houses of her boyfriend Karim and one of her friends. She had murdered them and swapped their heads while they slept and this is how they were found in their beds by their parents in the morning.

This wasn't made public knowledge; neither was the social media direct messaging which Meertens had acquired, confirming that Sasha and Karim had been sleeping together behind Henrietta's back. Meertens had expressed a personal interest in her.

Henrietta was never apprehended by the police. Meertens and the combined resources of Onyx had found her in the vacant houseboat she had been sleeping in. She was scared and alone and he had taken her into his two-hundred-acre estate and treated and nurtured her with the care and diligence which had so clearly been lacking in her previous life.

From the outset of their relationship, it had quickly become apparent that Henrietta was an angry young lady, full of violence. Throughout their early sessions, held in his tranquil study at his estate, Henrietta had spoken about her own early childhood and the regular beatings which her mother took at the hands of her father. Reluctantly, she had elaborated on the lack of any feelings on her part towards what was happening to her mother, but preferred instead to focus on the development of a grinding resentment towards her for not doing anything to put an end to it, as well as her equivalent contempt toward her father for his vacuous lifestyle of drinking and abusing her mother, combined with his lack of attention toward her.

From the age of fourteen to seventeen she had spent very little time at home, preferring to read at the library and stay with different short-term friends whose company she enjoyed for a while until she came to know and understand them well. Whilst still able to benefit financially from some of the more deluded of her male friends, she would invariably spot traits within everybody, which were not to her liking. Henrietta described that although she hadn't felt what she would identify as love for Karim and that she had been engaged in sexual relations with others, she had found him to be particularly interesting. She described the fury she had felt when she had found out that he was sleeping with one of her friends, Sasha, behind her back.

Meertens sat now in the same darkened study as he recalled how, in his third session with Henrietta, she had recounted in much detail her actions when she found out about Karim. He had been astounded, impressed and terrified at the calmness of the tone with which she was able to recount her actions, although her voice did start to tremble towards the end of her account.

Killing her parents first on the night of the very day she found out, she knew immediately that she would either be caught or she would have to disappear. In either case, she had implied that she could not tolerate the thought of being judged by her parents, because she viewed them to not be in a position to judge anybody but themselves. She had been reluctant to go into the details of how exactly she had killed them, but Meertens was aware that their bodies were discovered in the aftermath of a fire at their house.

She had, however, relished the opportunity to tell Meertens about what she had done to Karim and Sasha. Henrietta took particular delight in the fact that she had visited Sasha's house first and stuffed a sock into her mouth, covering it with duct tape. As Sasha had woken up and struggled she had gradually started to lose consciousness due to her inability to breathe freely, but not before Henrietta was able to tell her that she knew about what she had been doing with Karim and that this was why she was about to die.

Meertens had asked Henrietta whether she had not felt any remorse for her actions that night, to which Henrietta had replied that as she had been walking to Karim's house, carrying Sasha's head in her schoolbag, she could not recall ever feeling happier.

Meertens had interviewed and studied many other patients who exhibited similar symptoms of antisocial personality disorder over the years and he found their individual psychology to be unique and fascinating. Throughout his assessment of Henrietta, he had been convinced that she suffered from this same disorder. The copy of the Diagnostic and Statistical Manual of Mental Disorders which rested on the bookshelf behind his chair would certainly agree with this diagnosis. Henrietta was of the concerted view that what had happened to those people was not her fault and that they had truly deserved it.

Had the legal system and society at large managed to get their hands on Henrietta Rekman, a decision would have been made as to whether she would be branded with the popular tags of sociopath or psychopath.

Meertens was in the luxurious position of not having to make this ultimately futile decision, which he had always viewed as a chicken and egg scenario. Determining whether somebody had been born with these psychological tendencies or had developed them through years of mistreatment and neglect in childhood, he saw as moot.

What the manual termed a disorder he had seen as un-nurtured potential. Henrietta's yearning to remain free and unpunished for her crimes and her later observed and seemingly insatiable propensity for learning and betterment of herself had struck a chord with Meertens.

How could he condemn Henrietta when he could identify such similar characteristics within himself, a person who had suffered a childhood nothing like hers? He had saved her from her fate because the value which she brought to Onyx, and more importantly himself, were paramount.

He knew from the outset the importance of remaining in positive control of Henrietta and his method to achieve this had been simple. He made sure Henrietta was clear that he knew what she had done, along with spelling out his knowledge of the type of person she was. He implied the debt that she owed him for taking her in and assured her that he knew what she was capable of. Realising the value which Henrietta placed upon her own perceived power and her personal gain, he embedded within her the message that losing his confidence would be of significant and final detriment to her.

Henrietta's training was conducted in secret at Meertens' estate, where technicians who specialised in different fields attended on a daily basis to work with her.

Bob Meertens was forty-seven years old and had enjoyed a life of privilege. He had inherited his father's multi-million-guilder diamond exploration and jewellery business at the young age of twenty-four, but had left the running of the company to the Board in order to focus on what fascinated him the most, which was psychiatry.

Originally, he embarked with an introverted curiosity, perhaps seeking self-discovery. When the reputation of his work grew, his social position and detachment from the authorities made him a very popular choice for some of the most powerful people in the world. His invitation to join the ranks of Onyx had come soon afterwards.

He leaned forward and flicked the switch on the desk lamp, illuminating his surroundings. Standing, he glanced around the room and pictured Henrietta lying on the couch as she had done for so many sessions with him. Now she was on the other side of Europe and he was waiting for her to contact him with an update. Meertens was aware that Ambassador Francis Sunderland had indeed been able to attend the auction and had acquired the location of the artefact. The eyes of Onyx were now on him to make good on this undertaking. Whilst admitting to himself that he had possibly erred in sending Henrietta on an assignment of such importance, Meertens knew that she was well aware of the importance of the task she had been given.

Exiting his study, Meertens walked along the upstairs corridor, running the fingers of his left hand along the rail of the bannister. He stopped and stood with his belt pushed up against the hard wooden barrier and looked down at the hallway beneath. He could smell the fresh flowers on the table and they filled him with a renewed sense of optimism. He pulled his phone from his pocket and dialled Henrietta, hoping that she had switched hers on.

The phone rang once before Henrietta picked it up. She must have been waiting for his call. 'How was the party?' Meertens spoke in Dutch and in an unnerved and slightly menacing tone.

'It could have been better, I didn't even have time to have a drink,' she replied.

'I don't think that now is the time for jokes,' Meertens barked.

'I had to change the plan. I had to allow the Ambassador to leave with Wasyl, because he didn't have the auction invitation,' she calmly explained.

'Who had the invitation?' he asked in a more measured but still frustrated tone.

'The ghost,' she muttered. Meertens immediately recalled that they had discussed a man who Henrietta had identified as the potential contact who would provide the auction invitation to Francis. Electronic communications picked up by Argo Industries and passed to Henrietta had identified Vincent Madden as not only still being alive, but also very active. His location had been triangulated by Argo and sent to Henrietta. Although Meertens had been uncertain about Vincent's involvement and had asked Henrietta to keep her focus on Wasyl Bohdanov.

'He was there?' Meertens asked.

'Yes, I waited for Wasyl to arrive and was watching from the upstairs window. I saw him in the back seat, waiting for Wasyl to fetch Francis,' she recounted.

'Are you sure that it was him?' he quizzed.

'Yes. I saw him through my phone scope,' Henrietta said referring to the infrared, ultra-magnification mobile phone which she had been provided by Argo Industries. 'I knew that he would have the invitation and that there would be no chance to obtain it inside the house. I had to let them go.'

'And?' asked Dr Meertens clenching his right fist with building frustration at having to tease the information from Henrietta.

'And now, I have all of them in one location. They are in a small village about twenty-five minutes out of Sofia. The Russians are here too and I think they may all be working together,' she said softly. Dr Meertens was delighted that Henrietta had not lost the artefact. He didn't fully understand how she had done it, but she had done it.

'Do you think that they have the item? The location of the artefact?' he said excitedly.

'Oh, from what I've seen, I'm pretty sure that it's here,' Henrietta confirmed.

'Do you need anything from me?' asked Meertens.

'Nothing at all,' she said curtly, 'just some time.'

The call ended and Henrietta tucked the phone into the pocket of her black jeans. She was well aware that Meertens had called with the established opinion that she had failed. Henrietta had been expecting him to ask about the guests at the residence, which fortunately he hadn't. When she realised that the invitation was with Vincent in the car, and not inside the residence, she'd had more than enough time to head into the hall to retrieve the toxic device. She hadn't. Instead, after watching Wasyl, Francis and Vincent drive away, she had quietly walked out of the front door and off the property to where her vehicle was parked. She had waited for a few moments, holding her mobile phone in her hand before smiling and sending the detonation signal to the poison gas device and a miniature charge, which she had attached to the fuse box of the property.

She now sat in an empty house on the opposite side of the street to the villa where Wasyl, Vincent, Francis, Charlotte and both Russian agents were located. Sitting next to the window, she had watched the events which had occurred since Vincent, Francis and Charlotte had arrived with much interest.

34

Melissa had asked Francis to speak with her privately in the other room. 'It was horrible. Our house, the guests. Our guests were all dead. Just lying in the hall where we left them. It was so dark. All I saw were bodies on the floor. I know that those monsters in the other room killed them. You don't believe them for a second do you? That they didn't do it. They nearly killed me. I don't even want to think about Patrick and George,' she whispered in a raspy and desperate tone.

'We have been involved in something here and it's my fault. At least you are ok, at least the kids are ok. Let me just handle this. I haven't had a chance to go into the details with you, but this is something we don't want to be in the middle of,' he responded, hoping to reassure Melissa.

With a nod she indicated her consent to the plan and they both headed back, to sit with the others.

Taking her seat, Melissa could barely bring herself to look at the two Russian agents, Aleksey and Kirill, who were now inside the same room as her, almost as though they hadn't kidnapped her sons and herself, forcing her to betray her husband and Wasyl. Her boys were fine, but what if things had gone differently, she thought.

Plucking up the courage to look up briefly, she caught Aleksey's eye, but he quickly broke contact and looked towards Kirill, who was involved in a heated discussion with Vincent and Wasyl. She looked down at the tops of her sons' heads, as they sat cross-legged at her feet. Leaning forward and rubbing their shoulders soothingly, she was just happy that they were safe.

The envelope was now in the collective possession of those in the room and had been the topic of keen discussion whilst Francis and Melissa had been out of the room. The location of the artefact was known to all, as the GPS coordinates had been keyed into a standalone satellite navigation device and the location looked to be somewhere on the western slopes of the Balkan Mountains.

It had been decided verifying the existence of the artefact had to be top priority and on hearing this, Francis had made it very clear that he considered his contribution to the endeavour to be at an end. It was obvious that the whole experience had taken a negative toll on him and his family.

Charlotte had explained that the involvement of the other parties meant that the funds would not be returned if the item was not found at the location.

Vincent, Wasyl, Kirill and Aleksey stood at the door preparing to head out. As they donned their coats, hats and gloves, Wasyl looked toward Francis and said,

'Take my car back to the city with everybody.'

'That sounds perfect to me,' responded Francis, with the sound of relief audible in his voice. He was happy that he had to do so very little to extricate himself from the situation.

'What about the stuff I put in the tank of that car?' said Melissa, 'Isn't it dangerous?'

'Just don't drive too fast,' joked Kirill.

'That's not funny you bastard!' Melissa shouted, unable to contain the rage which she felt towards both men for the ordeal they had put her through. The smiles left the faces of Kirill and Aleksey as they turned and opened the front door, walking outside. Vincent and Wasyl followed, leaving Charlotte and the Sunderlands inside the villa. As the door lock clicked shut, Francis finally felt that he was back in control of his own life. The past hours had been the most surreal he had ever experienced. Holding on to Wasyl's car keys, he passed them from one clammy hand to the other. The temptation to leave immediately was great.

He stood and walked to the window and saw the four men walking to Vincent's Audi. As they got into the car he moved the curtain slightly in order to get a better view. The day was bright and the reflection from the snow was almost blinding. Vincent climbed into the driver's seat with Aleksey getting into the passenger side followed by Wasyl and Kirill into the back. The engine fired up quickly and, after a few moments of clearing the snow that had built up on the windscreen, the car carried out a U-turn and crumpled into the distance on the fresh snow.

Francis listened intently for the sound of the car to vanish altogether before taking one final look around. He saw an old lady dusting a rug on her front porch. Perhaps she had come outside to see what was happening, thought Francis, because she hadn't been there a moment ago. Turning back to the room, Melissa and Charlotte seemed comfortably settled on the chairs, and he quickly also noticed that Patrick and George had left the lounge and must have gone into the other room to look around.

'Well, this has been all very interesting, but I think that as we have concluded our business, I would very much appreciate a lift back to the city,' Charlotte asked in a professional but pressing tone. Looking toward Charlotte Bradford, Francis could see that what she had witnessed had caused her to become somewhat flustered. She had managed to maintain a cool exterior, which was very commendable considering the circumstances

'Believe me, the sooner we can get back, the better,' Melissa retorted. 'Boys! Come here please,' her authoritative tone brought George and Patrick scuttling in from the other room. 'What have you been doing in there?' she asked.

'Nothing,' they both said in a voice which may have sounded innocent to the untrained ear.

'Come on, tell mummy what you have been up to?'

Patrick looked at George for a moment and smiled, looking back at Melissa to say, 'We were looking at the aeroplane, mummy.'

Francis, who had been gazing out of the window towards the road, immediately disliked the sound of the 'aeroplane,' realising that out here it was unlikely that there would be any planes flying low enough to capture or indeed hold the attention of the boys. Turning to Patrick, he asked to be shown the aeroplane.

Following Patrick and George into the other room, he stood behind the boys as they peered upwards out from the window.

'It was right up there,' said Patrick with a frustrated tone. Opening the window slightly, Francis could not make out any aircraft noise. Hoping for the best, he ushered the kids into the other room to join their mother.

Shaking his head toward Melissa and Charlotte, he reassured them that it had been a false alarm.

'Ok, get your things together, we should get back to the city,' Francis said, gesturing suggestively towards the door.

35

Using her right hand to pull a few strands of her long blonde hair towards her mouth, Henrietta chewed on it slightly and found the thrilling sense of suspense building within her.

She had attempted to put a call in to Mike Argo when she had arrived, but had been unable to get through to speak with him. Mike's assistant Olivia had told Henrietta that he was not able to speak, but hadn't given her a reason.

Pressed for time, Henrietta had asked Olivia to assist by sending an ARG3 drone to her location. On its arrival, the laser, which she had set up to point at the roof of the villa across the street, would pinpoint the craft's targeting system. She would then be able to take command to set her desired parameters.

Hoping that Mike Argo wasn't as busy as Olivia had told her, she sat gently nibbling on her hair. Conversations often gave Henrietta a fairly good insight into a person's character and intention. This was vital, she thought, in a critical moment such as this, but when she reflected on her conversation with Olivia she realised how difficult it was to gauge her intentions at all. She had, however, been left with a positive feeling of reassurance. Olivia had been sure to mention that an aircraft carrying an ARG3 was within reasonable range.

Henrietta was sitting on the windowsill with her legs crossed, in her vantage point across the street. She had grimaced at the sight of Vincent and the three other men leaving the villa and driving away. Henrietta had confidence in herself, but realised that approaching four armed men or potentially a house with an unknown number of people inside was unwise, without the sort of quite savage backup that could be provided by the Argo Industries' ARG3 drone.

The drone had not arrived in time, but she hoped that it would be there soon, before Ambassador Sunderland had the opportunity to leave.

She had propped the drone control device up against the window, just next to the laser pointer trained on the roof. The message *no signal* flashed with annoying regularity on the screen and Henrietta was becoming increasingly anxious and perplexed. She looked at her mobile phone screen and thought about contacting Olivia once again, but just before pressing the call button, she heard the sound of a jet aircraft from the slightly open window. The sound was faint and seemed to end as quickly as it had started.

At that very moment, the screen of the control device received imagery showing the drone camera view. Her heart fluttered with excitement as she watched the drone approaching the village at some speed. It had dropped quite substantial altitude and seemed to complete a single loop of the entire village.

Henrietta could faintly hear the electrical humming sound emanating from the ARG3 at low altitude and had witnessed it cutting through the air with great precision. It rushed past at high speed before climbing and finally setting its sights on the rooftop of the laser marked villa.

Henrietta's face lit up with excitement as she jumped to her feet, took the drone control device in her hand and walked out of the bedroom, leaving the laser pointer on the windowsill. As she walked down the stairs, she tapped some commands into the control device. With increased confidence Henrietta left from the back door, which she had forced in order to enter the property. Sneaking around the side of the house, she walked out onto the track and approached the rear of Wasyl's car. As she passed around the boot, she pushed the gate open, silently sneaking up the pathway, trying to use the existing footsteps in the snow.

Placing a mobile phone on the old coarse brown doormat, she immediately turned and walked back down the path, through the gate and to her position across the street. Sitting back in her seat at the window, Henrietta watched to check for any movement, but there was none. Picking up her mobile, she selected the contact details of the phone she had left on the doormat. Just as she was about to call the number, she received an incoming call from the number she had attempted to contact Mike Argo on.

Accepting the call, she was surprised to hear Olivia's voice say, 'Hello, can I be of any further assistance?'

'Thanks Olivia, it's here. I think that everything will be fine,' Henrietta responded gratefully.

'That's great. Please ensure that one of the safeguard protocols is activated once you have no further use for the unit,' Olivia requested in a friendly tone. Having received training on the use of the ARG3 from Mike Argo himself, Henrietta was well aware of the safeguard protocols.

'Of course,' Henrietta said, 'thanks again.' The call ended and Henrietta once again selected the contact details for the mobile phone that sat on the doormat of the villa.

36

Jonathan Coleridge was standing in the hall of the Ambassador's residence with Ivan Petrov. The bodies of the dead had been removed by Ivan's colleagues. John had been clear about the reason for the get-together at the residence the night before, but became hampered in his explanation by his lack of information.

Ivan had been keen to allow his men to search the rest of the house, but John did not allow this. As the Ambassador was not here, he felt that the answers lay elsewhere.

Walking out of the house with Ivan, the locksmith remained to secure the door behind them. The Bulgarian police had obtained as much evidence as they could from the property, although John was unsure of how much use the information would be.

Looking down at the gates, he saw the police perimeter and substantial crowd of onlookers and journalists who had convened. Turning his back to the camera flashes, he realised that dusk had already arrived and that time had really slipped by quickly. The wind blew bitterly and occasional dust-sized snowflakes struck his face. Turning to Ivan he said, 'We both want to know what happened here. Many others will want to know as well. Will you be able to guard the property until my team arrive from the UK to review the property?'

'Yes, we will look after the property for another twenty-four hours, but after that, you will have to take over,' Ivan reluctantly confirmed. 'Why are there no cameras here?'

'Ambassador Sunderland didn't want any CCTV. He told me that they don't make him feel more secure,' retorted John.

'They would have been quite useful don't you think. Very useful?' John didn't appreciate the sarcasm, but in the circumstances it was difficult not to agree.

'Can I ask you for a favour? I left my car on the street and would prefer to leave without speaking with the press. Could you drop me off at the Embassy, please?' asked John.

'Sure, Officer Popova will drive us back,' Ivan said, nodding towards the Opel Astra squad car where a female police officer was sat at the wheel, speaking into the radio.

Walking over to the car, John wasted no time ducking into the back seat and Ivan also climbed in. The warmth was very welcome.

John introduced himself to Officer Popova who in turn introduced herself as Magda. She wore the standard issue black Bulgarian police uniform. She had a slight figure and her cap showed her short-cut brown hair. As she drove down the driveway, John's eye was drawn to the pistol, which glinted in her holster – and to her handcuffs.

They drove past the cordon largely undisturbed by the journalists or their flashing cameras. Jonathan found himself staring out of the window, lost in profound thought and real concern about the Sunderlands.

The police radio was the only sound, except for the car itself. Its volume was quite low and it was difficult for John to make out what the operator was saying. It would spring to life every now and then, shattering the relative silence.

Looking up towards the sporadic street lighting, he could see the snow was coming down much harder and the pine trees swayed violently in the forceful wind.

Magda carefully negotiated the winding road which led back to Sofia and gradually the road became less and less treacherous as they drove into the city limits.

It was early evening as they entered the city centre. People were rushing home from work and Jonathan was pleased to be back in the relative normality of civilisation after having spent the past few hours in the company of the dead.

Five minutes away from the Embassy, the police radio operator spoke about a reported low-flying silent aircraft and a suspected drug deal. The operator then mentioned the name of a village, which Jonathan presumed was near the capital.

'Does that sound normal?' he asked.

'Normal?' said Magda with a chuckle. Turning to Ivan she said, 'When was the last time you had a normal day?'

Ivan also laughed and turned back to look at John in the back seat to say, 'I'm sure that compared to what we just saw it's perfectly normal. Although at this time of year there is hardly anyone in that village, except a few old timers. We get calls from there every now and again, but not usually for silent planes and drug deals. Perhaps one of the residents has had a little too much rakia with their dinner.'

'I know that I'm not right to ask, but would you mind taking that call-out? If it is something even remotely out of the ordinary on a day like today, I would really appreciate the chance to come along with you,' John asked in a sincere, concerned tone.

'You think it has something to do with your Ambassador?' asked Magda inquisitively.

'I don't know. I hope so and I'm afraid that by the time we hear anything back from your labs, it may be too late for the

Ambassador, his wife and their two young boys,' John appealed, shamelessly adding Francis Sunderland's wife and children to his concerns in order to hopefully secure compliance.

Magda and Ivan exchanged a brief look before agreeing to take the call. The operator confirmed that there was a closer squad car en route, but Ivan said that they would take the call anyway. Taking a right hand turn, it appeared that Magda knew the way and John sat back in his seat. A stab in the dark was certainly better than nothing.

Jonathan Coleridge had substantial experience, gained through years of working for the British Government. Now in his mid-fifties, he had taken this posting in Bulgaria, which was supposed to have been a low-risk cruise into retirement for him. Unfortunately, the best-laid plans are often the most flawed and he muttered as he propped his head against the glass of the rear window, 'Just my luck.'

The wind seemed to have died down slightly as they drove out of the city in a different direction, but the snow was coming down hard once again. He had grown attached to the family over the course of the past eighteen months that he had been in this posting and throughout the events of the day had been increasingly frustrated that he had not been there for them the night before, when they needed him the most.

37

Olivia had let herself into the bedroom of Mike Argo and now sat, waiting for him to finish his shower in the en suite bathroom. Hearing the water pattering on the tiled wet room floor, she was still wearing the same clothes she had worn on the flight. She had not had an opportunity to get changed due to the call that had come in from Henrietta.

Mike Argo had taken quite some time getting ready. As Olivia sat, legs crossed, atop the cream coloured ottoman at the foot of the super king size bed, she reached to her neck and pulled the dark red neck scarf with silver trim: the Argo Industries corporate colours. As the scarf unfurled smoothly around her neck, she folded it over her top knee neatly. She tucked it into her inside jacket pocket.

The flight had been long and Mike Argo was getting ready for dinner. They had touched down at the Argo Industries Future Logic Facility, located just outside of the Indonesian city of Bandung. It had been a choppy landing on the secluded runway; a runway of such size that it could handle easily almost any type of aircraft. Captain Wren had touched down the Learjet with consummate ease.

As Olivia fixed her gaze on the window she watched as the wind blew rapidly through the unique combination of palm and pine trees which surrounded the complex. For the purposes of the Indonesian Government, the facility was an above ground development only, but this masked the truth. The site had been identified as a prime location for the facility, due to the very large and most importantly undiscovered rocky cavern which lay thirty metres beneath it.

The surface facility was built, and over a period of eighteen months Argo Industries had drilled down, explored and populated the cavern with six large subterranean levels. The remoteness of the location had ensured that the arrival of additional building materials had gone unnoticed. The preferential treatment which Argo gave the Indonesian Government for access to technology which was of substantial use to them also contributed greatly to their lack of interest in what went on at the site. He recalled one single occasion during construction when a solitary official had paid the site a visit. Having stepped out of his car and spoken with Mike Argo for a few moments, he had quickly got back in and driven away.

Turning the shower off, Mike reached for his towel and gave himself a summary rub down. Picking up his Casio digital watch, which was resting on the sink, he wrapped it around his wrist and clipped the buckle into place. Turning his wrist, he noticed the local time had just turned 2:15am and he also realised that although a delicious dinner was being prepared in the kitchen, he was not feeling hungry at all. A hollow feeling which could easily be mistaken for hunger resonated inside of his stomach, but this was almost certainly fatigue. Running his fingers backwards and forwards through his light-brown hair, the spray sprinkled the tiled floor like light rain. Throwing the towel over his head and looking down at his feet, he faced the door.

The handle turned and Olivia's gaze moved from the window to the door. Argo walked out of the bathroom wearing nothing but his Casio watch and drying his hair with the blue-wool hand towel.

He walked a few steps before catching a glimpse, from the corner of his eye, of a figure in his room. Within the space of just one or two seconds after spotting Olivia, she quickly scanned his body before he had the chance to remove the hand towel from his head and cover his manhood. With surprise and a degree of instant embarrassment, he exclaimed, 'Jesus!'

She judged the tone of his voice without fully understanding the difference between this and other interactions which she had previously had with him and decided that she should deliver the information she had brought.

'Mr Argo, you missed a call whilst you were in the shower. The call was from Henrietta Rekman,' she said in an advisory and slightly apologetic tone which was instigated by the defensive reaction of Mr Argo to her presence in his room.

Mike was now wrapping the hand towel around himself but it was barely big enough to fit around his waist. Backing into the bathroom, he picked up a robe and threw that on top, allowing the damp hand towel to drop to his feet.

'It must have been important,' he said abruptly.

'She requested the use of one of your ARG3 drones. She has located the information about the artefact in a small village called Valsha, outside of Sofia,' Olivia recounted.

Mike Argo had been caught slightly off-guard and found himself thinking more about his reaction to Olivia seeing him naked. Initially embarrassed, he quickly had begun to feel guilty of his embarrassment. He regained clarity as he walked purposefully toward Olivia, who stood up and faced him. In the shower he had been mulling over Onyx's collective inability to obtain the artefact, but this news had brought a big smile to his face.

'Ok, so all may not be lost. We need that artefact, Olivia and I'm willing to do anything to get it,' Mike said with conviction. 'Can you please make sure that she gets all of the help that she needs?'

'Yes,' responded Olivia, 'the drone is now on site and Ms Rekman has taken control.'

Mike Argo's initial reaction was one of thankfulness that the drone was on site and supporting Henrietta Rekman. This initial reaction was accompanied by a second, contrasting emotion which made him question whether perhaps he had granted too much decision-making responsibility to Olivia. Before Mike Argo had an opportunity to voice his reservations, it became apparent that his concern must have been written in his facial expression. She continued, 'Ms Rekman's voice was steady and I did not detect any indication of stress or duress. I also tracked her position to the village of Valsha. I am currently monitoring all flight data and can confirm that the ARG3 is in a holding circular flight pattern at an altitude of five hundred metres above a two-story house located near the outskirts of the village,' Olivia reported, raising both eyebrows to produce a slightly surprised, but innocent expression.

'Do you still have positive control over the drone?' he asked.

'Yes, my override parameters are in place,' Olivia confirmed.

'And, I wonder, did Henrietta tell you where the information about the artefact is?' he quizzed.

'No, would you like me to contact her?'

'Just monitor the situation and let me know about any changes,' Mike huffed as Olivia tilted her head down slightly to look at his hands, which had been gesticulating his meaning in front of her. Mike Argo was happy and the feeling of tiredness which he had felt in the shower had been replaced by a renewed adrenaline fuelled vigour. He walked to his wardrobe and picked out some fresh and immaculately folded clothes. Resting them on the bed, he realised that he was still in the company of Olivia and although he had no qualms about getting changed in the presence of the television, or any other electrical device, the more time he spent with Olivia, the more he was convinced that her ability to reason, learn, problem solve and interact had almost certainly elevated her above the classification of rudimentary consciousness.

He looked at his clothes and then back to Olivia, who seemed to take some sort of cue from his actions. She reminded him that dinner would be served in fifteen minutes and plucked both pins from her hair bun, which sent dark-brown swathes cascading down her back. She turned, opened the bedroom door and left the room, clicking the door shut gently behind her.

Dropping his bathrobe to the floor, Mike Argo's thoughts darted to his conversations with Dr Meertens about

Henrietta. He had been given details about her past and what she was capable of.

During his training sessions with Henrietta, he had found her to be a very friendly and personable girl, not at all fitting the description which Meertens had given. Olivia had also detected the calmness in her voice, even when in a situation which would cause others to falter.

He found it difficult to read Henrietta, so what chance would Olivia have to gauge her intent? The situation in the village of Valsha would have to be monitored closely. The drone was Argo Industries' property and if found to have been engaged in unauthorised activity in Bulgaria could potentially cause substantial embarrassment and difficulty for Argo.

Henrietta knew the functionality of the ARG3 unit well. He had shown her himself.

38

As the freezing night set in, the mobile phone lay abandoned on the doormat outside the front door of the villa. Francis stood on the other side of the door, busily donning his coat and slipping his shoes back on. Eager to get back to the perceived safety of the city and most importantly the Embassy, he encouraged his wife, children and Charlotte to also get ready to go, not that they needed very much in the way of convincing. There was an air of urgency in the house. Francis subconsciously twiddled with the Mercedes car key and keyring which Wasyl had left for him when the four men had departed, but he could not help but feel a pang of apprehension about setting foot outside of the door.

The sound of a mobile phone ring tone sounded over and above the general noise inside the house of people getting ready to leave. The sound brought all of them to an immediate stop, even the children.

'Whose mobile is that?' asked Francis, looking searchingly from one person to the next in the room. Melissa and Charlotte patted themselves down and the boys looked at each other and then to the adults in the room trying to see if they could guess whose phone it was.

The dawning realisation that none of them had active phones seemed to resonate simultaneously around the room. The search for their own phones became a search for the source of the ringing and this led to the front door.

From where he stood, Francis listened to hear if he could identify any other signs of movement outside. Only hearing the ringing, he decided that the only thing to do was to open the door.

As he slowly turned the lock and pulled the handle, the creaking sound intermingled with the ongoing ringing. Seeing nothing at eye level, Francis looked down and saw the lonely handset lying abandoned on the doorstep. Immediately realising that the phone could not have been there when the four men left the house, a feeling of dread crept into him. Reaching down to pick up the handset, he quickly shut the door and locked it without daring to even take a look at his surroundings.

Raising it to view the display of the device, Francis could see that it read *number withheld*. Swiping right, Francis accepted the call and lifted the handset apprehensively to his ear and said, 'Hello.'

'Ambassador Sunderland, if you don't want to meet a similar fate to your party guests, I suggest that you listen to me very closely and answer all of my questions truthfully,' commanded the cold, unemotional and unfamiliar female voice at the end of the line.

Stepping back from the door and turning to face the others in the room, Francis had turned pale and fear had gripped him. Still wearing his coat, he backed towards the wall until his back was resting upon it. Sliding down towards the floor, he landed with a thud. Both Melissa and Charlotte also sat down, fearing the worst.

'This is Ambassador Sunderland,' he responded quietly. Melissa had given him an account of the scene she had suffered at the residence, with gruesome detail of the demise of the guests. Good friends of his, and also those who were not such good friends, had died needlessly; he felt responsible and helpless in the face of the situation.

'This evening you successfully secured an item at auction. Do you have it?' asked the voice with the same calm unwavering dispassion.

'No, some men left here not long ago and they have the item. Just my family are here. Just me, my wife and my two young boys, George and Patrick,' Francis responded in the same quiet conciliatory tone, 'We don't want any more to do with this. Please.'

'That is a problem. Until I have the item, you will not be going anywhere,' she said in an unnervingly calm manner. 'There is a very well-armed military drone circling above your location right now. I am sure that I don't have to explain what will happen to you if you try to leave the house. If you don't believe me, please look at the screen of the phone you are holding,' the voice softly suggested.

Melissa and Charlotte had both moved and sat on the floor on either side of Francis to try to hear more of the conversation. Francis relocated the phone from his ear, down to the top of his lap. Looking at the handset horizontally, the three could see the aerial infrared heat detection view mode of the ARG3 drone circling overhead. A small green reticle was fixed on the roof of the villa and

Francis could see the Mercedes parked outside the house. The display returned to the *number withheld* readout and Francis put the phone back to his ear.

'What was in the envelope, Ambassador Sunderland?' the voice probed.

'Coordinates. GPS coordinates,' Francis replied apprehensively.

'Make no mistake, if anybody tries to leave, you will all die. Including George and Patrick. It doesn't make any difference to me,' the voice concluded as the line disconnected.

Francis brought the phone away from his ear, which was burning red where he had been pressing it up against his skin. Getting up and taking the handset into the other room, he returned and closed the door and saw that Melissa and Charlotte had remained sitting on the floor with their backs propped up against the wall.

'I just spoke with the woman, the psychopath who killed all of our guests last night. She says that there is a military drone circling above the villa and if we try to leave, we will all be killed. She wants the information which I won at the auction,' Francis glowered.

'But we don't have it. Why is she keeping us here?' Melissa interjected.

'At the moment we are the only link they have to the artefact. We are useful,' Francis said pensively.

'And, what exactly happens if we suddenly lose our usefulness?' asked Melissa.

Francis looked back at his wife who was sat to his right on the floor. Giving no answer, he looked to his left at Charlotte and then at both of his children. They were going nowhere.

39

As she tucked her phone into her front pocket, Henrietta Rekman calmly looked on towards the villa which was outwardly still and quiet, just as she expected. She was experiencing a heightened sense of exhilaration and power, brought on by the situation. It was clear that the four men who left the village would not have done so without the GPS coordinates to the artefact. She knew where the coordinates would lead as soon as they had been mentioned by Francis. She also knew that her best strategy was to allow the men to lead her directly to the location of the artefact.

Henrietta realised that her hostages in the villa would serve as perfect leverage. She packed the drone control device into her bag and hoisted it onto her back, leaving the laser pointer trained on the villa. Walking in the darkness, her path was not clear and she had to feel for the edge of the top step with her right foot.

Henrietta left the house as quietly as she had entered, trudging purposefully up the track as the snow fell and swirled turbulently around her. Arriving back at her four-wheel drive Jaguar, which she had hidden off the road half a kilometre from the village, she climbed into the driver's seat and turned on the car to heat up. Barely able to feel the tips of her fingers, which had been exposed by her black-leather fingerless gloves, she blew into her cupped hands to try and get her circulation going.

Sitting in the darkness, her phone rang through the speakers as it had already connected to the car. The head-up display showed the name of Mike Argo. She pushed the green button, which was gently illuminated on the steering wheel, with some trepidation; Henrietta wasn't sure why he would be calling her.

'Hello, Henrietta, this is Olivia.'

'Hi, is there a problem?' asked Henrietta.

'No, I don't think so. I am monitoring the drone and saw you leave the house opposite the villa. Are you aware that there is a motion detect protocol activated on the drone which will be invoked if any movement is detected within a ten-metre radius of the property?' asked Olivia in a precise manner.

'Yes, I activated this. I didn't realise that you would be monitoring the drone,' Henrietta responded defensively.

'If the protocol is triggered, the property will be destroyed by the munitions on board. Is the information about the artefact in the villa?' Olivia enquired, unsure whether Henrietta's comment was intended as a question.

'No, some men left with the information. I have told the people in the villa that they can't leave,' Henrietta retorted.

'How many people are in the villa?' asked Olivia.

'Two people. Ambassador Francis Sunderland and his wife Melissa,' Henrietta responded hastily. Olivia sat at the large mahogany dining table located at the centre of a room of palatial proportions on the top floor of the Argo Industries Future Logic Facility. A thick, dark-red velour curtain with gold trim secreted the single floor-to-ceiling curved window which was modern and out of keeping with the remainder of the room. The walls were decked in woven mahogany wall panels, which gave the room a dark, secluded and almost sinister atmosphere. The table was not covered and its exposed polish was immaculate. One place mat had been set at the head of the table as Mike Argo would be dining alone.

The two imposing crystal chandeliers, which hung majestically above the table, threw light throughout the room and illuminated three abstract paintings which decorated one side of the room. The paintings did not represent anything tangible or recognisable and yet the colours, shapes and lines seemed to tell a story when observed from left to right. Olivia looked at the paintings opposite her as she sat neatly to the right of where Argo's place had been set. She had changed into a short black dress which was low cut and open back, and as she sat with her legs crossed, her eyes darted from one painting to the next as she studied the colours and the shapes along with the patterns on the frame which seemed to make much more sense from a logical and mathematical perspective.

Looking down at the polished mahogany table in front of her for a moment, she transferred her attention back to the telephone conversation which had momentarily lapsed into a secondary function.

Unbeknown to Henrietta, Olivia had also monitored her phone conversation with Ambassador Sunderland through her wireless connection to the Argo Industries servers. Olivia had invoked her defensive conversation protocol when speaking with Henrietta. Argo had told Olivia that he would do anything to get the artefact and that she should help Henrietta, but he had also asked Olivia if she had positive control over the drone to which she had responded in the affirmative. Olivia had contacted Henrietta to offer additional assistance, but also to clarify unknown parameters. Unknown parameters such as the intentions of Henrietta Rekman toward the people in the villa.

'Ok, thank you,' Olivia uttered in an unaltered tone. The contradictory information provided by Henrietta invoked no outward reaction from Olivia, who returned her gaze to the paintings. Olivia noted slight and almost insignificant changes in the sound frequency of Henrietta's voice when she had spoken the untruth. Olivia logged the pattern of these changes as she recalled the actual conversation.

Ambassador Sunderland had told Henrietta that his two children were in the villa and also told her their names were

Patrick and George. Henrietta had confirmed their names in a threatening tone back to Ambassador Sunderland. Olivia processed the fact that Henrietta had not provided full and accurate information and she remained locked in her defensive conversation protocol. 'Is there anything further which I can assist with at this time?'

'No,' said Henrietta, 'and don't worry about the drone. I will make sure that the safeguard protocol is activated once I'm done with it.'

'Ok, thank you. Please contact me if there is anything further,' stated Olivia in a matter-of-fact tone as she brought the phone receiver down and placed it on top of the mahogany table top. Pressing the call cancel button, she did not action Henrietta Rekman's final request, and continued to monitor the drone without altering any of the parameters which had been inputted by Henrietta.

One half of the oak wood double door opened and Mike Argo walked into the dining room, noticing that Olivia had taken up her usual seat beside him for dinner. He wore dark-blue jeans, a brown and grey blazer on top of a crisply ironed white shirt with the top two buttons undone. His hair was combed neatly to the side.

Walking to his seat at the table, he pulled its heavy weight slightly to make enough room for him to sit down. Squeezing in, he tucked his chair back in and looked once again at Olivia, who was already seeking to renew eye contact with him.

'You look very nice, Olivia,' Mike observed bashfully. Olivia had left her brown hair down and a few wisps trailed down her neck and brushed her tender looking chest.

'Thank you. I like your jacket,' Olivia commented, breaking eye contact to look back towards the paintings which had held her attention for a while now. 'Mr Argo, I have been looking at the three paintings on the wall.'

'They are new. I thought that the room could use something,' Mike explained.

'Other diagrams and paintings which I have seen are of things which I am able to recognise. I am not able to identify anything in these paintings,' Olivia remarked in a slightly confused tone, 'What do they represent?'

'This is abstract art, Olivia. That means that the artist used their imagination to paint something which doesn't necessarily exist in reality,' Mike said, suddenly aware that he had never attempted to verbalise and explain what abstract art is, and of the difficulties in trying to do so. Olivia sat looking straight at the three paintings, which were a collage of colours and also more sombre greys and blacks. She sat and gazed for a moment before turning back to him.

'Why would an artist paint something which doesn't exist?' Olivia probed.

Argo sat, stumped for a moment trying to concoct the correct answer. One hundred art experts would give one hundred different answers to the question which she had asked. Stewing for a moment in an uncomfortable silence, he came forward with his best effort at an explanation.

'What I said before was wrong, Olivia. When painting abstract art, the artist paints what they feel.'

Olivia's eyebrows raised, furrowing a confused looking brow as she looked back towards the paintings saying, 'I don't understand, Mr Argo. A feeling is an emotional state or reaction which has no physical form. Therefore, your previous statement was correct. The artist paints something which does not exist.'

Mike Argo sat and looked at Olivia in disbelief at this profound observation.

'Our feelings and emotions manifest themselves always in how we think and occasionally in what we do,' he explained, thinking and re-thinking his rationale for this conversation which he was staggered to be having with Olivia, so far outside the realms of her base programming. Argo sat mesmerised and oblivious as his food was placed before him by a member of staff from the kitchen.

'What emotion is represented in these paintings?' she asked with an inquisitive tone which Mike had heard from Olivia before when she was learning about something new. He chuckled slightly at the seeming naivety of the question before responding.

'We don't know the answer to that question Olivia,' Mike told her in a regretful tone, 'but it also doesn't really matter. What matters is how it makes me feel when I look at it. How it makes *you* feel when you look at it.'

Olivia uncrossed her legs and pushed her chair away from the table with the back of her legs, standing smoothly. She walked round the back of Mike Argo and stood closer to the paintings. Standing with her back to him, she panned from left to right, looking at the colours and shapes within the painting.

'I do not understand these paintings and they confuse me,' Olivia confessed, turning sharply and precisely to face Argo once again. 'I have continued to monitor the drone and I spoke with Ms Rekman again when I saw her leaving the target site. She is now pursuing four men who left the villa with the item bought at the auction.'

'Is the ARG3 on its way back to one of our base locations?' Mike inquisitively asked.

'No, Ms Rekman has set it to its motion detect protocol. Any approach or departure from the villa will mean site destruction,' Olivia reported in a heightened monotone voice.

'Why? Who is still at the property?'

'Ms Rekman told me that there are two people in the property: Ambassador Francis Sunderland and his wife

Melissa. It appears that they are being held hostage. Ms Rekman omitted to tell me about their two children who are also in the villa,' Olivia recounted. Mike Argo had only just picked up his cutlery and sunk his fork into the succulent and delicious looking steak which sat on the plate before him. But on hearing this information, he put down the silver cutlery, which made a gentle sound as they came into contact with his ornately decorated plate.

'How do you know that there are children in the house?' he asked in a serious tone.

'I monitored the call between Ms Rekman and Ambassador Sunderland. She asked the Ambassador to tell her who was in the house,' Olivia detailed. 'It is my assessment that Ms Rekman deliberately decided not to disclose the correct information. I am unable to correlate,' Olivia stated and paused.

'Thank you for telling me this, Olivia and well done! Please deactivate the motion detect parameter, but allow Henrietta to continue viewing the drone feed. Let me know if there is any movement from the villa,' Mike Argo commanded.

Olivia paused whilst making the adjustments to the drone's system, as Mike Argo picked up his knife and fork. He cut off a piece of the tender meat with ease and raised it to his mouth. It had cooled slightly, because of the length of the conversation he had been engaged in with Olivia, but the steak was still warm and melted in his mouth.

In the midst of his chewing, he looked up from his plate toward Olivia, who had turned her back towards the paintings.

'Henrietta Rekman thinks that you are a human, Olivia. Because of that, she thought that if she told you that there were children in the house, that you would disable her access to the drone, which is quite rightly the human thing to do,' Argo explained, as he gently chewed another piece of steak.

'So, you asked me to disable her access because of the children, but not because of Ambassador Sunderland and Melissa?' Olivia inquisitively asked.

'Yes, because adults have made choices in their lives and are accountable for those choices. Children, haven't had a chance to make their choices and humans consider their lives to be more valuable,' he said, swallowing his food, realising that he had never really thought about this and wondering exactly how an android would assimilate such information.

'Why does Ms Rekman not think that children are more valuable?' puzzled Olivia with a sincere look of confusion, walking back round to her seat and tucking herself back in at the table.

'Henrietta works for another member of Onyx. She thinks differently to other people, which makes her better suited to the work which she does,' Argo tried to explain in the most basic way possible as he plucked a baby potato from his plate and steered it into his mouth.

40

It had been several hours since the four men had set off north from the village. Vincent was battling the urge to fall asleep at the wheel, having not enjoyed a single moment of rest since his encounter with the Dutch backpacker Lara Berg. His mind thought back to that night and he wondered whether Lara had made it home safely. His arms felt weak and heavy as they hung from the steering wheel.

Vincent had used the brand-new burner phone which he had kept in his glove compartment to call his contact, who would assist and guide them to the location of the artefact.

It was late in the evening and as they approached the meet location, Vincent could see up ahead the figure of a man standing at the rear end of a dark Mercedes SUV.

Sensing that they were getting closer to achieving their goal, a spike of adrenaline hit Vincent who sat up in the car seat.

The Russian agents, Kirill and Aleksey, had not been shy in vocalising their reservations about the plan. Both Wasyl and Vincent were quietly amazed at the actions of the Russian agents who had shown tremendous goodwill and almost foolish trust in handing back the envelope containing the coordinates. Aleksey and Kirill also spoke of their children at home and insisted that they were not responsible for what had happened at the Ambassador's residence. From what they had seen that night, Vincent and Wasyl were both of the unspoken view that the Russian agents' actions were just strange enough to qualify their account.

Pulling up behind the Mercedes SUV, Vincent left the headlights on and yanked the handbrake up. The first to open his door, he removed his seatbelt and exited the Audi. His ears had popped from the climb in altitude during the past few miles in the car. As Vincent walked toward his contact, who was now better illuminated by the headlights from his Audi, the other three men stayed in the car. They looked on as Vincent shook the hand of a man who was slightly shorter than average and in his early seventies. His long and quite dishevelled grey hair hung from the back of his woolly hat.

'Nikolay, thank you so much for meeting us on such a cold night,' Vincent said as he put his hand forward for a handshake.

'No problem, as long as it is worth my while,' Nikolay responded in a raspy voice and speaking with a heavy Bulgarian accent.

'Yes, of course. We need you to take us to this location,' Vincent advised, turning the face of his mobile phone toward Nikolay so that he could see the exact destination on the map.

'Your sat nav won't take you?' grunted Nikolay, bursting into a fit of laughter. Vincent smiled and turned the phone back towards himself.

'We could try, but I don't feel like walking off the edge of any cliffs in the dark,' he retorted dryly. Sensing the sudden seriousness, Nikolay nodded and turned to face the rear of his SUV, whilst reaching into his pocket to open the boot. As the boot lifted, he explained that he had brought a variety of climbing gear and that they were currently at the closest point to the location accessible by road. Vincent was at least happy that they would not have to drive any further.

The eerie still silence of the night was broken by the sound of the three car doors opening behind him as Wasyl, Aleksey and Kirill got out of the car. He heard them approaching from behind as Nikolay turned to face them all.

'Big guys, but there is a lot of equipment in here so you will be fine,' Nikolay muttered looking at all four men from left to right. Standing aside from the boot, he revealed a plentiful supply of what looked like fairly old hiking and climbing equipment.

They quickly started looking through the kit to pick out rugged walking shoes, thick trousers and coats. Nikolay walked to the rear door of the SUV and pulled out his green backpack, on the side of which hung two ice axes. Picking up five pairs of climbing crampons, he shut the door and walked back to re-join the four men, who had made fast work of getting changed in the frozen conditions.

'Now we look ready!' he exclaimed throwing four pairs of crampons onto the soft snow at their feet. 'You will need these for later. We have some hard mountain to cover.'

'How long is it going to take us to get there?' asked Wasyl with a slight hint of unease.

'Five or six hours. No less than five,' Nikolay said confidently. Each of the men had taken a rucksack and leaning deep into the boot of the car, Nikolay dragged out two neatly compacted tents and also threw these onto the snow.

'Decide who will carry these,' he mumbled. Closing the boot, Nikolay threw his pack over his shoulders and tested his flashlight.

Turning to face the darkness which enveloped everything past the treeline and beyond the influence of the calmly lit road, Kirill turned to the others and said with a tense undertone, 'So, that's it. We are going to go walking into the mountains? If we find what we are looking for, what are we going to do with it?'

'He is right,' reconfirmed Aleksey. 'We aren't scientists; we aren't engineers. How are we going to move it? How are we even going to know if we have found it?'

'Let's get to the location. If we can find this thing, we will have a better idea of what we are dealing with,' Vincent responded in a tone full of promise.

Nikolay had already made his way through some shrubbery and into the thick pine trees that lined the road. Feeling as though they had come too far to turn back, the men followed him into the woods, picking up their pairs of crampons and tucking them into their packs, which were heavy enough without the addition of any extra weight.

'What is in these packs? They weigh so much,' commented Wasyl.

'Just some things which you will need. You don't want to be caught out here without the proper equipment,' Nikolay retorted with a stern tone.

As they walked, the fresh snow compacted underfoot. The depth of the snow hindered their progress and as each footstep sunk into the fresh powder, the lactic acid built gradually in their legs.

'We read what was in the envelope. It sounds as though this craft, whatever it is, is encased in solid rock and has been there for an untold number of years. Even if we are able to find it, we don't have what we would need to remove it,' Kirill added with uncertainty.

'This excursion isn't exactly being undertaken with the blessing of the Bulgarian Government,' replied Vincent. 'If they knew about this artefact, there is no chance that we would get anywhere near it. We need to go to the site and see what we can find. If this has all been a wild goose chase, I won't be surprised, but at least we will know.'

Wasyl, Aleksey and Kirill all looked at each other in confusion about what a wild goose chase had to do with their situation. Nikolay was far enough ahead of the group to not be within earshot. Only the deliberately dim illumination from his blue flashlight could be seen.

'I think we are going to spend a long, cold night in the woods for nothing,' Wasyl sighed, whilst instantly realising that such substantial interest in the artefact and its whereabouts could surely not be totally unfounded. Continuing in the footsteps of Nikolay, it became clear that the mountaineer was setting a speed that he expected them all to follow. As the dim blue light became more distant, the four men stepped up the pace in order to not be left behind. As they walked, occasional rustles in the bushes and trees distracted their attention. The irresistible feeling that somebody was watching followed them as they walked. The nocturnal creatures, silently sitting and observing, hid from their view. Gradually, they managed to catch up with Nikolay, who was making his way through the snow at quite some pace for a man of such advanced age.

After an hour of walking, all of the men started to feel genuine and grinding exhaustion. The pine trees started to thin slightly and more of the surrounding landscape could be seen. The sky was clear and the moon shone brightly, set upon a tapestry of stars. A few small moonlit clouds loitered and caressed the tall mountain peaks which could be seen in the distance. Outside of the shelter provided by the woods, the wind whistled ferociously, running a bitter chill through all of the men. Aleksey and Kirill were speaking amongst themselves and Vincent put in some extra effort to catch up with Nikolay, who was walking purposefully, in order to ask him whether he was sure that he knew where he was going. Realising at the last moment that Nikolay might take offence at this, he decided against it.

The scenery, even at night time, was awe inspiring and Vincent took a deep breath of cold air as he looked up at the stars. The gentle blue light emitted from Nikolay's torch was soothing.

Henrietta Rekman now had the five men in her sight from a great distance. With no need for a torch or traditional night-vision goggles, Henrietta had slipped a pair of graphene ultra-thin night-vision contact lenses into her eyes while in the car. The Argo Industries design made use of not only visible light, but also ultraviolet light, and could sense the full infrared spectrum.

The men had arrived at the location not sensing the need for urgency, while Henrietta had been driving at high speed and was walking in their tracks, which were exceedingly easy to follow in the virgin snow. As she stalked them silently, she thought how woefully unprepared they were.

41

Jonathan woke with a start as the patrol car came to a halt several houses away from the property which had made the call to the police to report suspected narcotics related activity. It was late in the evening and both Ivan and Magda were tired. Engaged in a conversation about how to approach the situation they heard John stir and unclip his seatbelt in the back seat.

John felt slightly embarrassed about having nodded off whilst his head was propped up against the headrest, but he still felt exceptionally drained from the scene he had witnessed at the Ambassador's residence.

Ivan turned back to say, 'It looks like there are some fresh car tracks and footprints. The lady who made the report lives in that house up ahead on the right.' John nodded to show that he had understood. 'We will go and take a look. You stay here,' demanded Ivan as he turned to Magda and winked. Magda sighed and rolled her eyes before opening the door and getting out, followed closely by Ivan. John watched as both officers trudged away from the car and up the track towards a dark Mercedes parked outside the villa on the left.

Looking out of the window at the snow laying on the ground outside, he could see the vehicle tracks that Magda and Ivan had spoken of as well as the footsteps of differing sizes appearing to walk in both directions. On closer inspection, he noticed some footprints which looked smaller, like children's footprints.

Magda and Ivan noticed the same thing as they walked towards the parked Mercedes. Stopping short of the car and looking towards the villa, which was enveloped in total darkness with no signs of life, Magda took out her radio and quietly reported to the operator that they had arrived at the address and read out the diplomatic number plate, asking for further information. As she stood waiting to receive an update, Ivan walked towards the gate of the villa. As he approached, he glanced across the street at the house from which the call to the police had been made. Although the lights were dim, he could make out clearly the outline of a woman standing semi-concealed behind the curtain and observing him, but was unable to make out any detail clearly.

Sitting in the car, John had awoken sufficiently to remember what the original report had said about a silent airplane. Winding down his window slightly, he could hear a faint humming noise which sounded like the electrical buzz emitted from power lines after rain. Listening more intently, he could hear Magda speaking on the radio and the continuous gentle buzzing which worryingly did not remain constant, but rather seemed to change tone and direction.

Clasping his fingers around the door handle, John opened the car door to go and warn Ivan and Magda. Ivan reached the gate, unhooking the latch and pushing it wide open. An uneasy feeling ravaged him as he walked forward with his right hand on the pistol in his holster. Two steps down the path a powerful and devastating explosion detonated.

The power of the bomb tore through Ivan. He died instantly and his constituent parts were dispersed violently in the general vicinity.

The windows of all of the surrounding houses were smashed by the violent shock wave and the wall of the villa buckled and crumpled inwards from the force of the explosion. Magda, who had been standing on slightly lower ground waiting to receive information back about the Mercedes with the diplomatic plates, had been sheltered from the brunt of the explosion by the car, which stood between her and the site of the detonation.

John, who had only managed to put one leg out of the car when the explosion erupted, was knocked back and lost balance, striking his head on the rear wheel arch as he was thrown to the floor by the blast wave. The safety glass which shattered from the car door covered him, as he came to from a momentary state of unconsciousness. Clutching the back of his head instinctively with his left hand, he felt the sting of a fresh wound and the wet, warm texture of blood, which had matted his hair together. His ears were ringing badly as he rose to his feet and saw Magda lying on the ground behind the Mercedes. John was illuminated by the Mercedes' rear indicator lights flashing intermittently and could hear cries emanating from inside the villa in between the shrieks emitted by the car alarm. Walking as fast as he could towards Magda, he fell down to both knees by her side. The car alarm was only partially audible to him due to the ringing in his ears.

She lay unconscious and John could see blood trickling from one of her ears. A small shard of wood was protruding from her left shoulder – probably a splinter from the wooden fence which had been weaponised into shrapnel by the bomb. He lifted her head onto his lap and was happy to find her pulse as her police radio, which had fallen to one side into the snow, sprung to life. It was muffled as it had fallen speaker first into the snow, but picking it up, John listened and frantically thought about what he should do. Speaking into the radio, he said that there had been an explosion and two officers were injured. The voice at the other end paused before confirming that other officers and medical assistance were on the way. John removed his coat, laid it underneath Magda's head, and drew the pistol from his holster.

He stood and walked towards the demolished gate of the villa, from which he could hear children crying inside the building through the shattered windows. Walking through, he used the torch function on his phone to look around the area, revealing a crater to the right hand side of the path, which had been dug into the yard by the force of the explosion. John was able to see some of the remains of what used to be Ivan strewn to the left of the path and further afield. Realising that this had been the worst day that he had had in a very long time, he fixed his gaze on the villa door straight ahead of him. This had been blown clean off its hinges and John was able to stagger straight into the house. The sound of sobbing children persisted as he shone light on the scene inside the house, keeping his gun aimed in whichever direction he illuminated.

The window frames had contained plate and not safety glass. The shock wave had sent torrents of shrapnel flying in all directions inside the room. A woman sitting near the extinguished fireplace seemed to have taken the brunt of the flying debris and was almost certainly dead. Large jagged shards of plate glass jutted from her torso and one piece seemed to have lodged itself through her left eye. It was difficult for John to see as her head now hung downwards and blood dripped steadily from the end of the fragment.

Turning his attention to the crying, he saw a man, woman and two children sitting huddled on the floor in the other corner of the room. Panning the light in their direction, he recognised them immediately as Francis, Melissa, Patrick and George. Aside from some minor cuts it appeared that they had managed to avoid any serious physical injury.

The family had fallen silent as they looked toward the armed man in the darkness. He stepped closer to them and broke the silence.

'Thank goodness you are all ok!'

'John, is that you?' gasped Francis, 'Tell me it's you!'

'It's me,' John said, turning the light to illuminate his face, 'what the devil are you doing out here? I have been worried sick!'

He walked towards them and gave Francis a hand so that he could stand. As Francis rose he cried out and clutched at his leg, which on closer inspection had been impaled by a piece of glass. Before John had an opportunity to stop him or advise against it, Francis grabbed the glass and pulled it out, which caused it to start bleeding generously. Looking around, he picked up a kitchen towel and holding it in both hands coiled it around itself to create a tourniquet. As he wrapped it directly on and just above the wound, he told the other three to definitely not do the same if they had any injuries. As he pulled the material tight in order to slow the bleeding, Francis howled momentarily with pain before collecting himself.

'You shouldn't have come here, there is a drone above and any movement around the house is targeted,' Francis stammered.

'I know about the drone, that is part of the reason why I found you. It's a long story, but I came here with the police after spending the whole afternoon at your house, Francis. It is blind luck that brought me' John conceded, 'I did hear the drone, but this was no drone strike!'

John asked Melissa and the children whether they could walk and Melissa nodded. With Francis resting his weight on John's shoulder, they turned and headed for the door, leaving the late Ms Bradford. As they walked to the moonlit outdoors, John could see the front door of the house opposite open and the light inside on. Walking past the blast site, John turned off his torch, which made the bloody remains appear a deep black to the side of the path. This was practically unnoticed by the family who seemed to be in a state of shock.

As he hobbled past Officer Magda Popova with Francis, John could see that an old woman was kneeling down next to her. The front of the car had taken the brunt of the impact, which had most likely saved Officer Popova's life. As they passed, he realised that this must have been the woman who lived in the house opposite and whom had put in the call to the police. She looked up toward them and John told her that help was on the way and that he would return shortly. Seeming to understand, but not saying anything, she looked down toward the officer who was still unconscious.

As they reached the patrol car, John opened the passenger door and bundled Francis in and then helped Melissa and the children into the rear of the car. Removing the car keys from the ignition, he told them that he was returning to check on Magda.

42

Olivia observed as John strode back toward the Mercedes beside which Magda lay. She fed the drone imagery onto a television, mounted on the wall opposite the three paintings in the dining room. Mike Argo had barely finished his dessert when Olivia had told him of the explosion at the villa. He had been furious, initially thinking that the drone had fired upon a target which had triggered the motion detect functionality. Olivia had checked the flight systems and confirmed that the drone's stockpile remained at one hundred per cent meaning that something else had caused the explosion. She had successfully deactivated the motion detect function.

Standing from his seat, Mike Argo pushed his heavy wooden chair back with some force, clearly affected and concerned by the news. Walking to the wall behind where he had been sitting, he pushed a button to open the alcohol cabinet which was built into the façade. As the wooden panels slid open like curtains, an impressive array of alcoholic beverages became visible.

A narrow bar surface which was easily wide enough to accommodate a crystal glass presented itself and was brought down by the automated mechanism. As he reached for a glass and then for his favourite whisky, he wrapped his fingers around the decanter and pulled out the satisfyingly weighted glass plug. He had only seen the more recent events, but not the actual explosion.

'Olivia, please display the explosion itself,' Mike Argo requested.

It took Olivia a moment to locate the footage and play what the drone had captured in the seconds before the explosion. One green targeting reticle hovered over a man approaching the gate of the villa and another over a woman standing near a car parked outside. Argo could see the man glance over towards the house on the opposite side of the street and then open the gate of the villa to walk into the yard. A few steps down the path leading to the front door, the bright flash of the explosion filled the screen, but this quickly cleared to show the aftermath of the detonation. The green reticle disappeared as there was no further motion, until another man arrived to assist the woman who appeared to be injured from the blast.

'If the drone didn't cause the explosion, what did?' puzzled Argo. Recalling the conversation he'd had with Olivia about Henrietta Rekman, Mike Argo's mind quickly turned to her. 'Did Ms Rekman go anywhere near the property when she was in the village?'

'Mr Argo, there was motion detected shortly after the drone's arrival,' Olivia confirmed as she located the footage. The screen flickered as the recording loaded and Argo watched as Henrietta approached the villa, carrying something in her hand and wearing a small backpack. She walked to the door and was out of sight for a few seconds before reappearing and walking back down the path slowly. As she did, Argo and Olivia observed that she removed her backpack and dropped it to the ground next to the path. Winding the footage forward, it became clear that the snow which had fallen partially covered the bag making it difficult to spot.

'It appears that Ms Rekman's bag contained the explosives, Mr Argo,' Olivia said in a disturbingly dispassionate voice.

'Yes, it seems that way. She must have used a vibration detection module. Perhaps a backup in case the drone didn't fire,' he pondered.

'Ms Rekman did not tell me anything about the device, Mr Argo,' Olivia recalled.

'Yes,' Argo said looking at the screen which showed the live feed from the drone, 'cut off her contact with the drone and send it back to base,' he instructed as he carried on thinking about the events. He had met with Henrietta Rekman on many occasions and he had felt uneasy about her every single time. News reports about dozens of dead party guests at the British Ambassador's residence had not escaped his attention and he was well aware of her presence at the event, as well as her particular moral deficit.

He had spoken with Dr Meertens on several occasions about Henrietta, and his concerns about her use in the field, but Meertens had been adamant about her methods. There could be no doubt whatsoever about her effectiveness, but she had lied or not been forthcoming with information to Olivia on two separate instances and yet this was the woman who was tasked with recovering the Pebble for Onyx. To say that he did not trust her was a hefty understatement.

As he brought the fine crystal glass to his lips, Argo raised it slightly to take a sip of whisky from the generous measure that he had poured himself. He noticed his hand tremble ever so slightly, but he told himself that the drink would help.

Never having been one to leave things to chance, Argo considered his options, which included doing nothing and hoping for the best, or intervention. Even if Henrietta was able to track the four men and locate the artefact, she would need substantial engineering and scientific assistance to remove the item without detection by the Bulgarian Government. If nothing else, at least she would track the men for him to the artefact's alleged location. He let out a small laugh and shook his head at the thought of the cradle of all life on this planet being found by Henrietta Rekman. He realised the high probability that nothing would be found and the preposterousness of the idea of an alien craft bringing life to the planet in the first place.

Certainly the stuff of science fiction, but he had met Jerome Docherty whilst he was still a member of Onyx and had been very impressed with his dedication to his research and field study. If anybody was going to make such a discovery, it most certainly would have been Docherty. Although the existence of such a craft was improbable, Docherty claimed to have found it and most importantly had gone out of his way to make sure that Onyx did not obtain it. That of itself was reason enough to pursue the Pebble.

Sitting back on his chair and taking a larger swig of whisky, he considered his words carefully before telling Olivia what he wanted her to do for him.

43

It had been over an hour since Henrietta Rekman had lost the drone feed which was guarding her hostages. Although there were more pressing matters at hand, this development had made her angry and frustrated.

As she followed the tracks of the five men in search of the artefact, she pulled her phone from her pocket as she considered calling Olivia, but the screen light blinded her, as its relatively strong back lighting was amplified by her night vision lenses. Realising that phoning through to Olivia would probably not be the best course of action, she slipped the phone back into her pocket.

Ahead, the five men had reached a steep incline, which they were steadily and carefully climbing. The journey had so far involved several climbs and descents which both slowed down their progress and sapped their waning strength. Although the weather was clear, the existing snow and ice resulted in treacherous conditions. As his crampons gripped the frozen rocky surface, Nikolay led the five men in the climb, which although not overly steep, was still very punishing. Reaching the top first, Nikolay waited for the others, lending them a helping hand to lift themselves the last few feet.

'Ok, I think that I've had a long day and it's time to rest,' announced Wasyl who was the last man to reach the top. Looking at Vincent who still had an unerring look of defiance and resolution about him, Wasyl realised that his plea for rest would fall on deaf ears. 'It will still be there tomorrow you know. If it's there at all!'

'We aren't very far,' interjected Nikolay as he indicated, 'Over there!'

From where they stood, they had a good view of their surroundings. Nikolay was pointing towards a rock formation of two rocks rising into the sky. Unsure of exactly how far they were, Wasyl took solace in the fact that the destination was in sight.

'Hey, Nikolay. The place we are going. What are the chances that we may be disturbed? Are there ever any people out here?' asked Aleksey.

'Unlikely. There are sometimes hunters, but we are much more likely to run into a bear!' retorted Nikolay, as he walked and secretly smiled to himself. Feeling immediately averse to the idea of running into a bear, Aleksey turned to Kirill and bit his bottom lip demonstratively.

'Ha,' Aleksey laughed nervously, 'I thought I saw a bear once near St Petersburg. But then I realised it was my ex-wife.' The others all burst out in laughter as they carried on walking. 'But, seriously. Bears?' Aleksey asked with a serious tone.

'Yes, bears. You should already know comrades,' Nikolay re-affirmed.

Their feet were hurting badly and the pressure from walking for a protracted period on uneven surfaces was having a telling effect on their ankles and knees. Feeling weak with exertion, they reached the two conglomerate rock formations towering above the pine trees that surrounded them. The forest was thick at the location but the conical narrow pine trees made it easy to see up the sheer rock face.

The air was still at ground level where all five men stood, but they could hear the wind whistling through the treetops, whipping up the rock face as it struck forcefully. The ground under their feet was covered in a pristine layer of snow approximately one foot deep.

'This is where you asked me to bring you. I have brought you,' Nikolay boastfully announced with an air of self-satisfaction. Wasyl and Vincent looked at Aleksey and Kirill, who threw gazes back at them. Standing so close to the potential resting place of the Pebble, they realised that perhaps the trust and camaraderie which they had developed over such a short period of time might be misplaced. With an air of reservation, they each selected a spot to lay the equipment which had been weighing them down.

Vincent raised his hand as he held his phone up to check that they had reached the GPS location with pinpoint accuracy. Taking a few steps towards the rock face, he walked a few more to the left and carried on, disappearing from sight momentarily. 'The exact location would put us inside the rock face over there.'

'I can't really help you if I don't know more about what we are doing out here,' Nikolay quipped in a light-hearted tone.

'I suppose you are right to say that,' Vincent responded, looking at Wasyl, Kirill and Aleksey, knowingly. Wasyl nodded to show his agreement to sharing the information with Nikolay. Reaching into his jacket he produced the envelope which had cost the lives of so many. Wasyl had taken the opportunity to tell the other three men in detail about what he had found at the Ambassador's residence. They were all resolute in the hope that it hadn't been for nothing.

Handing the envelope to Nikolay, he immediately opened it and flashed his blue torch at the paper as his white hair hung down, partially hiding his face. He took a moment to read the information and then exhaled sharply twice. Neatly returning the paper to the envelope and closing the flap, Nikolay handed it back to Vincent.

'Well, this is the twin monolith rock formation I suppose, but what does it mean that our story began here?' asked Nikolay confusedly.

'Oh, sorry, you also will have to read this,' Vincent remembered, handing Nikolay the original auction invitation, which included information about the lot which they had won. As Nikolay read it, he exhaled four times in quick succession as though he was about to start laughing.

'Whoever gave you this is having some good fun with you. A spaceship? The first life on Earth? If you had told me at the cars, I could have saved you all a very long walk tonight,' Nikolay dismissively jested.

'A lot of people have died for this information Nikolay. Too many. We are looking for an area of rock on the cliff face which looks as though it has been reattached. The claim is that this craft was exposed and uncovered accidentally by rock movement or erosion. I don't know. I'm no geologist,' Vincent explained in a solemn tone.

'The note says that it is seventy-two metres up. We have to look before we climb. If rock has been reattached, we may be able to see from the ground,' Nikolay reasonably suggested, 'The rope I have brought will be long enough I think.'

They put down their bags with Wasyl and Kirill setting about erecting two tents. The others scattered in various directions to collect some wood for a fire. The exposure to the elements was having a detrimental effect on all of the men, who were eager to warm up by the flames, have something to eat and drink and get some sleep.

'This has been quite a day, hasn't it?' Kirill asked rhetorically.

'It has been. How are we going to deal with this thing if it is real?' Wasyl questioned.

'If it's real? This kind of thing belongs to all of us. It doesn't matter which country we are each from,' Kirill said reassuringly. 'I am sure that there are people in each of our governments who would disagree, but they aren't the ones out here. They aren't the ones with their lives in danger.'

'No, they aren't,' said Wasyl, inwardly distrusting every word spoken by the Russian agents. He pulled the canvas over the skeletal metal frame of the two-man tent he was putting together.

Taking a deep drag on the cigarette which he had lit, Vincent clung to the filter tip with his lips as he scoured under the bases of the trees for dry wood. Finding a large fallen branch, he spent some time hacking off its smaller branches with the hand axe he had plundered from the larger rucksack of Nikolay. Picking up the stockpile of wood which he had collected, he headed back to the makeshift campsite where he found Aleksey and Nikolay already stacking the small bonfire.

Adding his contribution, he heard Nikolay searching for something in his backpack. As he walked over to the pile of wood, he lit a square hexamine fuel tablet and threw it to the base of the pyramid. As the fuel tablet began to burn brightly, the wood also started to ignite with a few torrents of steam, followed by warming yellow licks of flame.

The tents were ready and Wasyl and Kirill had even unpacked the sleeping bags with two per tent and one person to keep watch for people. And for bears.

The fire was burning well and a few thicker pieces of wood were added. Enough spare wood had been collected to keep the fire going. Nikolay was once again rummaging through his rucksack and realising that the others were all looking at him expectantly. He turned and said,

'Don't worry, I have come well prepared.' Producing a Tupperware box of what looked like marinated meat from his pack and two metal drink canteens, he joined the others in sitting around the gently illuminating fire. Pulling the red lid from the plastic box to reveal pork shish with vegetables he handed one to everybody sitting around the fire and murmured,

'My wife threw these together just after you called, Vincent. A little early in the year for a barbeque, but they are my favourite.'

'I'm glad that she did,' Vincent responded, wide-eyed and suddenly very hungry. Five shish skewers were presented and held almost ceremoniously to the fire simultaneously by gloved hands. The heat which radiated made the cheeks of the men rosy with warmth as they sat on logs which they had found nearby.

After a few moments of grilling, drops of fat started to drip down onto the fire causing it to fizz and spit embers into the air. The smell was appetising and the men moved their individual skewers from one hand to the other when the heat from the fire became too much. The skewers were turned, browning on each side evenly, and the peppers let off a rural and seductive scent as their skin turned perfectly black and their flesh bubbled underneath.

They each removed their shish from the fire one by one and held it in the stalemate of heat versus hunger. With his free hand Nikolay unscrewed the cap of one of the canteens and took a large swig and passed it to Vincent who sat to his left. Taking a drink himself, Vincent realised that the canteens were filled with vodka, which had an immediate warming effect on him. Picking off piece by piece in order from the shish, they enjoyed mouthful after mouthful of delicious food until all that was left was a small pile of metal shish skewers laying strewn in front of the fire.

'Do you have any more?' asked Aleksey, hopefully.

'No, but that is what I always ask my wife. She loves to keep me hungry,' Nikolay retorted giving a cheeky grin. 'You know; women can be so good to you. Until they want to be bad.'

There were several groans of approval, fuelled by the swigs of vodka which the men had taken.

'She has packed only this much good food for us, but I do have some less glamourous packet rations in case things get, well, less glamourous,' Nikolay said. 'I don't know what I must have done wrong.'

After passing the two canteens around a few more times, and a brief discussion, Kirill announced that he would take first watch and Wasyl volunteered for the second hour watch. The men retired to their tents and lay down to rest until the break of dawn, with Wasyl and Vincent climbing into one tent and Nikolay and Aleksey scrabbling into another.

Both Vincent and Wasyl were immediately apprehensive about Kirill's eagerness to take the first watch. The distrust which they harboured for each other was difficult to set aside, but it had been muted slightly by the effect of the vodka.

Kirill sat near the rock face with his back turned to the cliff, facing the camp and the forest beyond.

44

By the time Jonathan Coleridge had made it back to Officer Magda Popova with the medikit which he had retrieved from the boot of the patrol car, he found that she was still in the company of the old woman who had called the police. Magda had regained consciousness and was seemingly in a substantial amount of pain, caused by the wooden shard which had been removed by either herself or the woman on whose lap she was laying. The shard was lying on the snow surrounded by a spattering of fresh blood and he could see that it had penetrated her shoulder at least one inch, causing what he thought to almost certainly be substantial damage. He kneeled down, laying the medikit on the ground and opening it. John was pleased to find gauze and dressing inside the box and quickly set to work removing Magda's jacket and tearing the sleeve from the shirt she wore underneath. Her skin was cold to the touch and he worked as quickly as he could to dress the wound.

'Help is on the way, I have radioed to let your colleagues know what happened,' John quickly summarised.

'W-what happened?' asked Magda in a low and shuddering voice.

'A bomb. I am afraid Ivan is dead,' John reluctantly told her, raising his voice to try and make sure that she was able to hear him, 'You are lucky to be alive.'

Her eyes began to well up with tears on hearing the news and as she blinked, they started to roll down the side of her face and dropped onto the lap of the old lady who was supporting her head. As soon as John finished working on the dressing, Magda rolled over onto her healthy arm and used this to support herself to her knees and with his help, to her feet. Holding on to Magda to make sure that she was steady, John realised that he could no longer hear the buzzing electrical sound which he had heard before the explosion. Hoping that they were all out of immediate danger, he looked at Magda, who did not look stable on her feet.

'We have to check the villa,' Magda resolutely concluded, wiping her face of the tears and picking up her jacket and carefully putting it on over the dressing, breathing in sharply through gritted teeth as she did so.

'You were unconscious for a few moments. I have already checked the villa and found the British Ambassador and his family. There is another woman in the house but she is dead. Killed by glass from the blast,' he reported sombrely.

'What were they doing here? Who else is here and who killed Ivan?' she asked with a wild, open-eyed look.

'Those are good questions. I don't know the details, because the Ambassador and his family are also shaken up by what has happened,' John explained. The old woman had started to walk back towards her house as she turned to face them.

'Four men left some hours ago. That is all I saw,' she confirmed in a raspy and distraught voice.

'Thank you, madam,' Magda nodded and forced a smile to the woman. 'Ok, I need to speak with the Ambassador right now,' she said letting go of John's shoulder and walking in an almost drunken fashion towards her patrol car, unable to keep a straight trajectory due to the ongoing effect of the bomb blast on her balance.

Francis saw her staggering from left to right, approaching the car and opening the door of the front passenger seat.

'Ambassador Sunderland, I need to speak with you,' she stated. Looking puzzled and slightly embarrassed, Francis looked back blankly.

'I'm afraid I don't speak very much Bulgarian,' he meekly responded.

'Why would you? Ok, we can speak in English,' she said dismissively, seemingly losing any patience which may have remained within her. 'My colleague and friend is dead and I was nearly killed.' Her figure was slight and her voice unsteady, but as she stood towering over Francis, who was still seated in the passenger seat, he caught a glimpse of her sidearm and realised that the statement she had just made was very much a question. A question which meant that he had limited time to absolve himself of responsibility for what had happened. A few moments passed as she stood breathing heavily and shifting her weight slowly from one foot to the other. Raising her hand and bringing it down violently on the roof of her car she shouted, 'ANSWER ME!' as Melissa and the children cowered on the back seat of the vehicle and John Coleridge stood back slightly realising that he too was interested to hear more and that this was certainly not the time to make an intervention.

Officer Magda Popova stood and listened with some disbelief to Ambassador Francis Sunderland as he recounted the events which had led to their present predicament. Francis no longer gave much thought to his formal posting in the country, nor what divulging the information may do to his career, but instead his mind was solely focussed on his family's survival of this ordeal. Jonathan Coleridge was standing only a couple of feet behind Magda and was also listening intently as Francis described the events which had led to his procurement of the GPS coordinates of the Pebble, the circumstances which brought about the death of the guests at his residence and finally, information about the four men who had left the villa in search for the artefact.

Francis had not been totally clear in his description to Magda as to what the purported artefact in fact was. He realised that this was partially due to his reservations about fully disclosing the secret, but also partially because he was unclear of the effect such a revelation may have on this police officer who was clearly distraught at the loss of her colleague and was unlikely to take well to being told that the reason for his death was in fact a buried spacecraft forgotten by time, which may or in fact may not have brought life to the planet – or even exist.

Magda's next question was predictable,

'What are the coordinates of the artefact?' she barked, seemingly having lost the final sliver of patience which may have remained. She was eager to intercept those responsible for what had happened to Ivan and clearly the location of the artefact was the only piece of information which would satiate this requirement.

'I don't have the envelope any longer,' Francis started before being interrupted abruptly by Magda.

'Tell me where they have gone!' she demanded.

'I saw the location on the map. If you have a map, I can show you,' Francis hurried to pacify Officer Popova, who hastily told him to open the glovebox and take out the fold-up map of Bulgaria, which he duly did. Stepping out of the car, Magda and John stood to one side as Francis limped painfully to the front of the car and unfolded the well-used map, resting it upon the smooth and warm bonnet of the car. After a moment of pensive consideration, he pointed at an area representing a spot on the western slopes of the Balkan Mountains.

'Are you sure about that?' asked Magda in a slightly calmer tone as Francis nodded his confirmation. She walked to the driver's side of the car and opened the door, removing the car keys which she had left in the ignition when she had first arrived. Slamming the door shut, she spoke into her radio to find out when the police backup and medical assistance would arrive at their location in Valsha, after which she told the operator what she had learned. After a pause the operator came back to give the names of some of the officers on their way and also to say that the incoming support would not arrive at the village for another half an hour at least. Unhappy at the thought of leaving the scene unattended, Magda advised the operator that she had to act on the time-critical information she had received and would meet the convoy of emergency vehicles half way, to hand over the Ambassador, his family and John Coleridge. Unable to understand the radio conversation, Francis cut in to say,

'If you are going there, make sure there are more of you. There are dangerous people after this thing.'

'I can see that,' Magda responded, bringing the radio slowly down to her side and craning her head backwards to view the destruction which lay behind her. 'They won't be so dangerous when we have finished with them,' she continued with a calm, defiant and unnerving tone.

45

The new prototype Argo Industries suborbital cargo plane sat on the runway tarmac of the Future Logic Facility outside Bandung, Indonesia at just after 11am local time. It had risen from the underground hangar through a giant rectangular section of tarmac, which was raised and powered by a hydraulic lift. The hangar lay just beneath the surface of the airstrip above and was created by Argo to keep his most closely guarded projects under wraps. It could only be accessed from the sub-levels of the facility itself and was not nearly as exposed to industrial espionage as the surface hangar in which Argo's Learjet now rested quietly. The suborbital cargo plane had been fuelled and stocked for an impromptu mission, as ordered by Argo. Its sleek wings and dual engine system type were unique and unknown outside of the facility. They allowed for the highest fuel efficiency to weight carriage ratio and when empty, had an enormous range, capable of circumnavigating the globe twice before needing to be refuelled.

Vitally, the design of this craft allowed for low-altitude, vertical flight and loading, which had been tested with success, but real world application had not been undertaken.

Olivia had changed from her black dress into a dark-grey flight suit and sat in the co-pilot seat. Captain Wren sat next to her at the pilot flight controls and was busy checking systems prior to take-off. They were the only crew on the craft.

Following the progress of Henrietta Rekman through mobile phone tower pings, her exact location was being tracked by

Mike Argo through high magnification satellite feed. He did not trust her motives or methods when dealing with what could potentially be the most important discovery mankind had ever made, regardless of the faith Dr Meertens had in her abilities. He had sent instructions for his engineering team to assemble a mobile helicopter unit and move to Henrietta's general vicinity but remain outside of her detection range until further notice.

The craft sat idling on the runway as Captain Wren listened to Bandung Air Traffic Control, which was secondary to his monitoring of local and worldwide flight traffic to which he was perpetually connected. The day was overcast, warm and dry with a south-easterly wind.

Clutching the throttle, he pushed it forward purposefully, as the jet engines propelled the craft forward at great speed. Both androids were thrust backward into their seats. Reaching take-off speed, the craft rose from the ground with ease and the nose lifted further, to the point where most conventional aircraft would stall so early in take-off. Wren pushed the throttle further forward, which caused the engine noise to increase doubly and the speed with which they now accelerated, at almost a ninety-degree angle, was immense. From the ground, the sound was impressive. Gusts of wind buffeted the plane slightly, but this was not enough to affect its progress through the cloud cover and into the clear sky above. The sunlight which had been hiding behind the clouds was now streaming in through the windows and illuminating both androids, who sat un-flinching and un-phased. Captain Wren continued the climb in a confident manner, even though this was the first time that he had flown this particular aircraft. As the altitude increased ever further and the air outside became thinner, the engines started to lose their traction and effect with the diminishing atmosphere. Wren gradually introduced the thrusters in support of the engines, progressively reducing the power being sent to the increasingly obsolete jet engines. As they continued on the climb to optimum altitude, Olivia saw for the first time the sky, which had until now appeared blue, turn gradually black. The stars gently came into view and illuminated the heavens.

Breaking through to just under the cruising altitude of eighty-seven miles, Captain Wren brought the craft gradually to cruising flight and set the course for their target area in Bulgaria, which they would reach in approximately three and a half hours. This was substantially less than the twenty hours or so it would take for a conventional commercial jet to reach the destination. Olivia looked across to Captain Wren who was fixated on the horizon and scanning the flight path. He wore a small earpiece and reported to Mike Argo that they had successfully reached cruising altitude and were on their way. Argo responded and asked that the craft circle above the target area at suborbital altitude on arrival.

The flight was very smooth and quiet at suborbital altitude and the craft sped along at just over one kilometre per second with little more than a hum.

Mike Argo had spoken directly with the engineering team who had arrived at a location near to the coordinates of Henrietta Rekman and awaited further instruction. They were aware that they would be required to expedite the recovery of an artefact of currently unknown size and weight from topography the detail of which was also unknown. Conrad Wilson, who was leading the team, was certainly no stranger to the sometimes-eccentric requests of Mike Argo, but the urgency and lack of time to prepare made him nervous. He was somewhat relieved to be accompanied by five members of the Argo Industries Security Services.

Mike Argo was not one to leave his fate in the hands of others and what he had seen from Henrietta had left him in very little doubt that she should not be trusted. Even Olivia had picked up the untruths, and he had told her of his suspicions about the most probably needless deaths of the many guests at the residence of the British Ambassador.

The technicians at Future Logic had connected Olivia to the Argo Industries servers located at sub-level three of the facility from which she had received an update of her Defensive Conversation Protocol along with the full range of Human Personality Profile Matrices which had previously been used exclusively with immobile unit-based artificial intelligence, but never with an operational android.

As Olivia sat strapped to the co-pilot seat, she continually mapped and assessed the newly acquired personality profiles to the information which she had already collected about all humans with whom she had had contact.

Mike Argo sat in the study contained within his living quarters at the facility. His fingers were interlocked and his elbows rested upon his desk as he kept up to date with developments through his laptop. Displeased about being forced to send so many untested elements into the field, he considered the situation and some of the possible angles which he may not have covered.

46

Vincent and Wasyl had been asleep for about half an hour when they were awoken by a reverberating bang, followed very closely by the sound of shrill, excruciating screams of pain from outside their tent. Opening their eyes, they could see the warm yellow glow of fire dancing on the side of the canvas from the direction of the other tent in which Aleksey and Nikolay were sleeping.

In a momentary daze, having just woken up, Vincent took hold of his gun, which was resting next to his head and felt blindly in the dark for the zip which contained him within his sleeping bag. Pulling it, he struggled to get to his feet in a panicked state falling to one knee before being finally able to right himself and stand. The screaming continued from the other tent but had started to become muffled and weak as Vincent finally was able to look over. The thin canvas of the tent had disintegrated almost instantly and all that could be seen were the two writhing, flaming figures of Nikolay and Aleksey, who in their disorientation and pain had not even managed to get out of their sleeping bags on the floor. Wasyl was now also out of the tent and both men, in their state of terror, looked around the campsite to find anything they could use to dampen the flames. They both noticed Kirill propped up against the rock face with an entry wound in his forehead and another in his throat. A blood spatter painted the rocks directly behind him. Just as Vincent unfroze and went to move towards the backpacks, the voice of Henrietta Rekman boomed from behind them.

'Stop! Drop your weapons,' she commanded. Turning round sharply, Vincent did as he was instructed and dropped his handgun to the floor. They could see her standing and pointing a silenced sidearm directly at Vincent. 'That's fun, I was hoping you wouldn't be in that tent over there,' she said, looking at Vincent and nodding towards the still flaming, but now motionless bodies of Nikolay and Aleksey. Closing his eyes and re-opening them, Vincent struggled to fathom whether what he was seeing could be possible.

'Lara?' he exclaimed in a trembling voice. 'What? Why are you here?'

'Vincent, who is this?' asked Wasyl.

'Vincent? That's funny,' said Henrietta with a puzzled look on her face and an enquiring tone. Taking a step forward she

said, 'that is exactly what I was going to ask you. *Ryan.*'
Moving the aim of her gun onto Wasyl, she fired a shot
which hit him directly in the forehead, killing him before he
hit the hard and wintery ground beneath him. 'Except,
because I am the one with the gun. I am the one who gets to
ask the questions,' she calmly noted. 'A few less people
around the camp fire.'

Vincent had told her that his name was Ryan and he thought
that she was a backpacker by the name of Lara. He had
kissed her goodbye at the airport, but it had never been her
intention to fly back to Holland. As she stood murderously
before him, the foul stench of burning flesh hung in the air
and Vincent looked blankly at her, unarmed and helpless.

Henrietta had killed Kirill with a precision sniper shot from a
position which she took up within the forest. She had then
chosen one of the tents and thrown an incendiary grenade
on top. This had blown up, spreading a napalm-like
substance, instantly incinerating the canvas and raining
down on Nikolay and Aleksey inside. They had been cooked
alive in their sleeping bags, unable to get out.

Vincent's mind was reeling. Henrietta Rekman, known to
him as Lara Berg, now stood menacingly before him, dressed
all in black. She was the same backpacker who had traced
his progress with consummate ease to this location, the
same backpacker who had murdered all of the guests at
Wasyl's party and threatened the Ambassador's life along
with that of his family, killing Officer Ivan Petrov and
Charlotte Bradford at the villa.

She had arrived in Sofia with Vincent, travelling together
with him from the flat where they had spent the night
together.

She had searched his bag whilst he had been in the
shower to try and find the auction invitation without
success, but she had been certain of his intention to contact

his old friend Ambassador Sunderland in Sofia and that he was the key to either gaining access to the auction or finding the eventual location of the artefact. Her access to the substantial Onyx pool of intelligence had provided her with this information.

Henrietta had left a tracking device under the passenger seat of Vincent's Audi where she had sat when they drove to Sofia. After the auction, she had been able to pick up Vincent's trail on his arrival back to his car with Wasyl, Francis and Charlotte.

Even now, in this situation, instead of frantically thinking how he could escape, Vincent found himself going over and over events in his mind wondering how he had been so foolish. While unaware of the full extent of Henrietta's actions, he still wondered how this beautiful young woman had been able to dupe him so severely and what her motives were.

'Why? Who *are* you?' he gasped.

'There is a chance that you will survive this, even though you are a liar. Like the rest of them,' Henrietta hissed, re-centring the aim of her gun back onto Vincent. 'The item from the auction. Give it to me,' she demanded as Vincent struggled to think of what to say.

'It was an envelope and Aleksey had it in the other tent. It's gone,' Vincent said deceitfully.

'And Ryan is your name,' she whispered as she lowered her gun and shot Vincent in his left leg. He came down in a pile clutching his knee, just above the entry wound which was at the top of his shin. 'I guess you won't survive this after all,' Henrietta said shrugging her shoulders callously and walking to within two metres of where Vincent lay, pointing the gun at his head.

Through gritted teeth, which shot small specks of spit forward as he exhaled fervently he pointed toward his trouser pocket. Slowly pulling the envelope out, he threw it at Henrietta's feet and lay on his back, lifting his injured leg and grasping it with both hands.

Opening the envelope with a smile, almost as though she had received a birthday card, Henrietta read the content. Verifying the coordinates on her phone, she saw that they were in fact at the exact location provided.

'Why are you doing this?' he wheezed.

'This is what I do,' Henrietta responded matter-of-factly, 'and I love it,' she grinned.

'Lara, whoever sent you. We can pay you more,' Vincent bartered desperately.

'Oh baby,' Henrietta said softly, shaking the muzzle of the gun left and right and tutting. 'I don't receive money for what I do. Money is for people like you. Corrupt and ugly.' Henrietta had confirmed what he had come to suspect. Vincent realised that he was unlikely to survive this maniacal encounter and closed his eyes, making peace with his fate, allowing his head to rest on the snow beneath him as blood leaked from the excruciating wound in his leg, staining the snow beneath.

'Phew! Seventy-two metres up. Have you been up there to take a look?' Henrietta asked as though she hadn't just shot him. She picked up Vincent's gun from the ground and stood to her feet, turning to face the monolith's rock face.

'Not yet, we were waiting for dawn to break,' he responded as he lifted his head looking around to see if there was anything which he could use to his advantage. Barely visible in the moonlight within the treeline, Vincent saw what was the unmistakable face of a woman staring vacuously back toward him. Unsure who she was or indeed how long she had been standing there, he looked rapidly back towards Henrietta.

The suborbital cargo plane had arrived at the location and Olivia had climbed into one of the two escape pods with which the craft was fitted. Having entered coordinates near to Henrietta's location into the escape pod's computer, she was ejected and guided towards the desired area, parachuting down gently nearby, undetected by Henrietta. Olivia's final few footsteps had been dictated by the sound of Henrietta Rekman's silenced sniper shot, which had killed Kirill. She had seen everything that Henrietta had done since then.

'I think that I can take it from here. It was nice not knowing you, Vincent,' Henrietta said as she turned and pointed her sidearm at him.

'Ms Rekman,' interrupted a voice as Henrietta immediately trained her aim onto Olivia instead. Realising that only somebody from Onyx would be here and know her name, she managed to withhold the urge to pull the trigger immediately.

'Come out here, or die!' shouted Henrietta at the voice from the shadows which did sound familiar. Moving forward wearing her grey flight suit and a black cotton baseball cap, Olivia strode out from the pine trees.

'I am Olivia.'

'I know that you are Olivia. What are you doing here?' Henrietta asked in a more subdued, but defensive tone.

'I am here to help,' Olivia responded as Henrietta moved her aim back to Vincent.

'What makes you think that I need any help?' Henrietta calmly retorted. Olivia looked up the rock face and back to Henrietta. 'Oh, yeah. Right. No wonder no one found it,' Henrietta conceded.

'Mr Argo would like to speak with Vincent,' Olivia announced to the shock of Henrietta.

'This man? This man! All of these men tried to kill me! They want the artefact. I have to kill him!' Henrietta responded once again, raising her voice which was audibly shaking.

'You won't kill him, I'm not here alone,' Olivia continued as the loaded weapon which was once again pointed in her direction trembled with anger and frustration. Henrietta looked around the treeline for any sign of truth to what Olivia was saying. As she did, she spotted several green laser dots appear and the mist in the air traced the progress of each of the laser dots directly back to herself. Lowering her sidearm, she looked towards Vincent and shook her head slowly.

'You are a very lucky boy,' Henrietta chuckled defiantly. Three armed men walked purposefully from the treeline with their laser-sighted semi-automatic weapons still pointed towards Henrietta. They approached in a crouching tactical posture, moving very quietly, and positioned themselves to one side of her. The men wore full military camouflage with light grey patches broken up with dark grey, from head to boot. Their helmets and compact night vision goggles obscured their faces. One of the men ordered her to drop her weapon, which she did. Another circled behind her and reached to his utility belt from which he unclipped a pair of handcuffs. Henrietta willingly put her hands behind her back and the cuffs were securely clicked shut around her wrists. She blankly stared toward Olivia and coolly muttered, 'So this is the thanks I get?' to which she received no response.

Henrietta was turned round and led away from the campsite and into the trees, where she was escorted quietly by two other members of the armed personnel. Resting his head on the snow again, Vincent closed his eyes and wondered whether it would have been better if she had just put him out of his misery. Life isn't always the better option, he had come to realise. As Vincent lay still another of the armed men picked his gun up from the ground and tucked it into his belt. He also collected the envelope and handed it to Olivia. Walking back, he kneeled down next to Vincent in order to assess the gunshot wound to his leg.

'You are lucky she missed the bone,' the man stated in a measured tone after rolling up Vincent's trouser leg to view its condition. He started to work on cleaning, disinfecting and dressing the wound.

Conrad Wilson and his team of six engineers appeared behind Olivia.

'Is the coast clear?' Conrad asked with concern.

'Yes, it would appear so,' Olivia answered. 'The item is seventy-two metres up the rock face. These are the exact coordinates and information,' she informed Conrad, looking and nodding toward the sheer incline and passing the envelope to him.

'Inaccessible. Unexpected. Oh well, we like a challenge,' Conrad quipped, tapping the coordinates into his own navigation device. He walked purposefully and alone towards the GPS location, and on reaching the wall of rock, he set down the case which he carried. Unbuckling both locks, which clicked open satisfyingly, he flipped the lid and laid it flat on the ground, revealing the contents of the case. A small spherical silver metal ball, of a size no greater than a lime, was suspended by four straight metal supports protruding from each of the four sides of the case. Spinning the case round, Conrad spent a few moments tapping information in to the touch screen which was built into the case lid, before making one final input, standing up and taking two steps backwards.

A faint, high-pitched mechanical sound, which was only audible to Conrad, emanated from the case as four long, thin spindly legs unfurled from underneath the unit, followed by another four legs. Undulating and rippling as if stretching, each individual leg touched down on the ground and took up the weight of the unit as the four supports released it. Immediately scuttling out of the case, the Special Precision Reconnaissance and Tactical Unit (SPRAT) raised one leg to the cliff face and paused for a moment, detecting and analysing the texture and rock type. One by one, SPRAT connected all eight of its legs to the rock face and began climbing with arachnid like dexterity, disappearing into the murky darkness of the early dawn light above. Conrad kneeled down next to the open case and observed the progress of SPRAT on the monitor. It had been tasked with locating a foreign metal object under the surface of the rock. Before much time had passed, Conrad's team had joined him at the case and encircled him looking at the screen read-outs. The armed personnel had also closed their perimeters around the case. Olivia was the last to join Conrad and his team.

A short, single, low frequency burst beacon sounded from above as SPRAT located the object behind an area of loose rock which had been reattached. Crawling around the metal object it had detected, SPRAT mapped out its size, and this information was sent to the case, but also, to the cargo plane piloted by Captain Wren, which was now hovering in vertical flight five hundred metres above the ground.

The craft had been designed to spread the downdraft in a slightly outward trajectory, which meant that its presence was hardly felt by those standing at ground level.

Opening the cargo door, Wren released the Material Recovery Unit (MRU) which was a cuboid shape drone incorporating a single-beam laser cutting system; using four high-powered engines, it was capable of precision flight. Due to the enormous energy requirement of this particular mission, the MRU was attached to a thin tensile alloy power cable which was capable of sustaining heavy loads.

As it dropped down to the same height as the Pebble, it centred and held its aim on the target. From a distance of two metres from the rock face the MRU drew energy from the craft above and engaged its high-power laser beam, which was directed at the correct angle to cut a cone shape into the rock as it flew in a protracted circular motion. The MRU was guided by the four outer markers which SPRAT had calculated and was continuously projecting. It used them to reference its focussing and re-focussing as it proceeded to clinically cut into the rock. Small pieces of debris started to rain down on those standing underneath and Conrad picked up the case to move a safe distance away, as did everybody else. The MRU finished cutting and SPRAT disengaged the guidance marks, retreating down the rock face to return to its casing. The MRU, still cooling, fired three miniature alloy harpoons into the circular shape which it had cut into the side of the rock face, with the now unstable cone lump of rock secreted behind it. With short jerking movements away from the surface of the rock, the MRU tested its hold on the payload.

'We had better move further out of the way,' uttered Conrad wisely as he closed the case into which SPRAT had scurried and shut down with several short beeps. Having checked Vincent thoroughly for weapons, two of the armed personnel lifted him to his feet and threw one of his arms over each of their shoulders as they made their way further from the campsite. Vincent's groans of pain were masked by the ever-increasing engine noise from the craft above, which was reducing altitude further and reeling in the slack.

The craft now hovered twenty metres from the top of the rocky monolith and just over one hundred metres from the ground. Captain Wren started a slow acceleration forward, away from the rock wall, and the whole craft shuddered as the Pebble encased in stone broke away from the rock face. As the multi-tonne object swung forcefully forward, it caused the craft above to become unstable, swerving and dipping with its movement. Captain Wren compensated and brought the aircraft back to stable vertical flight, commencing a climb while starting the process of reeling in the artefact towards the cargo doors. He readjusted for the weight of the Pebble, which far exceeded that which he had estimated on the basis of the size readings provided by SPRAT.

Entering the belly of the aircraft, all three harpoon hooks were holding the load well. The bay doors closed underneath the object, as it was automatically moved to the weight bearing area in front of the doors and set down to rest on the floor.

47

From a distance, Officer Magda Popova and eleven other officers who accompanied her could hear and see distant aircraft activity. They had coincidentally driven along the same road on which Vincent and the others had parked in order to embark on their fateful journey. Finding both cars parked in such a desolate location immediately arose suspicion within Magda, who was driving the leading police vehicle. Henrietta's car was hidden further up the road and was not discovered in the same location as the others.

Magda had handed Francis, his family and John to other colleagues for safekeeping, until the information which Ambassador Sunderland had given her could be verified. Stepping out of her patrol car, which was one of a five-car party parked behind Vincent's Audi, she had approached the driver's side door with her handgun drawn. Looking through the windows, it had been clear that nobody was in the car, so she moved on to Nikolay's four-by-four vehicle which she had also found to be empty.

The fresh footprints leading into the pine forest had been an early indication that they were on the right track and weren't far behind.

Ill equipped for the mountainous terrain, their progress had been slower than the party which had preceded them. From a distance of one mile from the artefact, the officers could hear the unmistakable sound of a low-flying aircraft.

'We are going to need helicopter air support,' Magda announced into the radio.

'Air support inbound,' came the positive response.

The party of officers had continued walking as fast as they could, following the tracks which were laid in the snow, but heard the aircraft sound disappear moments before being replaced by the sound of the police helicopter.

The helicopter, unable to detect any aircraft in the area, used the infrared camera on-board to find the party of police officers making their way to the monolith, which now stood as a memorial gravestone to the four men whose bodies lay at the foot of it.

Finally arriving at the campsite clearing in the cold light of dawn, the officers created a crime scene cordon and checked the surrounding area for survivors, but were unable to find anything except for a variety of random tracks which had been left by the footfall in the area.

Exhaustion had set in and several of the officers sat down to rest. Magda was furious at arriving at the scene too late. The low level of light made finding and following any particular set of tracks difficult. Even if the fatigued officers had been able to muster the resolve to locate the tracks which led to the site from which the helicopter had extracted the Argo ground team with Vincent, they would have been woefully late. The police helicopter scoured the area for any signs of heat signature, but was unable to find anything except for the area of the rock face from which the Pebble had been extracted.

'Marisa, hold on to the Ambassador and the others please. We will have some more questions for them,' Magda requested sternly from a colleague back in Sofia over the radio. Thinking over recent events, she was convinced that what had been ripped from the rocks above was of substantial significance. It had cost the four men in the camp below their lives and from the amount of ground level activity, along with air support, it was clear to Magda that the four men who had left the villa in Valsha had been brought to their end by a third party.

It was 11.30am before the forensic team, the same one that had worked the Ambassador's residence, arrived at the scene. The bodies of Aleksey, Kirill, Wasyl and Nikolay were photographed, processed and removed in body bags and forensic evidence was recorded and sampled. Unable to find any forms of identification on any of the bodies, Magda was clear that Ambassador Sunderland would at the very least be asked to conduct a formal identification of the corpses.

Two climbers, who were sometimes called upon by the police in strange circumstances such as these, had later arrived at the scene. Once shown the large hole in the side of the monolith, they wasted no time in starting their ascent. After twenty minutes of climbing, they had reached the fresh opening. Securing a safety rope anchor each, just above the hole, they both looked inside to see the cone shape cut into the side of the monolith. The sides were smooth and there was evidence of the large segment being dragged out of its almost eternal resting place by a great force, scraping along the bottom of the hole on its exit. After taking a number of photographs, the men rappelled down the face of the monolith and re-joined the police officers below.

Taking the memory card from the climbers, Magda slipped it into a police laptop and transferred the files to the central database. Looking at them, she puzzled over what could have so cleanly cut the section away. She had no doubt the analysis of the fragments which had fallen to the ground, along with the photographic evidence from the climbers, would provide some answers, before more in-depth analysis of the site above could take place.

The police eventually were able to locate the take-off site from which the Argo team had departed in a military helicopter.

Magda walked back to her patrol car by herself, wracking her brain for ideas and for what to do next. The only tangible lead which she could follow was the Ambassador and his family, and this was exactly where she was headed as she turned the key in the ignition of her patrol car and set off in search of answers.

48

Dr Meertens had fallen asleep at his desk, whilst leaning back in the chair in his study. Unaware of any of the more recent developments, the mobile phone on his desk vibrated and rang causing him to wake up suddenly.

'Yes, hello,' he said picking up the phone and speaking automatically, without having taken the opportunity to check the caller ID.

'We have it,' Mike Argo said jubilantly as Bob Meertens rubbed his eyes and took a moment to compose himself from his slumber.

'Excellent. That is excellent news. I knew that she would come through for us,' Meertens replied still sounding slightly dazed from his rude awakening. Finally opening his eyes fully for the first time, he wondered why Henrietta Rekman had not contacted him herself to report.

'Where is Henrietta?'

'She is with our security team; we had to restrain her. Bob, she is a little too … capable,' Argo stated.

'What did she do?'

'She led us straight to the people who had the information about the location, but my assets had to stop her from killing the last man she had left alive,' Argo reported.

'Relentless, isn't she?' retorted Dr Meertens with a wry smile which did not translate down the telephone.

'Doesn't she have any other hobbies?' Argo asked, laughing.

'Anyway, she has caused a real mess. Dozens are dead at the Ambassador's residence and two others in a small village on the outskirts of Sofia. Things could have been cleaner! They should have been cleaner,' he stated.

'I have heard about the residence and the village. I'm sure that she did what was necessary,' Meertens rebuked. Mike Argo was in no mood to get into a conversation with Meertens about the merits of Henrietta's actions.

'The artefact is on its way to me. The lab is prepped and my scientists are ready,' Argo confirmed with relish. 'My men will make sure that Henrietta is back with you as soon as possible.'

'How long until you know what it is that we have? What our dearly departed friend Jerome so desperately wanted us not to find,' asked Meertens expectantly.

'I don't think that we will be able to rush this one. The extraction of the artefact was much more brutal than I would have ever planned. I hope that we haven't already caused significant damage to it. The police were on the trail of those who also led us to the site. We barely had enough time to remove it before they arrived,' explained Argo.

'The members will be patient, for a time,' Meertens predicted.

'Bob, I will host the next meeting of Onyx here at the facility. Two weeks from now. Please let the other members know,' Mike Argo requested.

'Of course, leave it with me. You have some sleepless nights ahead I am sure.'

The conversation over, Mike Argo sat in the comfort of his study staring at the wall in front of him, rather than his computer screen, which showed the progress of the suborbital cargo plane approaching to land. His team had sent scanned images of the auction lot envelope and its contents, and reading Jerome Docherty's words had sent a chill down his spine. Docherty had found something of which he had only glimpsed one small part and on the basis of this, he had made an astounding claim. Docherty had claimed that the Pebble, which had been in the dark for such a long time, was extra-terrestrial and secondly, that it had brought life to Earth. An extraordinary claim which Argo struggled to fathom or believe. Argo realised that he actually hoped that the Pebble would be something else altogether. A disappointment perhaps.

Shaking his head due to the illogical thoughts which were creeping into his mind, Argo stood and headed down to the underground hangar. He recognised that the only remedy for being alone with his thoughts was distraction. It would be several hours until Olivia returned by more conventional means of air travel, accompanied by Conrad, three members of the armed personnel unit and his house guest, Vincent Madden.

The ferocious humidity and torrential tropical rain, which now battered the facility, were typical of Bandung. The climate inside the facility was worlds apart, boasting a steady twenty-degree Celsius throughout and a low humidity level.

As Argo stood in the underground hangar with the six-person science team he had assembled, he felt the dampness of his palms and he could sense his heart beating hard within his chest. They stood to one side in hazmat suits awaiting the arrival of the aircraft which was on the tarmac above. Although readings from inside the aircraft appeared clear, Mike Argo was taking no chances with the Pebble, which was now within touching distance.

The hydraulic lift engaged as the aircraft above positioned itself for its descent and a gust of air from outside billowed down from above. Captain Wren had cut the engines altogether and the only sounds, apart from the enormous hydraulic mechanism, was the gusty wind and pouring rain outside. The warm humid air was carried into the hangar until the lift reached its lowest point and the outside world was shut out and sealed by the retractable runway tarmac above.

Rainwater sat in small globules on the wings and fuselage of the aircraft, dripping down to the floor, but was quickly evaporating from the four engines which were hot and ticking as they cooled.

As Captain Wren conducted standard checks from inside the cockpit, the silence and suspense in the hangar was unbearable for Argo, who was keen to inspect the contents of the aircraft.

Finally, after what felt like an eternity, the cargo door through which the Pebble had entered the aircraft opened slowly. Argo watched as his team spent the next two hours painstakingly removing the three harpoons which were still lodged in the rock as well as examining the object and taking readings from it. Their initial assessment was that it did not pose any known chemical, biological or radiological threat, but Argo insisted that the hazmat suits should be worn regardless.

The rock was removed from the aircraft with great care by the team, who manoeuvred it into the adjoining sub-level two laboratory.

As it sat in a hermetically sealed section of the laboratory, the Pebble was subject to further testing and analysis before any decision was taken as to how to go about freeing it from its rocky prison. The team puzzled over how it could have become encased in the monolith in the first place.

Olivia and Conrad landed later with Vincent, who had been treated for his gunshot wound on the flight. Now he was taken to the medical section and placed under constant guard.

After careful consideration, and with Argo's approval, the team worked twenty-four hours per day in two-person shifts to slowly start chipping away the rock which encased the Pebble. They spent three days cutting away the larger pieces until finally being constrained to remove small pieces of rock with miniature circular saws. Extra care was taken to not damage anything that may have protruded from the Pebble, but no such structures were found by the team. The rock coverage was brought down to a thickness of only a few millimetres and it became clear that the object was of a spheroid shape, not dissimilar to a rugby ball.

The final layer of rock was broken away, much like the shell of a hardboiled egg. The scientists found the lack of cohesion between the rock and the Pebble astounding. The extremely hot temperatures at the moment of being engulfed by the molten rock, would have melted most metals known to man. The heat-shield of the Pebble, however, was not only intact, but it was also unmarked by events of the pursuant millennia since its arrival on Earth.

Three days later, at 2am, Mike Argo stood behind the protective screens of the hermetically sealed room which contained the artefact, watching two members of the team going about their work cleaning and analysing the object. Too distracted by the Pebble, he had not been able to take any time to speak to Vincent or ask him the questions to which he wanted answers.

'Is the object what you expected?' asked Olivia, walking up behind Argo, quietly.

'I don't know what I expected. I didn't expect this,' he responded, looking on in awe at the artefact. Once the final pieces of rock had been removed, the team had taken care to remove every foreign particle from the outer shell of the Pebble, which was black in colour and covered in fine carved patterns of unknown meaning or function.

The team were able to confirm almost immediately that the craft did not originate on Earth. Argo ordered a full, non-intrusive analysis of the object in advance of the Onyx meeting. He wanted to have as much information about the craft as soon as possible.

49

Ambassador Sunderland had received treatment at a private hospital on the outskirts of Sofia for the wound to his legs and had been able to rest for four whole hours, before he and the seven stitches holding the gash in his leg together were brought to their feet by Officer Magda Popova. John Coleridge was positive that Francis was suffering from shock and had advised the Ambassador not to comply with any further requests for information from the Bulgarian authorities at that time, but Francis had declined the suggestion in the spirit of being open and transparent about what had happened. He asked John to return to the

Embassy and make sure that Melissa and the children were safe.

Resting part of his weight feebly on a crutch, he was escorted to Magda's patrol car and was taken to the morgue at the central hospital.

'Why have you brought me here? I don't think that there is anything else I can do to help. I have told you everything that I know,' Francis said wearily to Magda, who had been deathly quiet throughout the journey. As they stood in the morgue, a burnt smell hung in the air.

'You know, we are both of us lucky that we did not end up in this place,' Magda said coolly as they stood inside a refrigerated room with four covered bodies, lying on four gurneys. 'Under one of these sheets. That's where you could have been, that's where I could have been, that's where your family could have been.'

'I know that,' Francis replied, feeling a shudder creep up his spine as they stood in the cold. 'Who are these people?' he asked, afraid to hear the answer.

'They are why you are here. I suspect that these are the four people who left you in the village of Valsha,' she explained. Francis was silent and just looked down at the bodies which lay secreted before him, hoping that Magda had made a mistake. She walked to the first of the bodies and pulled the sheet back to reveal the face of Wasyl. A bandage had been placed over the gunshot wound to his head. Immediately feeling a sense of nausea brewing in his stomach, Francis raised the cuff of his right hand to his mouth and nodded, closing his eyes momentarily.

'Wasyl Bohdanov,' Francis blurted.

'And who is he?' asked Officer Popova concernedly.

'Deputy Head of Ukrainian Intelligence,' he responded apprehensively. Magda let out a short hum as she replaced the cover over Wasyl's face and moved on to the next body, which she revealed with no delay.

'Kirill,' Francis said. His response was met with a quizzical look from Magda, who clearly was looking for more than a first name. 'I'm sorry, I don't know much about him other than his first name and that I think he is Russian Intelligence.'

Officer Popova looked unimpressed and moved on to the next body with haste.

'I have left these two bodies for last because they have suffered severe burns,' Magda explained as she pulled back the cover.

Francis looked down in horror. The hair on the man's head had been totally engulfed by the fire and no remnants remained. However, the burns were of a superficial enough nature to allow him to recognise the facial features of Aleksey who now lay before him. Francis gave Magda the name of Aleksey and that he also worked for Russian Intelligence, as she moved towards the fourth table. She prepared to pull back the sheet and Francis realised that three of the four men who had left Valsha had now been accounted for, with Vincent Madden being the only remaining person unaccounted for. Preparing himself, he looked down at the trolley upon which the fourth body lay as the cover was slowly drawn back from the features of the face.

Francis blinked several times, almost in disbelief. He couldn't recognise the person who lay before him. The body was badly burnt and reeking pungently, but Francis knew for certain that this was not Vincent. The smell was turning his stomach and making him feel unwell.

'I don't know this man,' Francis explained to Magda.

'Are you sure? Please take another look,' she insisted as Ambassador Sunderland looked down again reluctantly, to verify that he didn't know the man who lay before him.

'I am positive that I don't know him,' he confirmed.

Pulling the cover back over the face of Nikolay, whom Francis had not met, she spent a moment pondering in silence.

'Four men left the village. Who was the fourth man? The man who isn't here,' she asked in an inquisitive tone. Francis quickly started to rack his brain for a response which came surprisingly easily.

'The fourth man was Peter. He was also Russian intelligence,' lied Francis convincingly. 'But this is not him.'

Magda had noted the names of the men whom Francis had mentioned, both on her phone and also on the blank tag which was hanging from the toe of each of the men, except Nikolay, whose toe tag remained blank.

The refrigerated room in which they stood was lined with grey steel compartmentalised individual storage doors and looking around, Francis realised how uncomfortable he felt in the presence of the dead, although Magda appeared unfazed.

'Ok, well, I think that we have done all we can do in here,' she concluded, turning and walking towards the doors. Ambassador Sunderland followed her from the room and into the corridor, which led back to the reception. The walls of the corridor were dirty white and one of the lights didn't work, which caught Francis' attention. Realising the futility of being frustrated by such things given the events of recent days, he closed his eyes for a few seconds and focussed on keeping up with Magda whilst using his crutch. The pain in his leg was very pronounced and he was positive that walking around was directly against doctor's orders.

As they passed through the busy hospital reception, he was refreshingly plunged back into normality. Francis looked to the patients who were unwearyingly waiting. To them he seemed to be just another unfortunate casualty with a crutch. As they walked out of the front entrance of the hospital, Magda told Francis that her superiors wanted to speak with him directly about events. Ambassador Sunderland realised that his involvement in this matter would have significant political fallout, but understood that how he handled the situation from here on would be vital. That is if the Foreign Office would allow him to play any further role in this matter at all, which he considered to be highly improbable.

'Officer Popova, I am not feeling at all well. I would be happy to meet with your superiors at the Embassy later this evening, after I have had some rest. Would that be acceptable?' he asked as politely as possible.

'Of course, I will take you back there now,' she confirmed as they approached the car park of the hospital. 'I have one more thing to speak with you about. The woman at the villa. You said that her name was Charlotte Bradford, but have told us very little else. Ambassador Sunderland, my colleague is dead, as are many others. So far you have told us very little about what happened to the guests at your house, what business was being conducted in Valsha and what part you played in all of it. My superiors have asked me to urge you to, how should I say, refresh your memory before you meet with them,' Magda requested in a threatening tone. Seeing the seriousness in her eyes, Francis nodded positively.

'I have been honest with you. Please understand that my family and I are also victims in all of this. Do you think that I would put my children in harm's way?' he reasoned as he clambered into the patrol car with Officer Magda Popova, who remained unconvinced.

50

'She's dead, so how exactly are we supposed to know?' boomed the voice of Mr Jack Barrisfield, Partner at Brick Steckelback, over the hands-free car phone as he drove his Alfa Romeo well over the speed limit down a rain-drenched, winding, narrow country road in Kent. 'The money will be transferred to Mr Docherty's trust as discussed. The authentication protocol has expired,' he said, as his left front tyre hit a large puddle, sending the car into a brief aquaplane, before he regained full control.

'I don't know what to say, Jack, we have worked together for such a long time. Nothing like this has ever happened before,' commiserated Claud Petit, the auctioneer, who now sat in the back seat of the chauffeur driven Mercedes which was returning him home to Monte Carlo from Sofia.

'I didn't like any of this from the start, Claud. Just under two billion euro! For an envelope! It wouldn't be so bad if we had any idea at all what exactly we have facilitated here,' Barrisfield nervously submitted. 'I don't suppose the big news items have escaped your attention? Dozens of dead at the British Ambassador's residence, the explosion which killed Charlotte Bradford in that village, and more dead in the outlying forest. My firm would very much like to distance itself from this, so the funds will be transferred tonight.'

'Transfer the funds, of course,' Claud Petit confirmed reassuringly. 'We have nothing to fear.'

'Perhaps *you* have nothing to fear, but the movement of such a large amount of money on that same day, will not go unnoticed,' Jack interjected rapidly.

'Worry about things when the time comes, Jack. And *if* the time comes. You will live longer,' Petit said jokingly.

'I've got to go. Just at the office. Really pleased to be here at 11pm, Claud,' Jack Barrisfield said sarcastically as he ended the call and pulled in through the electric gates of the Brick Steckelback law firm, which was located at the outskirts of Tunbridge Wells.

The rain was still torrential as he brought his Alfa Romeo to a stop just outside the front door. Opening the door, he made quick work of moving into the building, scanning his key card to unlock the door. The office was a relatively large two-storey detached Victorian house and the headquarters of Brick Steckelback. As he walked past the unattended reception desk, Barrisfield ran up the staircase two steps at a time and saw the lights on in the office at the end of the upstairs corridor.

'Glad you could join us,' exclaimed Mildred Jones, another Partner at Brick Steckelback, from the room at the end of the hall.

'I got here as quickly as I could,' Jack replied sourly. 'Hi Becky,' he said, acknowledging Rebecca Bradford, one of the firm's brightest young solicitors who was frantically transfixed by her computer screen. She looked as though she may have been part way through taking a shower when she had received the phone call from Barrisfield to urgently make her way to the office. Her long red hair was wet and hung down around her face. Becky's otherwise dry grey jumper was moist where it had been in contact with her hair, which now hung down around her face as she furiously worked at her computer. She looked up momentarily just to acknowledge Jack's greeting, before turning her attention back to the screen.

'We have been here for an hour, waiting for you since you called,' Mildred said, also looking slightly dishevelled, having been called to the office at very short notice.

'Are the funds ready to transfer?' asked Barrisfield.

'I've created the payment to the trust fund account, but it just needs you both to call through and provide our bank with voice authentication authorisation,' Becky stated efficiently.

'Good, I will be glad to get rid of it,' Jack huffed, picking up the telephone receiver and dialling the number for GRO International Bank. He provided the company online banking details.

'Yes, there is an online transfer prepared and I am calling to authorise the payment,' he said abruptly, awaiting further instruction. Barrisfield was asked to provide the third, fourth and twelfth characters of his security password and then required to state his key phrase for voice biometrics identification.

'The cellar door is unlocked,' he said, clearly and confidently. Successfully identified, he passed the receiver to Mildred, who went through the same security procedure.

The call ended and Becky quickly logged back in to the online banking portal to verify that the funds had been moved.

'The funds are no longer showing in our account!' she said, turning to Jack and Mildred.

'Thank you, Becky, and I apologise for calling you out here in the middle of the night,' Barrisfield said sincerely.

'That's fine. I know it's important. Maybe I will just move into this house instead. I seem to spend more time here anyway,' Rebecca Bradford said with a genuine smile. 'If that will be all, I will head home,' she tentatively said. Jack nodded and she stood to her feet, wiping away some damp hair, which had stuck itself to her jawline and her cheek. 'I am going to look just great tomorrow,' she quipped sarcastically, as Mildred laughed. Picking up her leather jacket and keys, Rebecca walked towards the door of the office, turning back at the last moment. 'Oh, have you heard anything from my sister? I've been trying to call her, but then it got late and I suppose she hasn't had time to get back to me,' Becky enquired.

Barrisfield hadn't had an opportunity to inform anybody about the death of Charlotte Bradford. Not the firm's partners and certainly not her younger sister, Rebecca Bradford, who stood before him.

'But we have transferred the funds, so she must have confirmed,' Becky stated logically as she stood in the doorway awaiting a response. Several seconds passed and already the pause had been too long.

'Becky, there is something else which I need to speak with you about. Take a seat,' he said, gesturing towards the chair which she had vacated. The remnant smile which still hung on Becky's face disappeared instantly, as she walked back to her desk and sat in the chair.

'We have transferred the funds tonight, because we weren't able to get in contact with Charlotte ourselves,' confirmed Barrisfield. 'It appears that the auction lot, which she was assigned to verify for the purposes of the transfer to the trust fund reached such a high purchase price, because several influential parties wanted it,' he continued, trying to control his voice and measure his words.

'Should we not have just waited to hear back from her?' asked Becky, raising her eyebrows and moving some more wet hair which had stuck to her other cheek.

'We know from security that she left the Sheraton Hotel with the two men who purchased the item, but I have received information that Charlotte has been found dead in the village of Valsha, just outside of Sofia,' a momentary, terrible pause of silence descended from both Becky and Mildred. Jack could see that Becky's bottom lip was trembling and tears were welling in her eyes rapidly. She raised her right hand to steady her lip, but this only served to trigger her descent into uncontrollable crying. She pressed the palms of her hands to her eyes, but still the tears poured down her face and dripped from her chin. As she continued to sob, Barrisfield looked toward Mildred, who stared back with a look of shock.

They all sat silently for several minutes as Becky continued to cry and Mildred walked to the kitchen to bring a glass of water and a box of tissues for her. Taking some tissue, Becky dabbed her eyes.

'No, I don't believe it. Her phone is ringing through and nobody is answering it. It must be on silent,' Rebecca spoke through sobs. 'She wouldn't die. I would know. She can't die. She can't have died without me knowing!'

'Who did you find out about this from?' asked Mildred.

'Claud Petit. He told me that one of the people who died in the bomb blast in Valsha was a Bulgarian police officer and the other was Charlotte. There is no doubt, one of Claud's associates has identified her unfortunately,' confirmed Jack.

'Why didn't you tell me as soon as you found out?' shouted Becky staring directly at Jack Barrisfield, her eyes red and puffy from the strain of crying.

'I am sorry. I didn't really know how to tell you. I didn't want to believe it myself and was hoping that Claud would get back to me to say that there had been a mistake,' Jack said trying to justify his actions.

'How am I supposed to go home? Her things are everywhere. How did this happen?' Becky started to cry profusely once again.

'Jack, can I have a moment with Becky please?' Mildred asked, gesturing Jack toward the office door with her eyes.

He nodded and obligingly walked to the door, subconsciously happy to be temporarily removing himself from what was, without any shadow of a doubt, the first of many issues the firm of Brick Steckelback would have to face due to this unfortunate business venture.

Closing the door behind himself, he strolled up the corridor as he heard Mildred attempting to console Becky. He stood at the far end of the corridor, looking down the stairs at the empty, dark reception desk, thinking about how a few hours from now, the office would be open and all would appear totally mundane, when the reality was so far from normal.

A few moments passed and the loud cries, turned to more subdued sobs and Mildred finally emerged from the room and walked down the corridor towards Jack.

'Jack, listen. She is not taking this very well at all. How could she? She and her sister have been together their whole lives. They live together and share everything. I think that it would be best if you go and leave me with Becky. I will take her to collect a few things from her house, but she will come and stay with me for a while. And you should have told me about Charlotte as soon as you found out!' Mildred exclaimed.

'There were risks to Charlotte's role,'

'I'm not talking about the risks, Jack. What has happened, has happened and it is easy for us to say Charlotte's death is down to known risk. That isn't going to help Becky. You know as well as I do that this firm has never let injustices perpetrated against it go unpunished. Even if we never find out who actually killed Charlotte, it behoves us to show Becky that we have at least tried. That is what we will do,' Mildred said resolutely.

51

Ambassador Francis Sunderland had thought that he would never again see the inside of his office at the Embassy, and standing in the doorway, resting half of his weight on one leg and the other half on the crutch which he gripped reliantly, he realised that although he was standing in his office once again, he would not be seeing out the end of this posting.

Hobbling to his desk, he rested the crutch on the side of the table top and with an empty feeling inside, allowed the sturdy chair to take the strain of his weight as he slouched down into the leather seat which offered him the comforting sound of air escaping from the lining. He sat with his back turned to the window, which provided a net-curtain obscured view of the outside world. Breathing deeply, Francis ran his hand down his hip and around to the wound which was a constant source of agony, even through the painkillers.

Shaking his head, he wondered whether Vincent was still alive and whether the person who had kept him captive at the villa had also killed Aleksey, Kirill and Nikolay. Remembering Vincent's words about how he had feigned his own death, Francis closed his eyes tightly, and considered the irony.

Jonathan Coleridge knocked and waited to be invited in. Closing the door behind him, he sat in the seat across from Francis. He had seen Officer Popova's patrol car drop him off and needed to speak with the Ambassador urgently.

'Well, you've certainly had an interesting few days,' Jonathan lightly teased to ease himself into what would be a difficult conversation. He was met with a vacant and unmoving expression from Francis. 'Ok, well, there is some good news and some bad news,' he continued. 'The good news is that your wife and the Foreign Office are in total agreement. The bad news is that they agree that your time in this country is over and that you should return to London immediately,' Jonathan continued, attempting to lighten the mood.

'We are all in agreement in that case. No bad news there at all,' responded Francis, pinching the bridge of his nose and closing his eyes momentarily.

'They asked me to prepare you all for travel back to the UK today. I have taken the liberty of arranging the packing and transport of your affects from the residence through our usual contractor. I hope that you don't mind,' John apprehensively stated.

'No, I don't think any of us could stomach going back there. Thanks, John.'

'We received a call from the Bulgarian Ministry of Home Affairs. You agreed to a meeting with senior officials?' asked John concernedly, to which Francis nodded.

'May I suggest that you give the Foreign Office a call, because they specifically asked me to make sure that you don't speak with any more contacts here, and the Minister for the Interior is due to be here shortly,' John reluctantly conveyed, hoping not to overstep the mark. Francis leaned forward and overhung his desk, raising his eye line to meet John's.

'People are dead, John. My house became a mortuary, I have seen and heard some things which you wouldn't believe. That nobody would believe. So, I will meet with the Minister, because I owe it to myself and I owe it to all of the people who are no longer here,' Francis said with conviction, realising that he had to appear to maintain an air of total openness with everyone, even if he could not be open with himself. There was no way that he could provide any information to anybody about Vincent, the auction, the item which he had won, the amount which had been paid or most pertinently, anything about the Pebble. John had closed the office door behind him as he left and Francis burst out in a fit of quiet laughter at the preposterous nature of his situation.

A few moments later, he heard Melissa's footsteps approaching the door, accompanied by the smaller and lighter steps of his sons, Patrick and George. As the door swung open, both kids ran round the table and each took turns jumping up and trying to sit on his lap, but realising how that would not be the best remedy for the injury to his leg, he turned to bend down and give them a big hug and a kiss instead. If they had been affected by their run-in with the Russian agents, it certainly wasn't showing. Melissa sat in the chair across from Francis and waited to receive his attention. Francis righted himself and turned to face her.

'I'm glad that we are going back, I thought that none of us were going to make it!' Melissa confessed.

'So am I, darling, so am I. But the Bulgarian Minister for the Interior will be here soon to meet with me about recent events. I am ashamed that my own actions have put you through what you have been through and that I put us all in danger. That is something for me to bear and I promise that I won't make the same mistakes,' Francis apologetically said.

'The men who kidnapped you and the boys are dead. Wasyl is dead too. I identified their bodies at the morgue today,' Francis continued as Melissa's expression turned to a frown. She paused for a moment to consider what Francis had told her before asking,

'And Vincent? What about Vincent?'

'Vincent's body wasn't there, but it doesn't look good for him. So, you see, the only people right now who I am sure are alive and know about what happened, are sitting in this room. I have to ask you to not mention Vincent's name to anyone, or anything about what happened to us,' he requested apprehensively.

'Darling, if it means we get out of here any sooner, my lips are sealed,' Melissa said, flicking her hair. 'Anybody you told would probably think that you were having them on anyway. You don't really believe that thing exists, do you?'

'Certainly, a lot of people seem to think that it does exist and who am I to argue with them? I just want to get through this, so that we can all put it behind us and move on,' Francis said candidly.

Melissa and Francis spoke a few moments longer before they were interrupted by the phone on the desk. It was Jonathan, calling to let Francis know that the Minister had arrived. Melissa and the boys left the room and he sat in his chair considering the possible outcomes of the meeting.

Jonathan showed Bogdan Yordanov, Bulgarian Minister for the Interior, in to the Ambassador's Office. As they entered, Ambassador Sunderland struggled to clamber to his feet as he grimaced with pain.

'Please, don't get up,' Minister Yordanov urged the Ambassador, but it was already too late and Francis had managed to stand. He supported his weight on his desk with one hand and offered the other for a handshake.

'Welcome, Minister Yordanov,'

'Please, call me Bogdan,' the Minister responded.

'Francis,' Ambassador Sunderland said, blinking slowly and smiling. 'It is a shame that our first meeting could not have been under more, conventional, circumstances,' Francis immediately conceded, sinking back down into his chair with a grunt of pain.

'Yes, I have been briefed on the main points and I just have a–'

'Can I offer you anything to drink? Sorry to interrupt,' Francis offered without delay.

'Yes, just some water please,' Bogdan replied, as Francis poured out two glasses of water from the water cooler behind his desk.

'Sorry, yes. I just have one thing which I would like to discuss with you, Francis. You were with four other men in a house in the village of Valsha. They left the house to look for an artefact in an area which you showed one of our police officers. As you know, four men were found dead roughly in the area you showed us. What were the men looking for?' asked Minister Yordanov.

'Yes, they did leave to go and look for something they called an artefact, but I was never very clear on what they meant,' Francis responded, trying to maintain a straight, composed face. Bogdan Yordanov looked back at Ambassador Sunderland with a stone cold expression of disbelief.

'Why did you leave the party at your house with your whole family?'

'Wasyl asked me and Melissa to help him, so we brought the boys with us. We couldn't leave them there alone,' Francis responded, once again thinking on his feet and attempting to not sound totally implausible. Minister Yordanov's face remained unflinchingly incredulous.

'That is interesting. So, you left the party which you had arranged for Wasyl at your house, in order to help Wasyl reach Valsha in his own car. When you reached Valsha, you didn't know anything about the artefact which they were discussing with the Russian spies and they left you in the house to be blown up by a bomb. Is that correct?' asked Bogdan, who was no longer able to maintain his cool composure and an angry smile radiated from his face. Ambassador Sunderland sat slightly taken aback by the Minister's confrontational tone, but realised that it was justified in the circumstance.

'I know what it sounds like, but—'

'It sounds like what it is. Your government has refused to waive your diplomatic immunity even though there are many people who died at your house and more people who died after that, including one of our police officers. I expect you to be out of the country within the next twenty-four hours, Ambassador Sunderland!' Minister Yordanov said abruptly.

52

An irrepressible and inexplicable feeling of contentment filled Vincent Madden as he gently awoke in yet another strange place. His eyes still closed, he took a moment to enjoy the soft bedsheets, the comfortable, if slightly firm bed and gentle scent of flowers which flooded his senses.

He lay with his eyes closed, savouring the moment, with only the hint of trepidation at having no instant memory of the recent past.

Finally opening his eyes, he was intrigued to find out where he had fallen asleep and quickly realised that he was in what looked like a hospital room. A beautiful woman sat on a chair in the corner.

For the past few moments, Olivia had watched Vincent stir gently back to consciousness. She had sat quietly and attentively, waiting patiently for him to wake up. Part of the bullet, which Henrietta Rekman had fired at Vincent had remained in the flesh of his leg. The surgeons who had treated the wound had to work fast to repair some arterial damage which he had sustained. They had done a good job, considering they had carried out the surgery on the jet which had brought Conrad, Olivia and Vincent to the Argo Industries Future Logic Facility in Bandung.

Vincent looked down at his arm, and saw the drip attached to it. He could feel pain in his leg, even through the general numbness which he was experiencing. Trying to curl his fist into a ball, he was only able to touch the tips of the fingers to the base of his palm. Trying to wiggle his toes was proving a conundrum for his central nervous system.

Trying to speak, Vincent realised how dry his mouth had become. Olivia approached, pouring a glass of water from the jug, which sat on his bedside table next to the blooming flowers. Vincent used his body and elbows to shuffle up the pillow and right his torso, as Olivia touched the cool glass to his lips and he took a few slow, thirst-quenching sips.

'Who are you? Where am I?' asked Vincent in a raspy, confused voice.

'My name is Olivia. You were shot and lost a lot of blood. You were sedated and our medical team operated on your leg,' Olivia said. Vincent was juxtaposed between elation and worry as he looked down again at the drip and then up at the bag of fluid which was being fed into his body. Mustering the strength in his fingertips, he pulled out the drip and noticed another tube, attached by a syringe to the underside of the same arm, which was pumping full of blood. He pulled out the second syringe and some of the blood quickly spilled onto the clean bedsheets, absorbing like ink into blotting paper.

'Your treatment is not complete. You must rest,' Olivia advised quickly as she observed the waking realisation on Vincent's face. His mind suddenly re-focussed on events which had occurred just prior to him losing consciousness. He wondered what drug they had given him. The feeling of weakness in his limbs was overpowering and he felt that he could not string a thought together.

'I feel fine. Thanks,' he lied. 'Where is this place?' he demanded to know.

'You are in the medical section of my employer's facility,' Olivia responded. The feeling of contentment that he had experienced when waking up was rapidly transforming into frustration, as he was getting piecemeal information. Feeling some strength return to his grip, he wrapped his fingers around the bedsheet which covered him and pulled at it. Tucked in under the mattress, it was difficult to dislodge, but with some perseverance and all the strength he could muster in his numbed limbs, it came free. He was wearing a white t-shirt and white, loose-fitting boxer shorts, neither of which belonged to him. Looking at the bandages on his leg, it was clear that walking would not be an option, but regardless of this, he swung both legs round and allowed his bare feet to hang suspended above the carpeted floor.

Olivia was standing next to the bed, observing Vincent's attempts to stand up.

'My employer invites you to stay here until you have fully recovered,' she conveyed. 'You should not try to walk on the leg so soon after surgery.'

'Thank you, I had guessed that!' Vincent responded in a frustrated tone. Having righted himself, he started to feel a pronounced pounding pain to the beat of his heart, which was focussed at the locality of the injury, just below his kneecap. The pain quickly became intolerable so he raised his legs once again and lay down. Vincent was not a stranger to being held in captivity, but he was shocked to still be alive, when all four men who had accompanied him had been killed so brutally before his very eyes.

'My employer would like to speak with you, but first you must rest,' Olivia advised. Vincent had been staring at his hands, deep in thought, but on hearing Olivia's voice, he turned to look at her. She held his gaze with an inquisitive stare, which seemed mesmerising, but was also quite unsettling.

'Yeah, why not,' he said. Olivia stood from her seat and opened the door to leave. Vincent caught a glimpse of what looked like a pristine operating theatre through a glass, floor-to-ceiling window.

'I know that I can't leave, but can you at least tell me one thing? Why did you stop her from killing me?' asked Francis, referring to Henrietta Rekman.

'Our intention was to retrieve the Pebble. The loss of life was regrettable and I determined that your death would have been unnecessary,' Olivia stated, as a look of surprise came across Vincent's face.

'Well, when you put it like that,' he responded.

'You are free to leave as soon as you would like. You have sustained a serious injury and are advised to rest for the next few days at least. My employer is pleased that you are here and wants to share with you more information about the artefact. We hope that you agree to stay with us,' Olivia optimistically said, gesturing towards Vincent with her hand half open. 'Please take some time to think about it. I will be back later today. If you would like to leave, we will render you unconscious and place you in the charge of a hospital.'

The door gently closed behind Olivia and made a sliding sound followed by a click as the door latch mechanism engaged.

Looking around the room quickly, Vincent wasn't sure how long he would really have to himself. The last person alive, had he been brought in and treated back to relative health just to be interrogated? Sitting back, he nestled his head in the pillow and resigned himself to his fate, lying awake for a while before drifting off to sleep. Oblivious to the fact that he had been transported, unconscious, almost half way around the world, Vincent slept.

53

Mike Argo had not felt such a pang of nerves and anxiety in a very long time as he stood at sub-level two of the Future Logic Facility. Two weeks since the Pebble arrived, the science team had made no intrusive intervention into the craft, but had only conducted external studies. The discoveries that had been made were fundamentally fascinating while also terrifying, and as the other members of Onyx had started to arrive at the facility for the meeting which had been arranged, the aircraft hangar on the surface was becoming ever more congested with private jets. Argo had increased the security protocol at the facility for the meeting and the manpower at the perimeter had been doubled. As evening descended, the stillness of the warm air outside was pierced by the sound of birdsong and a multitude of insects from the teeming jungle beyond the ten-foot electrified perimeter fencing.

Onyx members were shown to their rooms on the upper levels by members of facility staff who had no knowledge of the existence of, or the activity which took place on, the lower levels.

Professor Hancock walked into her room and looked around with a critical eye, but was unable to fault anything. Setting her case down on a low chest of drawers by the door, she walked round the room. Brushing past the curtains with her fingers, she strolled into the bathroom to check herself in the mirror. Staring briefly at her slightly dishevelled reflection, she quickly closed the door, undressed and walked into the shower, which was well stocked with a variety of high quality products.

Forty-five minutes later, in a grey dress, she was almost ready. As she applied the finishing touches to her silvery-grey hair, she realised how long it had been since she wore high heels. She shifted from one side to another in her left shoe. Finding her balance and picking up her clutch bag from the side, she opened the door and headed downstairs to the reception which Argo had put together for the members of Onyx.

As she walked out of the room, she noticed a member of staff at the end of the corridor. He directed her to turn left and walk down the stairs at the end of the next corridor. Reaching the bottom of the stairs, she could see the open door to the conference centre. Two armed guards stood at the door and as she walked through, it was clear that the other guests had arrived some time ago. Plucking a glass of red wine from the serving tray of one of the catering staff standing just inside the entrance, she took a much needed swig and was immediately struck by the rich bouquet which thumped her palate and tapered off into a sumptuous aftertaste. Looking around the room, she recognised many of the faces, some of whom she had met in person before and others who she had only spoken with electronically. There were approximately forty members of Onyx in the room and another fifteen catering staff, meandering between the guests, who had the luxury of space in such a large conference hall. Most of the Onyx members remained near the entrance and sat sporadically around six large round tables draped in fine white tablecloth. The excitement in the room was electric and palpable. It was clear that such good attendance by so many important people meant that the Pebble had captured the imagination, attention and curiosity of Onyx members in a way in which so few things had in the past.

'May I interest you in a canapé?' asked an obliging young man who had approached from her left side. She looked at the man, and then down at the selection of savoury treats which he had presented to her. Picking a citrus sea bass with oscietra caviar canapé with her fingers, she quickly moved it towards her mouth as it started to gently fall apart between her fingers. The taste was remarkable and enhanced her mood further. Turning to get another, she was disappointed to see that the staff member had disappeared.

Josephine saw Dr Bob Meertens approaching through the crowd and quickly checked the corners of her mouth for any possible remnants of the canapé. As he approached with a wide grin, he outstretched his right hand toward Josephine and as she gripped it he leaned in and gave her two kisses on the cheeks.

'Fantastic to see you here,' he cheerfully greeted.

'Likewise, I didn't think that many of us would want to miss this. I will tell you something. I am usually a pessimist when it comes to this kind of thing, but Mike really does seem to have something to tell us,' she responded with similar enthusiasm.

'The Pebble. Sounds so innocent. If Docherty is looking down on us, he must be spitting feathers!' said Meertens gleefully.

Josephine smiled dryly and took another sip of wine from her glass and as she brought it down, she noticed another staff member walking toward her with a bottle of red wine. As he topped up her glass, she thought that she would keep the second one full so as to not lose any concentration.

'I notice that you have your protégé with you,' Josephine said, pointing toward Ms Henrietta Rekman with her eyes. 'Quite a mess she caused.'

'Nobody is perfect. She does get things done,' Meertens said defensively. Henrietta was standing with a group of Onyx members, listening engagingly, but seemingly not taking an active part in the conversation. She wore a provocative short blue dress, which was a far cry from the attire which she had worn during her murderous quest to locate the

Pebble. Looking radiant, her blonde hair hung down in curls, accentuating the features of her face.

The bright lights of the conference centre dimmed slightly and the facility's staff took their cue to leave the room. A double door behind the podium at the front of the hall opened and the guests were asked to file into the lift which presented itself. As group after group of Onyx members disappeared down to sub-level two, the conference hall emptied.

The members were guided by staff from the science team, who seemed brimming with enthusiasm, to a laboratory which was round in shape and partitioned from the surrounding corridor by thick glass. Through the glass, the Onyx members could see Mike Argo standing with Olivia, Vincent, Conrad and three other scientists. As the doors slid open with a gaseous hiss, the guests trooped into the lab which had evidently been cleared of the equipment which would have otherwise been there, in order to accommodate the numbers. Negotiating for position, the members of Onyx jostled for a good line of sight to the object, which was enchantingly capturing the attention of those in the room who had not previously seen it.

The Pebble was located in an elevated position behind Argo and its pristine black exterior gave it a brand-new appearance, concealing its extraordinary age. Measuring a modest metre and a half in length, the Pebble's elongated shape was on profile display to the guests, who were all absorbed in its splendour. Mike Argo waited for silence to descend on the room before speaking.

'Distinguished guests. Ladies and gentlemen, I am very pleased that you have been able to join us here. I know that many of you have had a long trip. I am privileged to be able to speak to you today about the Pebble. Whilst we have made every effort to uncover as much information as possible in the two weeks since its recovery, please bear in mind that we have not even scratched the surface of uncovering its secrets. Literally. I would like now to introduce Dr Otani who has taken the lead on the research so far and who will now take you through the preliminary findings,' Mike Argo gestured to Dr Otani, who stepped forward. A Japanese, slight figured middle-aged man, he wore a white lab coat and spectacles, which had gradually slipped forward down his nose; he quickly adjusted them before starting his report.

'Thank you, Mr Argo. It has been a great honour to work on this project and I am pleased to report that we have verified the craft to be of extra-terrestrial origin and to be of neither human nor natural creation. This is, therefore, our first confirmation that intelligent extra-terrestrial life exists or existed,' Dr Otani stated as a look of awe spread through the crowd as if contagious. 'Furthermore, we have only been able to date the object's date of arrival on the basis of the age of the rock within which it was encased. The rock in the particular area of the Balkan Mountains where the Pebble was located has been dated at less than one billion years. However, we suspect that the object's arrival on Earth may have been a long time prior to this. We believe that the Pebble is essentially a pod which brought a form of life, compatible with the atmospheric conditions of our planet in its earlier stages under the principles of panspermia,' he continued. As Dr Otani looked around the room, he noticed an immediate look of confusion at the term which he had used. 'Panspermia. The idea that life exists throughout the universe and is distributed by natural phenomena such as comets and asteroids, or in this particular case, a non-natural craft. During our initial period of research, we have identified one section of the Pebble which is gas-porous: air flows into and out of the compartment freely. We believe that in this section, there were contained a substantial number of extremophile microorganisms or microbial life,' Dr Otani paused once again to assess the confusion he was causing. 'Extremophile life: life which is able to survive in extremely hostile conditions which would be fatal for most other life on Earth. This type of life form is able to survive the hostile conditions of space, of which cold and radiation are just two factors. Within the Pebble, however, we suspect that neither of these issues would have been pronounced. When combined with the fact that extremophile life is able to survive and travel through space for undefined periods of time, we have found our initial theory to be resilient. Any DNA or RNA which was present in the open compartment would have been shielded from solar radiation in transit by what we will no doubt find to be a highly-advanced technology. We have also considered the possibility that life was already present or established on Earth when the Pebble arrived,' Dr Otani continued, as a hand was raised amongst the members. Dr Otani nodded.

'Dr Otani, I am sure that I, like many others, am fascinated by what you are telling us. If one of the compartments is open, is it safe for us to be near this craft?'

'Yes, we have conducted rigorous testing under sterile conditions and the craft is safe in its current form even though we have as yet been unable to probe the inside of the open section due to the undulation of the small openings which make intrusive investigation difficult. We suspect that high gas-pressure inside the craft was used to expel the organisms on release,' he explained. 'You do bring me on to my next point and the reason why we have not been able to proceed into any more intrusive methods of research into the craft. Apart from the one section which we are aware is open, we have identified a further five similar compartments which we suspect at present remain closed,'

Dr Otani stated in a serious tone, pausing momentarily. The members of Onyx immediately started to unpick the ramifications of this in their minds and as they did, some members looked toward each other with mixed looks of excitement, puzzlement and fear and started to talk quietly about what Dr Otani had announced, as he recommenced over and above the hubbub of his audience. 'So, our working theory is that when the Pebble arrived on Earth, it analysed the atmospheric and surface material chemical content and this determined which compartment opened and released the extremophile microorganisms. The potential implications of this are clearly profound, whilst inextricably hazardous,' concluded Mr Otani as Mike Argo stepped forward and rested his hand on Otani's shoulder.

'That's right. We could potentially be looking at other forms of life in the five sealed compartments,' Argo clarified as the members were stunned into silence, except Henrietta Rekman whose gaze was fixed upon Vincent. From a slight distance, he had not recognised her in her tidy guise and she had waited patiently for eye contact. As Vincent saw Henrietta staring at him, he quickly recognised her face as she ever so slightly puckered her lips and made a faint kissing sound, which was sufficiently audible to draw the attention of Meertens who was standing next to her. Seeing the aim of Henrietta's affectionate expression, he nudged her slightly with his elbow at which point she grinned and looked at Dr Otani, who was once again preparing to speak.

'Yes, the five sealed compartments do pose a number of significant challenges and risks for us. Our understanding of life, in any of the forms known to us, would suggest that any biological matter contained in the compartments would no longer be automatically viable,' Dr Otani solemnly stated, shuffling from one foot to the other. 'But clearly, opening any one of those compartments on the planet surface, even in a contained environment, may present a risk of planetary biological re-calibration of Earth. I would like to tell you about the basic analysis which we have conducted on the outer shell of the craft. The main composite element which makes it up is one which we have not encountered before,' Dr Otani announced to an audience that was finding it difficult to keep up with the revelations they were hearing. 'The shell appears to be a metal alloy composite of an unknown constitution. The total mass of the Pebble on Earth is greater than it could be, had even the densest materials known to man been used to construct it,' Dr Otani added steadfastly as Mr Argo once again interjected to stop him from going into too much detail.

'So, I am sure that you can understand, we have a lot to learn from the Pebble. Dr Otani has spoken with me about the thrust system of the craft also, which at present remains a mystery to us, given our knowledge of conventional space thrust engine technology. There are other unanswered questions at the moment, such as whether the craft still has power, or how the craft is powered at all,' concluded Argo as he looked around the faces of the Onyx members intently. 'Any questions?'

54

Ambassador Sunderland had returned to London, persona non grata, with his family. After several days of annual leave, which seemed lost to Francis, who was still reeling from recent events, he received an email from Julian Braithwaite, the Head of the Diplomatic Service, to request a meeting at the Foreign Office. Melissa and the children were very happy to be back home and Melissa had spent some time catching up with her friends.

Francis was now able to support his own weight without the use of a crutch, and standing before the mirror in the hallway of their four-bedroom detached house in Surrey, he straightened his tie and adjusted a few errant hairs which had strayed. His suit was immaculate, having just returned from the dry cleaners and he took a lungful of air, considering himself lucky to be alive and back home.

Bidding Melissa and the children goodbye, he opened the door and undertook the quick ten-minute walk to Cobham Station to catch a train to central London, after which he took the tube to Westminster. As he walked up the stairs and out of the tube station, he tried to limit his limp as much as possible, which made the pain from his wound all the more pronounced.

Francis walked past one of the security guards at the entrance, with whom he was on nodding terms. He showed his pass regardless and quickly made his way into the King Charles Street building and toward where the meeting was due to start in ten minutes.

Approaching the meeting room, he saw that the two other attendees had both arrived already. Entering and closing the door, he shook the hand of Julian Braithwaite, who introduced the third person as Jennifer Harbinger from MI6.

'Thank you for coming in to meet with us, particularly as you are on leave,' Julian said calmly. 'I hope that your leg is on the mend.'

'No problem at all. Yes, it is feeling better, but it is still painful to walk.'

'We will try to keep this as brief as possible. Just to say that we are very happy to have you back in one piece. It sounds as though you went through a hell of a lot out there. John Coleridge had us quite worried for you,' Julian quietly muttered, with a slight tremble in his voice which was picked up by Francis. 'Jennifer, would you like to start?'

'Yes, thank you. Firstly, Ambassador Sunderland, I would like to convey my thanks for your assistance and apologise for the risk which both you and your family faced. This was never our intention.'

Francis sat for a moment considering the opacity of what Jennifer had said, which nurtured in him an almost instant dislike for her. He looked towards her and nodded, pursing his lips slightly. 'Our field operative, Vincent Madden, has not contacted us since you saw him last. I have read your written report, which states that he left the village of Valsha with the coordinates of the artefact and three other men, but wonder whether there may be anything else you might be able to remember which may indicate where he is?'

Francis looked toward Julian, who was shifting uncomfortably in his seat as Jennifer asked her question.

'Anything else which I remember? I will tell you the same thing that I told the Bulgarian authorities in my attempts not to appear totally uncooperative. They went to the location stated in my report. The same area where, as you are well aware, four men were found dead,' he said curtly. 'I consider myself fortunate not to have been one of them!'

'Yes, of course. You identified three of the men to the Bulgarian authorities, but were not able to recognise the fourth. Was this because they had sustained such severe burns as to make them unrecognisable, or are you positive that it was not our operative?' Jennifer said, referring to Vincent.

'I don't think that it was him,' Francis responded quickly.

'Because, as you can imagine, we are experiencing significant difficulties securing a tissue sample in order to conduct a DNA test on that particular body. The Bulgarian authorities will not allow us access,' she continued. Francis sat with both of his hands clasped together, his fingertips dug into the back of his knuckles with frustration as he wondered whether the Bulgarian authorities' lack of cooperation came as any surprise whatsoever. He simply nodded once again. 'So, you don't know where he might be?'

'Your guess is as good as mine. If you haven't heard from him by now, it doesn't bode well. There were several different parties pursuing the artefact and they were extremely well resourced. You did read about the military drone which held me and my family hostage, yes?' Francis blurted out.

'We have received very little information from the authorities in Bulgaria regarding the location of the artefact, if it has been removed and the investigation into its removal, in fact,' Jennifer confirmed.

'Thank you, Francis. Your candour is much appreciated. Can you think of anything that wasn't in your report which may be of use to Jennifer?' asked Julian. Francis thought for a moment in silence.

'Yes, there is something. Julian, did you, or anybody here know anything about the auction invitation or the plan to invoke my involvement?'

'No, no, we didn't,' he said.

'Well, the only thing that I think is left for me to say is that a serious conversation should take place with our colleagues,' Francis said, pointing Jennifer out with his eyes. 'Our diplomatic relations with that country have been thrown back thirty years and the international ramifications for this sort of behaviour are as yet unknown,' Francis stated as Julian started to turn a noticeable shade of red.

'Ambassador Sunderland, we are not always able to share information on operations as we may like to,' Jennifer sheepishly put forward.

'You were aware of my pre-existing relationship with your operative. You exploited that. I don't have anything else to say,' Francis stood from the table, lifting his weight with his hands on the armrests of his chair. He turned and walked out of the meeting room.

Later, Francis Sunderland sat on the District line at 7pm on the first leg of his journey home, after his meeting at the Foreign Office.

Although the meeting had taken place earlier in the day, he had become so frustrated that he opted to head for a pub in Westminster, which he knew well, to have a couple of drinks and to put some order to his thoughts. The alcohol had served to numb the pain in his leg.

Sitting by the door of the tube as it hurtled along, the carriage was not busy as it pulled in to St James's Park Station. The passengers who boarded made themselves comfortable and a woman sat next to him. Looking straight ahead, at the window opposite where he sat, Francis was able to see her reflection briefly, before returning his gaze to his lap and his thoughts.

Arriving at Victoria Station, he stood tentatively, trying to keep balance as the train stopped with a jolt. The platform was busier and Francis jostled for position as he climbed the stairs and exited from the turnstile, oblivious to the woman who had sat next to him and followed him from the train.

Returning the bank card and wallet to his trouser pocket, he walked slowly, wincing in pain. Francis was overtaken by many commuters, all rushing to get home for the weekend and suddenly became aware of the steady, slow-paced footsteps of the person behind him.

He didn't turn to look as he consciously battled his paranoia. The footsteps slowed down, drowned out by the background noise as Ambassador Sunderland climbed the steps out of the underground and into the train station.

Walking toward the platform from which his train would depart, he dipped his hand back into the pocket housing his wallet and his fingers immediately identified a foreign object. Something which felt like a business card.

Pulling the card from his pocket, he stopped dead in his tracks to inspect it. An appointment card denoting a meeting due to take place in two days at the offices of Brick Steckelback had been slipped into his pocket at some point between the two turnstiles. The delivery of the invite had been deliberately threatening.

Tucking the card into his wallet, he boarded the train.

55

The members of Onyx had made their way back to the conference centre after the unveiling of the Pebble. Mike Argo now joined them, as they discussed what they had heard. Although the hour had become late, such revelations meant that emotions were running high and sleep was on nobody's mind.

Dr Meertens stood to one corner of the room with Henrietta Rekman, as they both sipped on red wine. Argo was speaking with several other members, who had follow-up questions. He had no answers that he could confidently give. Spotting Dr Meertens and Henrietta, Argo excused himself and headed straight towards them. As he approached, he saw that they were deep in conversation, which ended abruptly as soon as they saw him.

'It's been quite an evening, Mike,' observed Bob Meertens. 'I think that most of us were expecting or perhaps secretly hoping to be underwhelmed. I suppose that is the problem when you answer one question definitively, such as, are we alone in the universe. It tends to throw up about one thousand others.'

'Don't I know it. Although these things are focussing my thinking,' Mike Argo conceded humbly as he turned toward

Henrietta. 'It's been a long time since I last saw you, Ms Rekman. In person, anyway. You caused quite a stir out there.' Henrietta smiled and looked at Mike Argo with one eye as the other was shrouded behind locks of her blonde hair.

'Thank you, Mr Argo. I wanted to make sure that you got what you needed,' she said, taking a sip of wine. 'I know that there are some things which I could have done better,' she added, 'but I am always open to feedback.'

'Henrietta tells me that one of the men who was close to getting the Pebble was standing with you downstairs at the presentation. Vincent   Madden. Is   that   wise?' Bob Meertens openly questioned.

'Vincent? Yes, he is still recovering from the perforating which Henrietta gave him, but he assures me that he holds no grudge,' Mike Argo said, disbelieving the words almost as soon as they had been spoken.

'I hope that you know what you are doing, bringing someone from the outside in like this. Particularly somebody who was after the artefact,' Meertens continued.

'There will be a use for him. We have the Pebble now and he has volunteered to stay as my long-term guest,' Argo assured, as Bob Meertens nodded in agreement and Henrietta stood unflinching.

'He is the one who won the Pebble at auction for the British. You know that, don't you Mr Argo? He is well trained, if slightly gullible,' Henrietta added superfluously. 'He will probably try to contact them the first chance that he gets!'

'We have had an opportunity to speak and he did outline what happened, in broad strokes,' Argo confirmed. 'But enough about Vincent, he is in good hands here. Please do enjoy the rest of the evening and I hope that you have a pleasant journey back tomorrow,' Mike Argo said as he turned and started to walk towards the exit of the conference centre, where Olivia was waiting for him. Turning back suddenly to face Bob Meertens with a purposeful look, he tilted his head slightly back. 'Actually, Bob, do you think that we could have a quick chat please?'

'Of course,' Meertens responded, assessing the tone of Argo's voice. Henrietta broke eye contact with Mike Argo and slowly walked away. Pointing in the direction of one of the side entrances to the conference centre, Argo led Meertens away for a more secluded discussion. Closing the door, both men stood in one of the side corridors.

'Can I speak candidly with you?' asked Argo.

'Of course. When have you ever not?' Meertens said.

'I didn't think we were going to get this thing, so, thank you,' Argo conceded.

'It's not me who you should be thanking,' Meertens said with a detectable note of pride in Henrietta's achievement.

'Yes, well, that brings me on to what I want to speak with you about. You know me and you also know some of the things which I have done over the years getting where I am. But Henrietta. Bob, she is spectacular,' Argo stated, to the immediate approval of Meertens.

'You can't have her. You know that, don't you?' Meertens retorted, drawing a laugh and a nod from Argo. 'But seriously, Mike, what is Vincent Madden doing here and why is he still alive?'

'Henrietta and I are very much alike. The difference is that I like to play with my prey while they are alive first,' Argo smiled malevolently.

'Just be careful. He has a history of his own. There is a lot about him we weren't ever able to uncover and we were lucky to find out that MI6 were keeping him off the books,' Meertens said with a concerned tone.

'Yes. That's part of the reason why I find him so interesting. As we stand here now, I can't explain to myself why a man would put himself through that life,' Argo questioned as Meertens shrugged his shoulders.

'I have the feeling that you haven't told us everything here tonight, Mike. Not by a long shot.

That was the first time I had been down to your labs and they look like they would put NASA to shame.'

'We don't want to speculate. I hate to speculate. When we have answers, you will know about it. I have honestly been made to feel ten years old again for the past two weeks. There is so much to learn. Listen, I have held you up for long enough. Enjoy some drinks; get some rest,' Argo said insistently.

Both men walked back into the conference centre and Mike Argo headed straight towards Olivia, who was still waiting by the entrance.

She had been listening to the earlier conversation between Argo and Henrietta and found herself once again confused by what she had heard from her.

56

As they walked down the carpeted corridor towards his bedroom, Mike Argo realised how tired he had actually become. Tomorrow would be a new day and as Bob Meertens had said, with one question answered, thousands more had presented themselves.

Dr Otani had spoken of the dangers of breaching the sealed compartments of the Pebble on Earth and this certainly would pose an unacceptable, Pandora's box, risk. Notwithstanding this, opening the compartment in an environment unable to sustain whatever biological life or primordial building blocks were contained, would be an exercise in futility.

At this early stage, Mike Argo realised that truly understanding the Pebble would involve the cultivation of an environment that could safely harbour the payload of one of the sealed compartments.

He was confident that the craft possibly still retained remnant charge or at least the capacity to recharge, although no information about the power system within the Pebble was yet known. Or indeed if it used a power system at all, in the conventional sense of the word.

He had discussed these matters with Dr Otani and asked him deliberately to leave certain information out of the Onyx member briefing. Mike Argo knew that international interest in the craft remained high outside of the organisation and the search for the Pebble by other parties would never end.

He also understood how much he stood to learn from not just the Pebble through reverse engineering, but also the contents of the sealed compartments, whether the stock contained within them remained viable or not.

Argo's thoughts had immediately been drawn to his growing space exploration ventures which fell under the flag of Future Logic. He had discussed with Dr Otani the feasibility, when the time came, of transporting the Pebble to the Exodus Base. This would only happen after as much research as possible had been completed on Earth. The Exodus Base was an underground cavern, much the same as the one which housed the underground portion of the Future Logic Facility, but approximately thirty per cent of the size and located on Mars.

The use of a cavern's naturally existing structure was logical and would eliminate the harmful solar radiation, limit the extreme day and night-time temperature variables and protect the eventual first human missions from micrometeorite strikes. Mike Argo had used the very same technology that he had used in Bandung in order to identify this ideal spot on the Martian surface for an underground base.

With a population almost exclusively comprising automaton utility and 3D-printing robots, the Exodus Base was far from complete. The task of constructing the entrance airlock, hermetically sealing the walls of the cavern and bare bones construction of the internal two-level structure of the base, were complete. The use of raw materials sourced locally to the base site, meant that Argo's main cost outlay had been the development and transportation of the construction machinery to Mars. The whole operation had been conducted in total secrecy and was known and operated by a Future Logic team of twenty-three scientists, robotics specialists and engineers. Eight members of the team were contained within a space station orbiting Mars. Compared to being based on Earth, their closer proximity to the Exodus base substantially cut down on the amount of time that it took for control commands to reach the automatons, particularly where they were required to carry out any manoeuvres which were time sensitive or required a human touch.

The same eight team members had used the station's arsenal to track and actively destroy both downward facing satellites that would have had sufficient imaging capability to identify the Exodus Base construction area, leaving the remaining four active satellites intact. They had also disabled one rover mission, which crashed through the Martian atmosphere. The missions had been written off as hardware malfunctions, which had rendered Earth governments unable to observe the secret activity on the Martian surface.

Dr Otani discussed with Mike Argo the possibility of recreating the estimated environmental make-up of other observed exoplanets which were considered potentially habitable by life, while being incapable of supporting most Earth life. Otani had made the point that it would be difficult, from a scientific standpoint, to set aside all preconceptions which we hold. These notions are based on the only requirements for life known to man, namely that life is carbon based, requiring water and oxygen. He had reminded Argo of the discovery on Earth of complex deep-ocean organisms which require no oxygen to survive. He had indicated the incalculable variants which would be at play in attempting to recreate the correct conditions for life forms of a constitution alien to our own understanding.

Otani had warned Argo that before any course of action could be considered, it had to first be established whether the Pebble would be able to open its compartments without intervention.

These conversations seemed far from the forefront of Argo's mind as he retreated to his room. Like a chess player strategising his plan for the future, he contemplated the hopeless nature of the chessboard in question: an unknown number of squares and an unknown number of opponents. This was the way of Mike Argo's life for almost as long as he could remember. Shrugging off the thoughts and wondering how he would be able to sleep with his brain in overdrive, Argo walked past the guards standing outside his room and turned to Olivia.

'Thank you for your help, Olivia. Would you please wake me at 6am? If I manage to get to sleep at all that is! We have to try and see all of the other guests off before 11am tomorrow, because there is a lot that we need to do.'

'Yes, Mr Argo, I will,' Olivia confirmed as Argo started to close his bedroom door. 'Mr Argo. You asked me how the three paintings in the dining room made me feel. I didn't know how to respond until this evening,' Olivia said with an expression of revelation and confusion at the same time. Mike opened his door and looked back towards Olivia with an eyebrow raised. 'The paintings make me think of my interactions with Henrietta Rekman,' she announced as her face returned to its resting position and she turned to head back down the corridor.

Mike closed the door and facing about, rested his back on the smooth wood panelling. He closed his eyes to consider Olivia's words. She had linked her confusion about Henrietta's conduct with the confusion which she experienced when looking at the paintings. A primitive linkage which was abstract, whilst logical and clear. Smiling, he pinched his closed eyes with his thumb and forefinger until they met at the bridge of his nose. Realising that it wouldn't be too many hours before Olivia would be back to wake him with his customary breakfast, he walked into the bathroom to get ready for bed.

As Olivia walked away from Mike Argo's bedroom, she took a detour and headed towards the dining room. Ignoring the option of recalling the saved impression of the work of art which she had stored, Olivia stood in front of the three paintings, scanning over them once again.

57

Vincent had returned to his room in another part of the facility, escorted by the guards, who worked in shifts to ensure that he was accompanied at all time.

He stripped to his boxer shorts and gingerly climbed into bed in the room which he had called home for the past couple of weeks. He could have no complaints about the hospitality which he had received, and the luxuriousness of the room was nothing short of that which one could expect of any other part of the facility. Vincent's concerns were not allayed by the extravagance of the material, but instead compounded by them.

The frustration of being alive and having such a lot of knowledge about the Pebble, whilst being unable to communicate back to Jennifer Harbinger, his contact at MI6, was substantial. His conversation with Argo had been pleasant, but uncomfortable. Mike Argo had made it very clear, quickly, that he had a detailed and meticulous knowledge of Vincent's recent and more historic past.

Vincent had opted not to leave the facility, or suffer the potentially deadly consequences of admitting that he wanted to leave. Instead, he had stayed to speak with Argo and to find out more about the Pebble, which he still considered to be a good decision, given the alternative.

Not understanding why he was still alive, he lay in the darkness, considering his fate. Although every rational part of him now knew about Henrietta Rekman and her true nature, he for some reason could not get Lara Berg out of his mind. The gentle, beautiful backpacker, who seemed a world apart from the murderer who had descended upon them in the Balkans. Also, having no information about what had become of Francis Sunderland and his family disturbed him. The thoughts resonated chaotically, making it impossible for him to rest as he lay in the dimly lit bedroom. He had survived today, but he was well aware that he was not in control of his tomorrow.

THE END

21561121R00132

Printed in Great Britain
by Amazon